$20

Reader ... own
series by JACOB Z. FLORES

When Love Takes Over

"Jacob has a way of writing that puts you in the story and just won't let go."

The Novel Approach

"The author had a ... in ... interested in what he is going to pull out next in the sto... you feel humor, drama and hotness throughout the story."

—Love Bytes (The Blog of Sid Love)

Chasing the Sun

"I have to say that when it comes to man on man intimacy Jacob Flores has a peculiar way of taking you in a wild ride no matter the genre of the book. I quite love his men…"

—MM Good Book Reviews

When Love Gets Hairy

"I absolutely loved this story! I was rooting for these two to the point where I literally couldn't put the book down."

—Hearts on Fire

"This addition to the series is just as lively and fun to read as the last two."

—The Romance Reviews

When Love Comes to Town

"I couldn't put the book down."

—Rainbow Golden Reviews

By JACOB Z. FLORES

3
Being True
The Gifted One

PROVINCETOWN
When Love Takes Over
Chasing the Sun
When Love Gets Hairy
When Love Comes to Town

Published by DREAMSPINNER PRESS
http://www.dreamspinnerpress.com

BEING TRUE

Jacob Z. Flores

Dreamspinner Press

Published by
DREAMSPINNER PRESS

5032 Capital Circle SW, Suite 2, PMB# 279, Tallahassee, FL 32305-7886 USA
http://www.dreamspinnerpress.com/

Being True
© 2014 Jacob Z. Flores.

Cover Design
© 2014 Paul Richmond.
www.paulrichmond.com
Cover Photo
© 2014 JTownsendPhotos.
www.jtownsendphotos.com
Cover Models
© 2014 Nick C. & Nicholas S.
Cover content is for illustrative purposes only and any person depicted on the cover is a model.

ISBN: 978-1-63216-379-0
Digital ISBN: 978-1-63216-380-6
Library of Congress Control Number: 2014945076
First Edition September 2014

Printed in the United States of America
∞
This paper meets the requirements of
ANSI/NISO Z39.48-1992 (Permanence of Paper).

To Amy and Rhys

You both know all about being true. I love you.

Chapter 1

RANCE PARKER slammed my head against the tile of the boys' gym shower where he'd cornered me. "Fucking fag!" He spat in my face and shoved me. I tripped over the three-inch-high barrier separating the showers from the locker room and fell on my back. Hard. The impact knocked the wind out of me and caused the world to spin.

My heartbeat thundered in my ears, and my breath escaped in ragged pants. I tried to get up, to scramble somewhere where Rance's meaty paws couldn't get me, but my sneakers slid across the slick green tile that smelled like mold and ripe feet.

"Where the fuck do you think you're going?" Rance asked behind me. His steps were slow and measured. He was in no rush. And why would he be? We were alone.

Javi wasn't here like Claudia said he would be. I'd only found Rance, getting dressed in a fresh pair of shorts after a workout. When he saw me enter the locker room with the camera Claudia had loaned me, the storm of hate that had brewed within him all day was unleashed.

And now I was on my knees trying to crawl toward the second shower exit a few feet away. There, salvation waited in the form of a dry concrete slab where my feet would find the traction they needed for a rabbit sprint out of this musty foxhole.

Rance wasn't about to let that happen.

He lifted me by my shirt collar. He then clutched my shoulders and hoisted me until I dangled about four inches from his face. His hot, rancid breath plumed across my cheeks, and a nauseating mixture of onions and sweaty ass assaulted my nose.

He evidently preferred beating up on the new kid to addressing personal hygiene.

"You're gonna wish you never came to my school. Or called me a douche," he said as he shook me from side to side. A sneer broke across his hard features, and his brown eyes turned black. The sadistic prick enjoyed this. But was that really any surprise? "And what kind of a fucking name is Truman Cobbler?"

This, from a douche named Rance? But irony was typically lost on the bullies. Most couldn't even spell the word.

"And who the fuck was your dad, you weird-looking little fuck?" He flicked my big ears, which had been the subject of a popular taunt throughout the years. "Donkey from *Shrek*? Is that who your dad was, you fucking cocksucker? Does your mother fuck donkeys?" He laughed as if he'd told the funniest joke in the world. "She must, because with your big-ass ears and horse teeth, there's no way your dad was a real man like me."

"My dad was more of a man than you'll ever be," I said without thinking. I knew better than to talk back when getting beaten up. Giving lip only made them punch you harder. If you kept your mouth shut, they eventually got tired and left.

But my dad was a raw nerve. And I'd just made a comment I'd hopefully live to regret.

"What did you say, faggot?" Rance asked as he shoved me backward. My feet slipped from underneath me again, and I landed on my ass. Flares of pain shot through my legs, but I didn't have time to nurse my wounds.

If I didn't get out of there soon, I'd likely never feel anything again.

"Do you think I'm gonna let you talk back to me again?" He drew closer, his bare, sweaty chest heaving like he was a mad bull and I was the matador's red flag. "No one talks back to me. Gives *me* shit. Those who do learn to shut up real fucking quick." He cracked his knuckles, the universal sign that the beating was about to begin.

I scooted backward like a crab, trying to increase the distance between us. Rance was practically twice my size, which wasn't saying much. I was just over five and a half feet tall. Still, my brand new, sandy-haired, brown-eyed tormentor was probably the biggest bully I'd ever encountered. His fist most likely struck like Thor's hammer.

But big guys like Rance usually cornered no better than a semi. My small size was an advantage against big oafs. I had speed born from years of survival. All I needed was a diversion.

Like the one Ms. Garcia had given me earlier this morning.

"ALL RIGHT, that's enough," Ms. Garcia had told the two boys who shoved me against the lockers. I had been walking the halls of Burbank High, my new school, no more than five minutes before I attracted the attention of haters.

When they stopped to gawk over their shoulders at her, I grabbed my book bag and darted through the sea of students who stopped to watch the show. Many had amused expressions on their faces like a ringside audience at a boxing match. Only the kids at the top of the food chain grinned at such sights. They'd obviously never been on the other end of the fist.

Some of the other faces I blew past appeared almost grateful, as if they were relieved someone new had arrived to take the heat off them in the shark-infested waters of high school. They were like me. At the bottom of the food chain. The minnows off which the predators thrived. The only difference between me and the other outcasts was my newness. They could school together for protection while I was left to float on the surface like chum.

I ducked into Ms. Garcia's office, which reeked of bad perfume, just as the first morning bell buzzed, and sought shelter in the corner. Her office wasn't the standard high school counselor sanctuary filled with books, plants, and soothing colors. The walls had been painted a burnt orange, which was the spirit color for BHS, and dozens of posters from the school's various athletic booster clubs hung on the walls. Judging by the sheer number of baseball calendars, Ms. Garcia preferred the diamond to the football field.

"What's the matter with you two?" Ms. Garcia asked the two boys who stood just outside the office door. Her tone was more annoyed than angry.

"He looked at us funny," one of the guys said.

"And he's funny-looking," added his friend.

Was Ms. Garcia actually chuckling? That didn't bode well. I'd had some experience with high school administrators who, for whatever reason, sided with the bullies over the bullied. Perhaps they resented the weakness I represented or reminded them of the kids they'd once tortured in their youth.

"Do you want to end up in ISS?" she asked.

"Fuck, no!" one yelled.

"Aw, come on, Ms. Garcia," the other pleaded. "I just got out of in-school suspension last week."

"I know. And unless you want to end up there again, I suggest you lay off the little white boy."

What a bitch! If my mother were here, she'd tear into Ms. Garcia. Just like she'd laid into the principal of the school I'd just transferred from. She'd practically shredded Mr. Meyers to pieces for not keeping me safe.

The scraping of sneakers against the linoleum floor announced the boys had agreed to her terms and were headed to class. A few seconds later, Ms. Garcia entered her office to find me seeking refuge in the corner.

She sighed. If she'd have been any more aggravated, she would have shoved me against the lockers as well.

But now that I got a good look at her, I understood why she found me distasteful. The school-educator exterior hid an aging former high school cheerleader.

She'd done her best to hold on to her youth. Her face was pulled tighter than a snare drum, which caused her eyes to bug outward and her pencil-thin eyebrows to arch farther across her forehead than God had intended. Her platinum blonde hair, which looked like a home dye job, also had a body wave added to it that reminded me of a coat on a cocker spaniel.

She fought time tooth and nail. She had perky, full boobs that were likely only two years old, and the six coats of cherry red lip gloss likened her to a sixteen-year-old. The turkey wattle neck, though, revealed she was fighting a losing battle.

"Take a seat," she said as she rounded her desk and sat down. I did as instructed, eyeing my open academic file on her desk. She'd been reading all about me. And what a fun read it must have been.

"Six high schools in four years is quite the record," she said as she sat back.

I nodded. It wasn't exactly an achievement to be proud of. Moving from school to school because I kept getting my ass kicked hadn't exactly been a treat. As it was, my mother was at her wit's end. I had to find some way to make this school work, find some way to fit in. I was seventeen and only had a few months before graduation. I would survive until then if only for her.

She'd been through enough, and she needed a break. So did I.

But I wasn't going to tell Ms. Garcia any of that. She didn't care. This was just a job she endured to pay for her plastic surgery.

"Your file says you've had a rough time of things at your other schools. Being bullied and such."

I nodded, but she kept staring at me as if she expected a blow-by-blow account of every beating I'd taken throughout the years. Was she a sadist or something?

When it was obvious I wasn't going to elaborate, she added, "And I'm sorry about your stepdad."

So was I. But not for the reasons she thought.

I was sorry Bart Cox had ever entered our lives.

"You do speak, right?" she asked. "Nowhere in your file does it say you're a deaf mute."

"Yes, ma'am," I finally uttered. I made sure my voice contained equal measures of respect for her position and apology for not immediately responding. Why couldn't I just tell her to jump into a lake of fire and burn in hell for the condescension that poisoned her tone? Or for the look of disgust that sneered her lip? The reason was simple enough. I was the perennial good boy, or Goody Tru as I'd been called since my class read *The Scarlet Letter* my junior year at high school number four. "I'm just nervous and ready to get to class."

She sighed again, no doubt displeased that her fishing expedition had turned up nothing. "I'll walk you to class," she said as she rose. "To avoid any further hallway disturbances."

I appreciated the gesture even though it was obvious she'd rather sit at her desk filing her nails.

As she led me toward my first period precalculus class, I tried to hold my breath. Why did every high school smell like a musty unfinished basement where stale farts hung in an invisible cloud?

"Get to class," Ms. Garcia scolded a pair of mousy girls lingering in the stairwell. They glanced at me out of the corners of their eyes, most likely recognizing a fellow loser, before they scampered away.

We reached the top of the stairs and entered the main second floor hallway, which had been waxed to a fine sheen. The fluorescent lights that lined the ceiling gleamed off the polish, making the area so bright, I had to squint. Not even the ambling bodies of unmotivated students deflected the shine.

Ms. Garcia, though, got most of them moving. When they saw her coming, they ducked into their classrooms. Was this Hogwarts, and was Ms. Garcia really Dolores Umbridge in disguise? They sure as hell reacted as if she were an agent of Voldemort.

But a quick glance around revealed I hadn't been transported into Harry Potter's world. I'd landed at an impoverished San Antonio high school, where silver metallic lockers stood sentry along the halls.

As I passed, I eyed the many dents along their worn fronts. How long would it take before my head added to the collection?

"WELCOME TO Burbank," Mr. Rodriguez, my new precalculus teacher, said shortly after Ms. Garcia handed him my transfer papers before slipping out of the classroom without so much as a good-bye.

As he scanned the information, I surveyed the room, which reeked of sweat and desperation. That was typical of an advanced math class, as were the unhelpful posters about signs and cosigns that were plastered everywhere.

The classroom, and most of those I'd passed on my way here, clearly indicated I now attended a poverty-stricken school. My last school, Reagan High, had been located in a more affluent neighborhood, and the classrooms had had all the bells and whistles wealthier taxpayers could afford, like flat screen computers, smart boards, and plasma televisions.

This room had big, bulky desktops, a chalkboard, and a television sitting on an old rollaway cart.

I'd secretly hoped that by transferring to a school where other kids were just as economically embarrassed as I was, I'd perhaps find company in financial misery. All the rich kids saw was poor, white trash. When was I going to learn?

I still existed at the bottom of the totem pole as I had everywhere else. The judgmental eyes of my classmates proved that. As they silently scrutinized me, I did my best to avoid their gazes.

I'd learned quickly that making eye contact led to disaster. It was as if locking eyes with someone began a struggle for dominance that only ended in spilled blood.

High school and the wild had a lot in common. Everyone traveled in packs and gathered at the same watering hole. As long as you did your thing with those like you and kept your nose down, you'd live another day.

If you dared to do more than that, a pair of unseen jaws took you out.

My problem, though, was that I'd entered their habitat uninvited. Packs had already been established, and unless I found a group of losers willing to take me in, I'd be skirting the periphery and fending for myself the rest of the year.

"Queer!" someone coughed into his hand. The comment created a ripple of hushed laughter in the room. All of which escaped Mr. Rodriguez's attention. He was either deaf or just didn't care.

Either I was growing tired of being the butt of everyone's private joke or I was suffering a brain aneurism, but before I could stop myself, I coughed "douche" in my hand as a reply.

The class grew deadly quiet.

A few seconds later, a low whisper caught my attention as one of them pointed at me before more muffled laughter filled the room. They were probably making wisecracks about my ears, my messy hair, or my jacked-up clothes.

They weren't exactly dressed in name-brand jeans and tops. Their clothes came from department stores like JCPenney. Mine came from the Goodwill clearance bin.

One girl, a cheerleader dressed in her burnt orange and white uniform, giggled to her cheerleader friend while sticking her finger down her throat in a gagging gesture. They both had their long dark hair pulled into ponytails so tight it made them look slightly Asian.

I pretended not to notice their theatrics.

Adjacent to Gag-arella, which was what I'd call her from now till the end of time, sat a row of jocks. Naturally, they took up the entire back row, forming a wall of tight denim, muscled bodies, and letterman jackets. What was it about jocks and the back row? Was that, like, in their playbooks or something? As if the farther away they sat from the teacher, the cooler they were? Whatever!

Anyway, the jocks sat there glaring at me when they weren't trading sideways glances at each other. Or trying to get the attention of the meanest-looking jock of them all. A snarl seemed to have taken permanent residence on Mr. Badass's upper lip. His sand-blond hair, dark eyes, and beefy arms certainly made him the strongest and most attractive of the group, but the way the guys around him looked to him for guidance marked him more importantly as an alpha among his pack. I'd been around enough Big Men on Campus to know the drill. Being tortured was in my immediate future, especially if he was the one I just called a douche in front of the class. I'd either suffer through yet another swirly in a urine-filled toilet or get pissed on as I exited the shower in gym class. Oh, joyful day!

There was only one face among the entire class who stared blankly at me. No harsh judgments wrinkled her face, which was caked with white powder, and no friendly twinkle lightened her almond-colored eyes. Either she was an emotionless void, or she just didn't give a rat's ass. Based on her all-black clothing and the purple streaks in her hair, which definitely set her apart from the carbon-copy clones around her, it had to be a little bit of both.

"So, Truman," Mr. Rodriguez said as he rose from behind his desk and patted his tiny belly covered in brown plaid. The mention of my name elicited laughter, which Mr. Rodriguez ignored, from my future tormentors in the back row. Everyone except Mr. Badass apparently found my name knee-slapping hilarious. The big, dumb, predictable jerks! "Why don't you tell the class a little bit about yourself?"

"Why?" I asked. "They don't care."

Mr. Rodriguez rankled at the appraisal. Although I hadn't meant to come off as disrespectful since I'd just been stating a rather obvious fact, Mr. Rodriguez had no doubt already placed me on his shit list. The man crossed his arms in front of his birdlike chest and gazed at me over his glasses. "You're not making a very good first impression, young man."

Yeah, well, neither was this class. But I didn't have the balls to make such a rebuttal. Instead, I apologized. My apology took some of the bluster out of Mr. Rodriguez's sails; his arms fell to his sides, but it also resulted in further derision from the class. They rolled their eyes at the lame-ass geek they'd already pegged me as being. Only Emo Girl's expression remained unchanged.

"What do you want to know?" I asked, trying my best to sound like the dutiful student I really was. I couldn't alienate the teachers. They were the ones who'd end up saving me in the hall.

"Anything you'd care to share," Mr. Rodriguez said with a smile at the class. He no doubt believed he had successfully shamed me into compliance.

Before I could launch into the speech I'd given countless times throughout the years, the door behind me opened and shut. Mr. Rodriguez's triumphant sneer broadened into a hearty smile, and the entire class underwent a metamorphosis. Even Emo Girl lit up a kilowatt or two. Who the hell had just walked in, Leonardo DiCaprio?

I glanced over my shoulder. At the door stood the most beautiful boy I'd ever seen in my life. He had big, ebony eyes, flawless skin, and a full head of rich, jet-black hair. The Burbank Bulldogs baseball team T-shirt he wore spread nicely over his full chest. Strong arms clutched at the backpack he'd just shrugged out of, and a lopsided grin tugged at his lips as he wiggled his big bushy eyebrows at the class.

This kid certainly knew how to make an entrance.

My cock apparently agreed. It had awoken and filled my briefs in an effort to snake out and introduce itself. I lowered my textbook in front of my groin and glanced around. No one had seen the tent in my jeans. Thank God.

Most kids already teased me about being gay because of my odd yet delicate features. Popping a boner for the hot jock in the middle of math class would only add unnecessary fuel to that fire.

"Sorry, I'm late," the tardy hunk of lean muscle said as he exhaled a lungful of air out the corner of his lips. The sudden rush of air caused his dark locks to briefly flutter on his forehead before once again settling into perfect alignment. "But coach wanted to run a few things by me before practice this afternoon."

Mr. Rodriguez's snort told everyone he didn't appreciate the tardiness. "Well, I will speak to Coach Moore about this, Mr. Castillo. That's the second time this week."

The young man shrugged in response to Mr. Rodriguez's reprimand, as if being tardy was beyond his control and nothing to worry about. Had this guy ever worried about anything in his life? Most likely not. He was not only insanely good-looking, but he carried himself with a devil-may-care attitude that obviously swept up everyone in his proximity.

Mr. Rodriguez hadn't interpreted his shrug as a discipline problem, and the class apparently thought he was the emperor of ice cream since they practically clung to his every word like eager little kids.

How did someone my own age pull that off so effortlessly? Hell, it had never occurred to me to shrug off a teacher's comment before.

"You can take it up with him after class," said Castillo. He pushed himself off the door upon which he'd been leaning and suddenly noticed me standing slack-jawed in the middle of the room. His eyes caught mine, which made my dick jump within its denim prison, and for the briefest of moments, time slowed to a standstill.

Gazing into his eyes was heavenly and momentous, like watching a comet streak through the night sky. It also unleashed a flurry of sparrows in my stomach, which decided to take flight at once, flapping their tiny wings with all their might. If they flapped any harder or faster, I'd likely soar above the classroom, which, even though that would be pretty darn cool, would probably just alienate me further from my classmates.

I wouldn't be that cool kid who could fly. I'd be that weirdo who couldn't keep his feet on the ground.

"New kid, huh?" he asked as he crossed over to me.

I nodded. What else could I do? My lips could only tremble, and I had to keep my cock from burrowing through the book to the other side.

"I'm Javi." He extended his hand, and his lips broadened into a genuine smile. I'd been on the end of supposedly friendly greetings from popular kids before. They claimed to want to be my best friend and show me the ropes when all they were doing was setting me up for an embarrassing prank that every asshole in school played on the new students.

But I could tell that wasn't what Javi was about. It wasn't anything I could put my finger on. It was just sort of a feeling. You know the kind I'm talking about. It's how you just know a random dog you spot on the street won't bite you. That was the same gut feeling I had with Javi's smile and his offered hand. They told me I could trust him implicitly.

"Truman," I finally responded, and when I took his hand in mine, an electrical current coursed through my fingers, up my arm, spread through my chest, and down into my balls. "But friends call me Tru."

I winced at my stupidity. Now that I'd made that little revelation, everyone would make certain to address me as Truman. No one wanted to be the new kid's friend.

"Nice to meet you, Tru," Javi said without missing a beat. He gave my hand a friendly squeeze before withdrawing. He spun around to the shocked looks on the other students' faces. They couldn't have been more dumbfounded than I was. Javi didn't even acknowledge their collective horror. Either he didn't see it or he didn't care.

He chitchatted with Gag-arella before heading to the back row. He took his seat beside Mr. Badass, who glared at me as if I'd stolen his best friend.

Why did I have a feeling I'd be paying for that, whatever *that* was, later?

MUCH TO my surprise, most of my day had gone pretty much without incident and played out how my first days at a new school usually did. I ate lunch by myself in the outside quad on a bench far away from everyone else. I shuffled from one class to the next, where I was either scowled at or ignored. Most of the negativity came from the Jock Brigade and Mr. Badass, who had been in every class I had except physics and English.

Who exactly had I pissed off in an earlier life to be that unlucky?

I tried my best to be as invisible as possible, to lessen the serious hate-on they'd had for me since precalc. I didn't answer questions when called on. I didn't talk to other students. Hell, I didn't get up to go to the restroom even though I'd had to pee since fourth-period US History.

My efforts had all been in vain.

Nothing seemed to stop the relentless piercing stare Mr. Badass shot at me every minute of every class, or every time we passed each other in the hall. My standard demeanor of head down and averted eyes hadn't done its usual trick.

It only seemed to infuriate him more.

By the time sixth period rolled around, which was the only class I had actually looked forward to, I had become a bundle of nervous energy. The hairs on the back of my neck refused to go down, and I was about ready to jump out of my skin.

Only thinking about Javi Castillo settled my nerves.

Whenever I wanted to bolt from the classroom, I'd remember how warmly he greeted me. The memory of his friendly gaze and electric touch kept me from the agitated twitches that occasionally took control of my body in times of high stress.

The only negative side effect had been the never-ending wood I had to conceal.

My attraction to Javi wasn't a big revelation that I was gay or anything. Hell, I'd known I liked boys since Carl Delacruz kissed me in second grade. After that, it was pretty clear where my preference lay.

Besides, it wasn't like I was a typical boy who ran like a battering ram through life.

I was always more delicate. More sensitive.

My parents had always suspected I was gay. At least that was what my mom told me when I came out to her a couple of years ago. She hadn't been surprised, and she didn't really care either. She said my father had asked her if I might be gay when I was, like, four or five. And when I say father, I mean Alexander Cobbler, my real dad, not the jerkhole, Bart.

Apparently, I used to put string on my head and pretend I was a girl with long hair. And I'd begged for a tea set and an Easy-Bake Oven one Christmas. My dad had been taken aback by it, but according to Mom, it hadn't mattered. I was his son.

Somehow, knowing that, knowing I had my parents' support— even my dad's from the great beyond—made being who I was a lot easier to bear.

At least when I wasn't hanging naked upside down with my face shoved inside a toilet.

So when I finally got to my sixth period journalism class with Mr. Avila, I was a nervous wreck. Thankfully, Mr. Avila proved to be a decent human being. He was the only instructor who welcomed me with a smile instead of an apprehensive frown. He hadn't seen me as a potential troublemaker or mistaken my extremely shy nature as social deviancy. Why did most teachers think I was one trench coat away from becoming a mass shooter?

"So, tell me, Tru," Mr. Avila began. "Can I call you Tru?"

It was awesome to be greeted with familiarity, so I nodded eagerly as my gaze swept across Mr. Avila's desk. It was littered with copy for *The Harvest*, the school newspaper. While most people might think the pile of papers a disorganized mess, I could see the order amid the chaos. To the right were the articles that had been approved. They were stacked in a small tower with notes legibly handwritten in the margins. The rejected articles lay strewn to the left. Huge, red circles enclosed words and sometimes, whole paragraphs, and the marks in the margins were roughly written. Had Mr. Avila been upset when he wrote those comments? It appeared to be the handwriting of someone about to fall off the edge.

It was an emotional state I could relate to.

"What do you have experience in?" Mr. Avila asked. "Writing copy or taking photos?"

"I can do both."

His arched eyebrows indicated skepticism.

"I've done pieces on the school cafeteria, dress codes, you name it," I said. "I took my own photos for each one."

"And you know your way around a DSLR?"

I nodded. Mr. Avila was testing to see if I had any clue what the acronym stood for. "I've worked with a digital single-lens camera at most of my schools. I also know my way around Photoshop and InDesign. I'm also pretty good at web pages too."

Mr. Avila stared at me for a few more seconds before asking a student named Trevor to get someone named Claudia out of the Mac lab. After Trevor disappeared, Mr. Avila's attention returned to me.

"If what you say is true, and Claudia will be able to tell better than me, then I might just have use for you at both the newspaper and the yearbook."

"Really?" I practically twittered with excitement. I'd spent so much of the day trying to appear as if I didn't give a damn about anything, it was nice to not only let myself feel but to express it as well.

A wide grin spread across Mr. Avila's lips as he nodded. He obviously enjoyed my enthusiasm.

"You sent for me, Mr. Avila?" a girl said to my right. It was Emo Girl from precalc. She had also been in a couple of my other classes, but this was the first time I'd heard her speak. Her voice was actually quite pleasant. Based on her gruff appearance and attitude, I'd expected her to speak in a low rumble. Instead her sweet, melodic tone served to counter the big red sad face on her T-shirt, which read "Don't know" at the top and "Don't care" at the bottom.

"Claudia, this is Tru. He claims to be both a writer and a photog. Care to take him for a spin?"

She studied me with her wary, dark brown eyes made darker by the heavily applied black eyeliner. The sweetness of her voice did not extend to her gaze. "Sounds too good to be true," she said. "No pun intended."

I laughed. It wasn't like I hadn't heard that line before. With a name like Tru, I'd heard that and much worse. But I figured laughter might somehow make me more appealing. I should have known better. I'd forgotten that when I laughed, I bared my full set of horse teeth.

Claudia rolled her eyes and then abruptly turned around.

So much for that. My one chance to be involved in something I really enjoyed, and I'd blown it. After all, those who embraced the emo lifestyle preferred the dark and brooding. If I'd played it smarter, I might have been given a chance to prove myself.

"If you're waiting for an invitation, you'll be standing there with your thumb up your butt until the zombie apocalypse."

Claudia had paused outside the doorway that most likely led to the computer lab. She waited for me to join her.

"Really?" My voice cracked with excitement. Could I be any more of a dweeb?

Claudia sighed and stepped over the threshold. Before she could lock the door behind her, I sprinted across the room and followed her inside.

"NOT BAD," Claudia said as she inspected the typographic layout I'd created. I'd even inserted a couple of photos into the design just to impress her. Since her face lit up with genuine surprise, she'd obviously expected me to fail. That was nothing new. Pretty much everyone except my mom had low expectations of me. Most people only saw a skinny little screw-up with a weird face and God-awful clothes.

No one really took the time to get to know the person underneath.

But now that I had impressed Claudia, who scanned me up and down with a begrudging pale smile, perhaps she'd be one of the first.

"But can you write as well as you design?" The smile disappeared from her face. Clearly, she still had doubts. Since she was the editor for both the newspaper and the yearbook, she had a lot on her plate, as she had told me while I'd worked on the computer. She didn't have time for people who didn't know what they were doing.

"I like to think so," I said.

Once again she studied me apprehensively. Her lips hooked up to the left as she pondered whether I was telling the truth. I certainly wrote better than I lied, but she didn't know I couldn't fib to save my life. And I really didn't see the point in deception either. Wasn't it just better to be honest?

"Give me a chance and I'll prove it to you. You can even give me an assignment. Due tomorrow. And I'll write it up and have it ready for you first thing in the morning. Then, if you don't like it, well, it's no skin off your back. But if you do, then maybe you'll let me on your staff."

She scrutinized both my words and me in silence. Whenever people took that much time to look at me, when they appraised me on my appearance, it rarely boded well. "There's just something about you—"

"I know I don't look like much," I said. I tried my best not to come off desperate even though I was. Working for the newspapers at my other high schools had been the only way I'd felt connected. As if I actually belonged somewhere. "Lots of people don't think I can do a whole lot because of the way I look. I'm kinda odd, and my clothes aren't exactly the best, but I'm a good worker. I make good grades, and it's not like I have friends, so I could devote pretty much all my free time to what you'd need from me. Think of me like an indentured servant."

When I stopped speaking, Claudia's demeanor changed. Her shoulders tensed, and she bit her lip. What unseen toe had I just stepped on?

"I'm not some shallow bitch who judges other people based on the way they look. Don't put me in the same category as Lucy Canales or Rance Parker." I'd come to learn that Gag-arella and Mr. Badass from precalc were Lucy and Rance, who made up one of the most popular power couples on campus. Like that was any surprise. "I don't give a flying fuck what people look like. I judge people on how they act. What kind of people they are. So don't go judging me either, Tru." Even though she muttered my name with disdain, I couldn't help but notice she'd called me Tru. Not Truman. Not Goody Tru. Or any other awful name I'd been saddled with.

"I'm sorry. It's just that—"

"And another thing," she said, cutting me off. "You've obviously had a tough life. I sure as hell can spot misery in someone else. Believe me, I've had experience with life crapping all over me. With people seeing me as some devil worshipping, homicidal, depressed drug addict because I like to wear black. Which I'm not by the way. *Any* of those things." She arched her eyebrow to punctuate her statement. I nodded. I wasn't about to interrupt. "And it sucks when people do that to me, so I don't do that to others."

After she stopped speaking, I waited a few moments to see if she would start up again. I'd pissed her off enough and didn't want to add more gasoline to the blaze of indignation I'd unintentionally ignited. And even though she was obviously upset, Claudia's displeasure offered comfort. She might be the friend I'd always wanted.

"I'm really sorry," I said when it became apparent she'd finished talking. "I didn't mean to be an asshole, but you're right, I assumed you were judging me. And even though it happens to me a lot, I guess I can't go around thinking everyone is going to do that to me, huh?"

She snorted. "Oh, people are gonna judge us every fucking day of our lives. We just have to learn not to give a shit what others think or return the favor by being shitty to others."

I couldn't disagree with her, so I didn't even try. I merely nodded. "So you think we could be friends?"

"Well, before you interrupted me with your judgmental crap, I was about to say there was something about you that made me want to trust you." I about fell over. Only my family had ever said those words to me. "And I'm not a trusting individual. Ask anyone around this godforsaken school. I don't let most of these dipshits within five feet of me because I know what kind of assholes they are. They've taught me that most people will betray you in a heartbeat. Which is why I prefer animals. They have good hearts. Not like humans who just suck balls."

Normally, I suppressed my laughter since most people made fun of me when I brayed like a donkey. But I couldn't hold it in. It forced its way out of my throat, and I gave myself to the moment. It wasn't like Claudia had said anything that was hilarious. It just felt so good to not only carry on a conversation with someone my age but to talk to another teen who appeared to be a kindred spirit.

Claudia squinted at me dubiously. She was no doubt trying to determine if I was making fun of her, or if I'd just lost my mind. I opened my mouth to assure her I wasn't laughing at her, but when I tried to speak, the giggles and guffaws strangled the words, making them completely incomprehensible.

"You're very bizarre," she finally said before rolling her eyes. The smile that stretched across her lips was one of the most welcome sights I'd seen in a long time.

After I got myself under control, I wiped the tears from my eyes. They were among the few I'd shed out of joy and not sadness. "You have no idea," I finally uttered through one final snicker.

"Okay, enough fun and games. It's time to get to work. That's if you're serious about working for me. And before you answer, you should know when it comes to journalism, I'm the biggest bitch there is. When I say move, I expect you to already be halfway gone. Understand?"

"Yes, ma'am," I answered with a salute.

"Dumbass," she teased. Now that was a name I'd been called plenty, but Claudia was the first to not really mean it.

She walked over to a cabinet in the corner and took a camera from one of the shelves. "Here's what I want you to do," she said before placing the equipment in my hands. "I want you to head over to the gym after last period. Our baseball team went to state last year, and we're hoping for a repeat this year. I've gotten quotes from all the major players on the team, even that dipshit Rancid." I chuckled at her nickname for Rance Parker, formerly known as Mr. Badass. "But I haven't been able to get a quote from the star himself. And I need one."

"Okay," I said with a nod. "Who is that?"

"Javi Castillo," she answered with a glint in her eyes. "Remember him from precalc?"

Remember him? How could I forget the boy who'd given me a hard-on all day? "Of course," I mumbled, hoping my soft speech hid the excitement that coursed through me.

"Get me a quote and a photo for the paper. He's not fond of doing either. Think you can do that?"

I nodded. Oh, I'd get them both. Especially since Javi had been super decent to me this morning. I anticipated no problems whatsoever.

OBVIOUSLY, I had never been more wrong in my life.

I'd gone to the gym looking for Javi but found Rancid instead.

My cheek exploded with fire when Rance's fist collided with my face. I stumbled backward, my jaw feeling as if it had unhinged, before I slammed once again onto the hard tiled floor.

"Who the hell said you can come into my locker room?" He once again lifted me off the floor by the collar and shook me like a dog with a chew toy. He bared his teeth and practically barked, "You think you can come in here with that camera of yours and snap pics of our cocks? Is that what gets you off, you dirty little perverted fuck?"

"I'm here for *The Harvest*," I mumbled. My words didn't form correctly. My cheek throbbed and had grown to at least twice its usual size, so my attempts at communication came out garbled.

"You're here for the hairiest?" Rance asked in disgust. "Fucking fairy!" He then shoved me out of the shower area and back into the lockers. "Let's see how many pictures you take once I break your thumbs."

I had nowhere to go. Rance's big body blocked the exit, and based on what I saw reflected in his eyes, only my death would be acceptable to him.

"What the hell is going on here?"

Coach Moore's voice caught us both by surprise.

When Rance turned to gape at the coach, I sprinted past them both and out of the locker room. And I wasn't stopping until I got home.

Chapter 2

WHEN I made it back to The Projects, which was what our government-subsidized housing complex was called, I didn't rush inside. No comfort could be found within its strange, cracked walls and crumbling brick façade, where cockroaches on the hunt for stray food outnumbered us.

How could I find solace amid the stacks of boxes or the contents of our lives strewn across the floor? No pictures of my family hung on the walls. Only disgusting brown streaks decorated the interior.

This place wasn't home. It offered no unseen embrace of familiarity with which I could lose myself.

Apartment C at 603 Esperanza Street had nothing I needed. Not even my mother was home.

After tossing the camera Claudia had given me on the couch, I hopped on my bike and pedaled as fast as my legs could go.

I had no clue where I was going, and I didn't care. I just needed to get as far away from the hell my life had become as possible.

I sped down streets lined with trash and weeds and broken concrete. I zoomed around potholes big enough to swallow cars and by alleys filled with shadows and graffiti.

Cars horns blared as I darted through intersections, not caring to look if the coast was clear. What would it matter if one hit me anyway? My life had stripped the ignorance of death from me already.

Yet my heart pounded in my chest like a rabbit that had just escaped a pack of hounds, and fear held me tight and refused to let go.

So I pedaled faster, pumping my legs in a vain attempt at wiping the image of Rance's hate-filled, glazed-over eyes from my mind.

I'd never been that terrified before in my life. I'd been beaten up before several times, but this was the first time I'd actually believed I might not make it out alive.

All the other times it had happened, there'd been witnesses. Rance had had me cornered in a secluded area where he could have done anything to me, and no one would have been the wiser.

Skidding tires drew me from my thoughts. A quick glance over my shoulder revealed a brown Honda fishtailing to a stop six feet to my right. The driver laid hands on his horn and shouted curses at me out the open window.

But that didn't stop me. I continued onward until sweat dripped down my forehead and stung my eyes. I only slowed down once the dull ache in my side grew into a blinding, stabbing pain. My lungs pleaded for air, and I realized I was wheezing and on the verge of passing out.

I stopped pedaling and coasted. The blur my surroundings had become cleared, and I realized I had no idea where I was.

Just how far had I gone?

The rundown buildings that made up my neighborhood had disappeared. Actual houses surrounded by chain-link fences now lined both sides of the street. Cars were parked in driveways and not on the lawns. And they even had all four tires. They weren't resting on cinder blocks.

These homes weren't the residences of the well-off. They were obviously owned by those of the lower working class, but considering where I lived, they might as well be mansions.

"Hey, you!" someone behind me shouted. "Stop."

Panic once again crushed me as the unmistakable clank of a spinning bike chain came from behind. I didn't waste time looking back. What followed me could only be further torment at the hands of another bully. So I rose off my seat and put my full weight into each pedal.

"Hey, man. Wait up!"

Yeah, right. For what? Another jock beatdown? No, thank you.

Up ahead, at the top of a small hill, stood a set of uneven train tracks. If I didn't slow down, the tracks and my momentum might send me tumbling to the cracked asphalt. Such a spill could probably split my skull open. But getting caught by whoever pursued me would likely end the exact same way.

I pedaled faster.

The lights atop the crossing gate arms flashed red in warning before lowering, and the horn of an approaching train blared three times.

If I could beat the train, I would be safe on the other side. There was no way the guy behind me could make it before it hit the intersection. It would give me the time I needed to take a side street to safety and then circle back around.

The apartment might not be home, but within its moldy walls, I'd be relatively safe.

"What the hell, man?" the voice asked through panting breaths.

I had to give the guy his due. He was nothing if not persistent. And from the sound of his voice, the gap separating us had decreased.

It had to be one of the Jock Brigade. That knowledge caused me to piston faster and harder as I reached the bottom of the hill. The train's horn thundered again as it bulleted toward the intersection. It was so close I could make out the tiny head of the engineer in the first car.

I maneuvered the bike around the crossing gates, skidding to regain my purchase on the road, and then aimed my bike toward the tracks that would either offer me safety from further beating or bring everything to a bone-crushing end.

As I rode over the tracks, the heat of the approaching train buffeted my flesh, and the roar of the horn drowned out all other sounds. A few seconds after, the train flew by.

I glanced over my shoulder to verify I hadn't been followed, and the coast was clear. I had made it.

I'd never been more relieved in my life. At least until I turned around.

My trajectory over the tracks had set me on a collision course with a huge decorative stone in the yard of the first house on the downhill side of the tracks. I tried to correct, but it was too little, too late.

I struck the rock hard, flying over the handles of the bike and the boulder before skidding to a stop on my face.

I HAD no idea how long I lay there on my stomach. It could have been a few seconds or ten minutes, but my face exploded with fresh pain when I regained consciousness and opened my eyes. As if getting smacked around by Rance Parker wasn't bad enough, I now had to contend with losing a fight against a rock and the ground. My luck fricking sucked.

Maybe that was why I couldn't stop the tears. Or why I dug my fingers into the grass. I couldn't take much more. Something had to give. My life had to change. If I didn't find light at the end of the tunnel soon, I feared the darkness might whisk me away.

The rhythmic hum of the train flying across the tracks grew more and more distant, and the warning clangs at the railroad crossing ceased. The intersection was now clear. A few seconds later, a bike skidded to a stop a few feet away before frantic footfalls crunched across the dry grass. "Fuck, man!" Someone suddenly said at my side. "Are you okay?"

Great! Thanks to my carelessness and complete inability to dust myself off and get back on my bike, my pursuer could now kick me while I was down. But why did I hear genuine concern in the strangely familiar voice?

"Just leave me alone," I said, not wanting to turn around. It was bad enough to be lying facedown in the dirt. To be crying like a baby only made matters worse. I prided myself on never letting my tormentors see my tears. I couldn't control the fear, but I was damned if I'd ever let them see me reduced to a blubbering mess.

"Yeah, well, I'm not gonna," he said. For some reason, whoever this was sat on the hard-packed ground next to me. What the hell was he waiting for? For me to stop crying so he could then kick the crap out of me? But if that was his motive, why join me on the grass? "You took a nasty fall, Tru, and I'm not leaving till I'm sure you're okay."

Who the hell was this guy?

Reluctantly, I opened my eyes and glanced over my shoulder. Staring back at me were the gorgeous ebony eyes that had captivated me this morning in precalc. "Javi?"

He nodded. "Well, at least we know the fall didn't cause amnesia." The right corner of his lips tugged into a half grin. The tears that had previously streamed down my cheeks and blurred my vision dried up. How could I cry while basking in the warmth of such a smile?

"What are you doing here?" I asked as I struggled to sit up. If that was going to happen, though, the world needed to stop spinning.

"Take it easy," Javi said. He placed his hand on my chest and gently nudged me back onto the grass. The weight of his hand sent shivers across my flesh. "You still look a little shaky."

That was no lie. My breathing had increased, and my blood pounded in my ears. If I tried to stand now, I'd likely resemble a newly born fawn unable to find his footing. But it wasn't the fall that had caused these reactions. It was Javi.

For a few moments, I said nothing, and neither did he. He sat cross-legged in the grass, gazing around the neighborhood. Every now and then, a car passed by. Sometimes, the driver honked and shouted a greeting at Javi, who raised his hand and waved in reply. Javi's popularity apparently followed him beyond the hallowed halls of Burbank High, which wasn't all that surprising.

But while Javi studied his surroundings, I simply watched him. His long onyx hair fluttered about his forehead whenever the humid September breeze stirred the early-evening air. Every time he heard a bird chirp, he'd scan the trees and whistle back. Sometimes he'd receive a response and carry on a conversation with his new feathery friend. And the whole time, a big, cheesy grin lit up his face. As if speaking bird was the coolest thing he'd done all day.

"Are you a bird whisperer or something?"

Javi laughed before tearing his gaze from the cardinal he'd been chatting with in a neighboring pecan tree. "I don't know. Maybe. I've just always been able to mimic birdcalls. Just one of my stupid childhood talents I've never outgrown."

"I don't think it's stupid," I said as I sat up. "It's neat."

"My friends don't think so. They used to give me a hard time about it. So I really don't do it as much as I used to when I was a kid."

"That sucks."

He shrugged. "Yeah, but what can you do? High school's tough enough without being known as the weird bird boy."

I couldn't help but stare at Javi as if a third eye had suddenly opened in the middle of his forehead.

"What's that look for?" he asked.

"I find it hard to believe that high school, much less anything, would be tough for you."

Javi's eyes caught mine. "Yeah, well, you'd be surprised." The confident, carefree boy I'd met earlier today vanished almost entirely even though his half grin still blazed a trail across his lips. The guy who sat next to me now seemed lost and alone. The smile couldn't hide that. But as suddenly as some unseen barrier had fallen, it immediately rebuilt itself. The lighthearted sparkle returned to his gaze before he glanced away and surveyed the trees again.

"You never answered my question."

"What question is that?" he asked before sending a bird whistle out to the neighborhood and receiving another enthusiastic reply.

"What are you doing here?"

"Well, that's a silly question. I live around here."

"I'd already guessed that," I said. "What are you doing here with me?"

Javi danced his bushy eyebrows across his lightly tanned forehead. He wrapped his sculpted arms around his knees and pulled them to his chest. Although he still wore his baseball shirt from class that morning, he'd abandoned his jeans for gym shorts. "Now you've gone from silly to strange. I'm here because you almost killed yourself. First with the train, and then when you learned you couldn't fly over the rock you hit on the other side."

"I don't understand why you care," I admitted. No one outside my family had ever showed this much interest in my well-being. Why was Javi taking the time to be nice to a loser like me?

"Jeez, kid," he said. When he raised his hand, I flinched. I'd grown accustomed to quick hand gestures ending in a punch to the face or gut. I certainly hadn't been prepared for Javi to rub my shoulder. "You must be having a really tough time, huh?"

Tears welled in my eyes again. This time, it wasn't because I was in pain or being bullied. They were falling because someone had finally noticed me.

AFTER I'D dried my tears, Javi invited me back to his house. He claimed I needed to get cleaned up after my face's introduction to Mrs. Sanchez's yard, but I didn't buy it. He'd seen how emotional I'd gotten, and he evidently didn't want to leave me alone while I was in such a fragile state.

I'd never met anyone like Javi Castillo before in all the schools I'd attended. How did someone so popular and good-looking get to be so considerate and kind? It had always been my experience that kids like Javi were the biggest assholes on the planet.

I kept waiting for the other shoe to drop.

In fact, my natural caution almost made me decline the invitation. I suspected I was being lured into a false sense of security. That Javi was perhaps leading me to some dark alley or secluded lot where Rance and the Jock Brigade laid in wait to finish what Rance had started in the boys' locker room.

But after walking our bikes a few blocks—the collision with the rock had knocked the chain off the pulley and made riding my bike impossible—we finally arrived at Javi's house.

It wasn't a grand house, but it sure beat my crappy, rundown apartment. It had been painted in warm earth tones, and white shutters framed the street-facing windows. A white rail extended the full length of the porch and over to the wooden poles that framed the carport, where a blue Lincoln Town Car sat on the driveway. Dark green grass covered the well-cared-for front lawn, and the branches of a huge Magnolia tree crisscrossed its heavy branches overhead. Young trees and hearty rose bushes, surrounded by painstakingly placed bricks, spotted the yard.

The Castillos took excellent care of what was theirs.

"We're here," Javi said as he dropped his bike on the grass. "You can leave your bike next to mine."

I nodded. My nerves made me capable of nothing else. I'd never met a friend's parents before. Hell, I'd never had a friend before, and the fact that Javi was fast becoming a friend, had my head spinning worse than my recent tumble. What would I do if Javi's parents hated me? Everyone else seemed to instantly dislike me. If the Castillos followed suit, they could forbid Javi from hanging around the poor white trash he'd literally found on the side of the road.

"You just gonna stand outside or what?" he asked from the front door. I'd been so lost in thought, I hadn't noticed Javi cross the lawn to the house.

"Maybe" was all I replied.

He shook his head and laughed. "Get your ass in here."

And once again, I did as Javi commanded.

The interior of the house proved to be as inviting as the outside. It wasn't the furniture that was neatly arranged with the sofa and recliner facing the television set. Or the shelves along the far wall filled with books and knickknacks. The possessions were merely possessions.

What I found so welcoming was the atmosphere. It smelled like a home, not some place that was merely occupied for the moment, and on the air wafted a mixture of cinnamon and tortillas.

"What's that wonderful aroma?" I asked as Javi closed the front door.

"My mom's cooking," he said. "She always lights her cinnamon candles while she makes supper so the house doesn't smell like *caldo*, *carne guisada*, or whatever she happens to be making."

I breathed deeply. I loved caldo. I hadn't eaten Mexican beef soup in years, and last time I had the stew was longer than I cared to remember. "Well, I like it."

He grinned. "Me too."

"*Mijo*, is that you?" A woman asked from the kitchen. I'd learned enough Spanish over the years to know it was Javi's mother. Who else would address him as my son?

"It's me," he yelled back. He then turned and said, "Wait here. I'll be right back." He headed across the living room and through the doorway to the right, where his mother prepared dinner for her family.

While I waited for Javi to return, I inspected the dozens of pictures that adorned the living room walls. Most were of Javi throughout his childhood. In one, he sat in a stroller, waving a rattle in his hand and grinning at whoever snapped the picture. Everything about him was pretty much the same except his hair, which lay across his head in short dark wisps. In another photo, he was dressed in a tiny suit and sat on his mother's lap while his father stood protectively over his family. His hair was buzzed short in that one. The rest of the pictures were of Javi dressed in his baseball uniform, standing on the pitcher's mound, or holding a trophy while surrounded by his teammates.

When I spotted a picture of Rance with his arm around Javi's neck, my flesh crawled. How the hell could a guy like Javi be friends with an asswipe like Rance? It defied explanation.

It was too much to think about right then, so I turned around and found a picture of the Virgin Mary lovingly placed above a table to the left of the front door. On what could only be described as an altar stood two lit candles, some prayer cards, and a crucifix, around which hung a beaded rosary.

"Mom, this is the new kid I was telling you about," Javi said as he reentered the living room with his mother. "His name's Tru."

I turned to greet Mrs. Castillo, readying myself for the disapproving gaze I'd grown accustomed to. I was not prepared for what happened next. Her plump lips drew themselves into a big O, and she rushed over to me. "*Ay dios mío!*" she cried to God. Her hazel eyes narrowed in worry. "What happened to you?" When she spoke in English, her accent was thick, but not as deep as the concern in her voice. She even gingerly glided her hands over my cheeks as she inspected me for broken bones.

"I told you he fell off his bike," Javi said from immediately behind his mother. It was obvious from his tone he was slightly annoyed.

She turned around and playfully smacked her son across the head. "And you neglected to tell me he fell on his face."

"Gee, thanks, Mom," Javi said. His cheeks flushed a deep red. "Way to make a good first impression on my new friend here."

Mrs. Castillo continued chiding her son as she took my hand and led me through the living room and toward the medicine cabinet in the bathroom. I stood in stunned silence as she wiped the blood from my face with alcohol and gauze. I didn't hear any of the questions she asked or her banter with Javi.

The only word that still resonated in my ears was the one Javi had spoken: friend.

AFTER CLEANING me up and bandaging my cuts, Mrs. Castillo insisted I stay for dinner, especially after she learned my mother wouldn't get off work until midnight. The offer was too good to pass up, so I accepted after convincing her to allow me to help set the table and clean up.

"I didn't know you were such a brownnoser," Javi playfully teased as I set the yellow kitchen table for four.

"*Cállate*," Mrs. Castillo reprimanded from the stove. She was making chicken mole, Spanish rice, and refried beans in her white apron embroidered with yellow daisies, which draped over her blue pants and yellow-and-blue striped shirt. She commanded Javi to be quiet, but the glint in his eyes revealed he wasn't planning on obeying. "It's nice to have someone around here who wants to help," she said with a wink at me. Javi's mom had to be somewhere in her forties, but you couldn't tell that from her smooth skin or her long, thick locks. It was obvious where Javi's full head of hair came from.

"You're making me look bad," Javi said. "You know that, right?"

I glanced at him, sitting on his ass and drinking a Coke. "I think you're doing just fine with that all on your own."

Mrs. Castillo laughed at my retort. Javi scowled and then let fly the loudest burp I'd ever heard in my life.

"*Cochino!*"

Javi grinned broadly at his mother's attempt at embarrassing him. Clearly, he didn't mind being called a pig. He seemed to rather enjoy it.

"So how was your first day at Burbank?"

I'd been in the middle of placing the last plate on the table when Javi asked his question. I froze. I didn't know how to respond. Rance and Javi were friends. If I told the truth, what would that do to our new friendship? It wasn't like I could expect Javi to choose me over Rance. We'd just met, and Lord only knew how long he and Rance had been best buds. I decided being vague was my best bet. "It was interesting."

He snorted. "Yeah, right. There's not much interesting about BHS."

"Don't talk badly about your school," Mrs. Castillo said. She shook her wooden spoon at Javi to make her point. "It's been good to you. You might even get a baseball scholarship to college because of it."

"Yeah, yeah," he said as he rolled his eyes. This subject was obviously a bone of contention between them. "There's more to life than baseball."

"Like what?" someone suddenly asked.

I turned to see a man, who looked like an older version of Javi, standing at the entrance to the kitchen. Besides being slightly taller and thicker around the middle, Javi's dad also had skin about two shades darker and a full moustache across his top lip. He wore a button-down short-sleeved shirt and brown pants. Unlike most of the people he spotted in the neighborhood wearing dirty work overalls, Mr. Castillo apparently worked in an office somewhere and not in a garage or doing shift work.

Javi rose from the table and greeted his father with a hug. Mrs. Castillo then followed suit.

"And who's this?" he asked as he walked over to shake my hand.

"I'm Tru," I answered as I took his hand in mine. His grip was strong and confident while mine was loose and tentative.

"True?" he asked. "Like true or false?"

"Dad!" Javi complained.

Mr. Castillo glanced at his son as if he had no idea why he was being fussed at. "What?" he asked. "I just asked a question."

"Tru is short for Truman, sir," I answered, trying to save Mr. Castillo from his son's teasing.

"Ah, like President Harry S. Truman," he said.

I nodded. "Except Truman's my first name."

Mr. Castillo nodded. "You *bolios* sure pick weird first names," he said with a playful wink.

"*Dad!*" Javi clearly didn't appreciate his father's teasing or addressing me as a white boy. Like Mr. Castillo was the first who'd ever called me that. In the barrio, I heard it on a daily basis.

"It's okay, Javi," I conceded. "My name's pretty weird. And I am a bolio."

"See," Mr. Castillo said as he gestured at me. "Some boys know how to take jokes."

"And how to help set the table," Mrs. Castillo added.

"Really?" Mr. Castillo glanced at his wife. When she nodded, he turned back to me and smiled. Javi only groaned. He must have sensed what was coming next. "Perhaps we need to swap sons," he said as he messed up his son's hair. "The only thing this one concerns himself with is baseball and his hair."

"Dad, stop!" Javi squirmed underneath his father's playful gesture. "You know I hate it when my hair's messed up!"

"I know," Mr. Castillo grinned at me. "That's why I do it."

I sat there transfixed as Javi and his dad playfully tussled with each other in a perfectly choreographed dance. The ease with which they interacted revealed this was how they truly acted, and they weren't putting on a show. No wonder I'd been overcome by a general sense of welcome upon entering this house.

True love lived here.

It wasn't like my mother didn't love me. Or that she didn't do her best to make a nice life for me. She was just so busy working, trying to make up for the hell we'd gone through since Bart Cox entered and exited our life that we passed like proverbial ships in the night.

Seeing Javi and his family made me miss the family I'd once had even more.

"Okay, enough playing in my kitchen," Mrs. Castillo said as she swatted her husband on the behind with her wooden spoon. "If the mole burns because of you two, there'll be hell to pay."

Both Javi and Mr. Castillo immediately ceased their horseplay. In the kitchen, Mrs. Castillo was the undisputed law.

"Okay, enough," Mr. Castillo agreed as he released his son from a bear hug. Javi's long exhalation revealed he couldn't have been more relieved. "I'm going to wash up, and then over dinner, Tru can tell us about the fight he was in."

How the hell had he figured that out? I glanced nervously at Mr. Castillo and then to Javi and his mother. I couldn't tell them about what had happened. If I did, I might lose Javi's friendship. And after being alone for so long, I couldn't bear the thought of losing the one friend I'd just made.

"Tru fell off his bike, Dad," Javi said. His mother nodded in agreement. "He wasn't in a fight."

Mr. Castillo paused next to me and placed his hand on my shoulder. "Is that true?"

I nodded. "I did fall off my bike, sir."

"Told you," Javi said with a hint of smug righteousness.

"I believe you." Mr. Castillo, however, refused to break eye contact or take his hand from where it rested. "But were you also in a fight today?"

I opened my mouth to lie, but I couldn't do it. How could I bring deception into this house? Besides, Mr. Castillo already knew the truth. I could see it in his eyes. "Yes, sir. I was."

Mrs. Castillo gasped.

"What?" Javi asked as he stood from the table. "With who?"

I didn't want to answer. It would ruin everything. I was stuck.

"Not now," Mr. Castillo answered for me. He patted me on the back to let me know it was okay. "For now, we all wash up and eat."

He nodded at me and then at his family, who stood in silence. When he realized there'd be no more questions, Mr. Castillo exited the kitchen and left me standing there with my mouth wide open.

Somehow, Mr. Castillo had sensed I wasn't ready to answer, and he'd come to my rescue.

And I hadn't even had to ask for help.

CRAMMED AROUND the small kitchen table, we ate, and it was perhaps one of the best meals of my life. My mother, God love her, excelled at many things. Cooking was not one of them. Her idea of a meal consisted of Hamburger Helper or any other boxed dinner.

So naturally, I ate everything on my plate. Being a bolio, as Mr. Castillo had so kindly pointed out, I'd never had homemade chicken mole before. How had I lived my life without it for so long? I even ate a second helping Mrs. Castillo deposited on my plate without my having to ask.

"You've got a good appetite," she said after I picked the second chicken breast clean.

The familiar burn of embarrassment flushed my cheeks. "I couldn't help myself," I said. "It was delicious."

Mr. Castillo patted his full stomach and nodded. "My Maricela is the best cook ever, even though she tries to make me fat."

She huffed. "There'll be no skin and bones in my house," she said with a proud jut of her chin.

And Mr. and Mrs. Castillo definitely weren't skin and bones. They weren't obese or anything. Just pleasantly plump. Next to them and Javi, who appeared to be all lean muscle, I was a string bean.

"So tell us about yourself," Mr. Castillo said as his wife cleared the dishes.

"Not much to tell, really," I replied as I stood to fulfill my end of the bargain with Mrs. Castillo. I placed Javi's clean plate atop mine and crossed to the kitchen sink. "I'm just your average, boring kid."

I turned on the faucet to rinse the dishes, hoping breaking eye contact would dissuade Mr. Castillo from continuing his interrogation. I hated talking about myself. Who wanted to hear a sad story after such a good meal? Besides, my tale ended with Javi's best friend smacking me around the locker room. That could potentially put Javi and me at odds.

"I don't believe that," Mr. Castillo said. The scraping of his chair on the linoleum indicated he had backed away from the table. A few seconds later, he was at my side with a dishtowel in hand. "Everyone has a story."

I nodded. "True. Others are just more interesting than mine."

"Why don't you let me be the judge?"

I peered over my shoulder to find the kitchen empty. Sometime during the conversation, Javi and his mother had left us alone. When I turned around, Mr. Castillo's kind brown eyes smiled down at me. They were the same dark ebon as Javi's.

"I had a feeling we should have this conversation in private," he said with a wink.

"You asked them to leave? But I didn't hear you say anything."

He grinned slyly. Just the way Javi had the first time I laid eyes on him. "In this house, words are sometimes not necessary."

I turned my eyes down to the soapy water. It always made me uncomfortable telling my story. Not like anyone had ever really asked before. Just the therapist I'd briefly seen shortly after the specter of Bart Cox had been exorcized from our lives.

Mr. Castillo's hand rested reassuringly on my shoulder. "I sense you are a good boy, Tru. Someone very different from the friends Javi typically brings around. And to tell you the truth, I kind of like that. His teammates are nice, but they are not respectful. And are often unruly. In just the short time I've known you, I can tell you have a big heart. Probably bigger than most people I know."

I blinked back the tears. How could Mr. Castillo see all that when not many others could?

"But I see something more," he said, lightly squeezing my shoulder. "There's a lot of pain there too. Probably more than I've seen in any one person. Especially someone so young. Your life should be an open road, filled with possibilities and adventure. But something holds you back. Something has darkened the road."

I sniffled. He was right. My life had been one late-night drive down a pitch-black highway with two broken headlights.

"But I want you to know, I'm not going to push. I won't force you to tell your story. You're a man, and a man shouldn't be forced to do anything he doesn't want to do. But a real man, a true man, recognizes when he can't go it alone. When he needs to lean on someone else for a little while. And I'm here to tell you it's okay to do that. If you'd like to talk, I'd be happy to listen. But you should also know my Javi is a good boy too. He's there for his friends. No matter what."

And what would Javi do if he learned his old friend was responsible for beating up his new one?

"Do you understand?"

"Yes, sir," I answered with a nod.

"Good. Now let's finish these dishes. Then we can get your bike all fixed up so you can get home."

"Sounds like a plan," I said as I resumed washing. And while we finished cleaning up, Mr. Castillo told me stories about Javi. How he'd been a pitcher since he was a toddler, when he used to hurl his pacifier across the room. Or when Javi had his first girlfriend, or the time they all drove down to Corpus Christi and spent a weekend camping on the beach.

By the time the dishes were done and put away, and Mr. Castillo, Javi, and I had worked to fix my bike on the front lawn, it didn't seem like I'd stepped into the Castillo house a few hours ago. It was like I'd known them my whole life.

Chapter 3

WHEN MY alarm went off the next morning, I hopped out of bed and into the shower with far more enthusiasm than I'd had in years. The usual dread with which I greeted each day didn't descend upon me with bone-crushing weight. I even sung in the cramped shower, which was so not like me. I typically got ready in somber silence, as if preparing for a funeral.

And perhaps I was.

I'd been going through the motions for so long, I'd been pretty much dead on the inside anyway. I'd certainly forgotten what hope felt like. But this new outlook kept me light on my toes, and the world around me glowed like a bright summer day.

It felt good to be alive.

"Breakfast's almost ready," my mother called at the bathroom door.

"Okay," I responded with an unusual cheer in my voice. "I'll be right out." No doubt my mother stood on the other side of the door with a puzzled look on her face. My standard answer to breakfast was a sigh, because it meant the school day was about to begin.

Even though the threat of Rance waited for me at BHS, his presence was offset by the knowledge that Javi would be there too. In fact, he'd promised to drop by this morning so we could ride our bikes to school together.

I immediately accepted the offer. It certainly was better than making the almost two mile trek alone and on foot. Sure, I could take the school bus, but I'd suffered enough bloody noses in the back of a bus to cure me of ever getting on one again.

And that was when I remembered my face. I hadn't looked at myself since Mrs. Castillo cleaned me up and put aloe vera salve on my wounds. She'd promised I'd be better in the morning. If she was right, it would spare my mother a lot of pain.

I took a deep breath and gazed at my reflection in the bathroom mirror. A big purple bruise spread across my left cheek, thanks to Rance's fist, and a red skid mark cut an angry path across my forehead courtesy of falling off my bike. But what was far more apparent than the reminders of the pain I'd endured yesterday was the smile that spread across my lips.

Not even seeing my big teeth bothered me.

Today was going to be a good day.

I turned off the cracked bathroom light and headed to the kitchenette, where a plate of scrambled eggs and toast waited for me on the small table we'd owned since I was a kid. It was one of the few pieces of furniture from her marriage to my dad Bart had allowed my mother to keep.

"Good morning," I told my mother, who stood at the tiny sink washing a pan. Her light golden-brown hair, which was the same hue as mine, was pulled back into a ponytail, and she still wore the waitress uniform from her late-night shift at IHOP.

My positive tone made her freeze. Then, she turned slowly around. Most likely trying to verify I was indeed her son. When her chestnut brown eyes fell upon me, she cried out and dropped the pan with a clang. "Oh, Tru," she said as she pulled me into an embrace. Under the hint of maple syrup that clung to her, I could still detect the cherry blossom fragrance of the perfume I'd given her for Christmas last year. "Not again. And on the first day too."

"I'm all right, Mom. I'm fine. I really am."

She stepped out of the hug and studied me from head to toe. I gazed at her with my dad's baby blues, hoping to end her scrutiny. I should've known better. She gestured for me to spin around, so she could get a good look. After I obeyed, she placed her slender hands on her slim hips and locked onto my eyes. It was her standard posture when she wasn't buying what someone was trying to sell her. "Just look at you," she said, as if that alone made her point.

"That's right," I said. "Look at me. Look past the bruises and the cuts."

She averted her gaze. A tear slowly slid down her cheek. "I can't," she said. "Not when my son has been hurt."

I grabbed her hands. When she still refused to look at me, I tugged on them as I used to when I was a kid trying to get her attention. She reluctantly turned her gaze to mine.

"What do you see that's different about me?"

"You mean beyond the obvious signs that my son was tortured again? *Those* weren't there when I sent you off to school yesterday."

She was being difficult, but that wasn't so unusual these days. She'd become a tougher, harder woman since Bart. What other choice did she have?

"And you don't see anything else?" I asked, making my smile as broad and obvious as possible.

She wiped the tears from her vision. "Well, I also see that fake smile of yours. But you're just trying to make me feel better."

"Fake?" I asked. How on earth did she think the smile was fake? My fake smiles stretched flatter and thinner than a pancake. When was the last time she could actually count my teeth?

That realization slowly dawned on her as she truly observed the smile. She dropped her hands from her hips and plopped down at the table. "Okay. Tell me what happened."

And when I opened my mouth, I told her about falling off my bike. But mostly, I talked about Javi.

AFTER I'D finished filling in my mother on yesterday's events, she sat up in her chair. Her droopy, tired shoulders no longer slumped, and a hint of hope glinted in her eyes. "You made a friend?" The question almost brought her back to tears.

"Yes," I answered as I patted the hands that clutched desperately onto mine. I hadn't seen my mother this encouraged about anything in so long. It only verified I'd made the right decision not to tell her about Rance or the boy's locker room.

It just didn't seem important any longer.

"I need you to get me the Castillo's phone number. I must thank them for being there for you yesterday." She surveyed the kitchen. "Maybe I can bake them a cake."

"I thought you wanted to thank them," I said with a grin. "Isn't that more like punishment?"

She looked at me with eyes which were a far richer golden brown than I'd seen in some time. "Well, well. Someone makes one friend, and all of a sudden he's a smarty-pants."

"I am my father's son," I added with a grin. My mother had told me many stories about how much of a tease my father had been. He used to rag her endlessly about her horrid cooking.

A nostalgic grin lit upon her lips. It was the same smile that brightened her face whenever she thought about my father. I hoped to someday find a love like that. "That you are," she finally agreed with a nod.

Someone knocked on the front door.

"It's Javi!" I sprinted out of the kitchen. I was so excited my heart practically burst from my chest, and my feet couldn't get me to the door fast enough. When I finally swung the front door open, Javi stood on the petite front stoop. His long black hair was wet from his morning shower, and it was slicked back instead of dangling in wavy locks across his forehead. Instead of his baseball T-shirt, he wore a green-and-brown-striped collared polo and jeans that clung to his lower half quite nicely. The half grin that seemed to constantly dangle from his lips was still there, though, as bright and entrancing as it had been yesterday.

"Good morning," he said. The half grin grew broader till it stretched across his face. "Glad to see you don't look as awful as you did yesterday."

I stuck out my tongue at him. When was the last time I'd done that? "Yeah, well, skidding on your face does that to a person."

He shrugged. "I wouldn't know. I have the grace of a gazelle."

With anyone else, I'd likely roll my eyes. But Javi was probably right. He seemed just about perfect to me. And to my cock, which had once again awoken.

"So you must be the Javi I've heard so much about."

Flames of embarrassment licked at my cheeks because of my mother's comment. Her presence also immediately deflated my erection. Nothing was better at killing a boner than the sound of Mom's voice. But why did she have to go and say that? She made it sound as if I was some teenager crushing on the high school jock. Which I probably was. But she didn't need to let Javi know that.

"Nice to meet you, Mrs. Cobbler," Javi said without any indication he'd caught on to what my mother had unknowingly revealed. Thank God! He extended his hand to my mom, and they shook.

"I can't thank you and your family enough for taking care of Tru yesterday after he fell from his bike."

"No biggie," he said, waving away her thanks as if it was nothing. And to Javi, it probably was. To me, it meant the world. "I'm always there to help out after someone realizes their face is a poor substitute for their feet." He grinned broadly at me. I'd most likely be teased about this for the rest of my life, and I'd never been happier. But I wasn't going to let Javi in on that.

"Jerk!" I said, pretending anger.

Javi's smile practically extended from ear to ear.

"Well, you're always welcome around here," my mother interjected. "For dinner or a sleepover."

"Mom!" I'd never been more mortified. A sleepover? Really? Had she mistaken me for a ten-year-old girl? I was seventeen, for crying out loud.

"What?" she asked. The look of surprise on her face told me she had no clue what she'd done. Javi, however, did. He was trying hard to suppress his laughter but failing miserably. It was escaping him in measured snorts.

"Okay," she said, raising her hands in surrender. "I've obviously made some parental faux pas, even though I have no clue what I did wrong. I was just trying to say you're always welcome here, Javi."

"Thank you, Mrs. Cobbler," he managed after one final snort. "I appreciate it."

"We better head to school or we're gonna be late." I had to get us out of there before my mother said or did something even more embarrassing.

Javi nodded. "Yeah, you don't want to be late for precalc. Mr. Rodriguez hates tardiness."

I eyed Javi. This from the boy who'd been late most of the week for that class?

"What?" he asked, pretending he had no clue what my expression meant.

I shook my head in reply and unlocked my bike from the front porch rail. "Let's go."

"Forgetting something?" my mother asked.

Oh Lord. Was she really going to make me kiss her in front of Javi?

From the hand she'd just placed on her hip, she obviously was. I dismounted and crossed to her. Thankfully, Javi had suspected what was up and respectfully faced the street on his bike to save me from more awkwardness.

I delivered a quick peck to my mother's cheek and then bounded down the steps back to my bike. "While that was very sweet and much appreciated," she said, "I was referring to this." She held the camera Claudia had given me yesterday. I'd completely forgotten about it, and the picture and quote I was supposed to get from Javi for my first assignment.

"Oh my God!" I exclaimed as I hopped off my bike and let it fall onto the grass. "Claudia would've killed me!"

"You're welcome," she said, handing me the camera. She glanced at Javi with wet eyes. She appeared to be more pleased about me meeting him than I was. "Have a good day."

"Thanks, Mom. You too." I strung the camera over my neck by the strap.

"You working for the paper?" Javi asked as he prepared to mount his bike.

I nodded. "I was actually supposed to get a picture and a quote from you."

Javi looked around. "Where do you want me?"

"Really?" I asked. "Claudia said you were difficult to pin down for photos and quotes."

"I hate doing that stuff," he admitted. "Seems silly to me. I play for a team, yet the newspaper only seems to ever want to talk to me and not the other guys. It's not really fair, if you ask me."

I got off my bike, checked to make sure the camera was ready to shoot, and said, "Well, Claudia says you're the star."

Javi chuffed. "I'm not a star. I'm just me."

And that sounded like the perfect quote to me. "Okay, then," I said as I framed the shot. "You ready?"

"I don't know," he said. "What do you want me to do?"

"Just be you."

Javi thought about that for a minute. If he'd had his dad's moustache, he'd be twirling the edges right now. An idea must have struck because a devilish grin danced across his lips. "Come here," he said.

"What? Why?"

"Do you want a pic or not? And before you answer, don't forget about Claudia. She's a nice girl, but when it comes to the paper, she's a real ballbuster." Grinning sheepishly, he glanced over his shoulder to see my mother still standing by the front door. She shook her head in response to his assessment of Claudia. "Sorry about that, Mrs. Cobbler."

My mother smiled and closed the swollen front door.

I walked over to Javi. "Okay, so what's your big idea for the shot?"

He wrapped his arm around my neck. "Now take it."

My cock snapped to attention. It was obviously ready for its close-up. "You want me in the shot?" I asked, hoping he didn't find a reason to look down. "The write-up is about the team. I'm in no way involved with the team."

"Are we friends?" he asked.

His dark eyes, which reminded me of a clear night sky, locked onto mine and threatened to sweep me away. I swallowed hard and nodded.

"Then you are involved with the team. As my friend."

How could I argue with that? So I turned the camera around, doing my best to make sure Javi and I, minus my erection, were in the shot. "You ready?"

"Just take it already," he said.

So I did.

WE LOCKED our bikes at the rack in front of the school as teachers and other students slowly filled up the parking lot in their cars. Since I'd left all my stuff in my locker before I ran home yesterday, I needed to get my book bag before heading to class. The idea of not being with Javi for even a few minutes caused my skin to crawl.

What would I do if I ran into Rance?

It wasn't like Javi and I had any other class together besides precalc, while Rance and I had practically the same schedule. Maybe I could get Ms. Garcia to do a schedule change. If she wasn't too busy applying lip gloss.

"You coming?" Javi asked as he stood at the top of the steps leading to the front door.

"Sorry. Just thinking."

"About what?"

What could I say? That I was worried Rance would try to attack me again today? Javi still didn't know all the details, but maybe I should tell him. That was the advice Mr. Castillo had practically given me after dinner last night. But my fear of Rance wasn't the whole truth. I craved being around Javi.

"Am I talking to myself or something?"

"I was just wondering why you ride a bike and don't drive a car to school," I lied.

Javi's knitted eyebrows indicated he didn't believe me. What else could I expect? I wasn't exactly good at misdirection. "For one, my parents can't really afford the expense. But the real reason is my dad. He doesn't believe in giving me responsibilities that should be earned. If I want a car, I have to pay for it. And the insurance."

"But how can you do that and play baseball all the time?"

He grinned at me. "And now you know why I ride a bike."

"Tru Cobbler, tell me you haven't disappointed me," Claudia said from a few steps behind us.

She ascended the steps toward us. Today, she wore black denim and a gray T-shirt with Stewie from *Family Guy* on the front. He was dressed in black emo garb with a red streak cutting a swath down his pitch-black hair. A dialogue bubble above his head read "Damn Emo Kids."

"I have not," I proudly announced as I pointed to the camera, which still hung around my neck. "Got both the photo and the quote."

The light of her smile outshone her dreary wardrobe. "I'm pleased to hear that," she said, grinning. But as she drew closer, her smile waned. "What the hell happened to you?"

How many times was I going to be answering that question today? "I fell off my bike."

The suspicion in her eyes couldn't have been more apparent. "And what? Landed on someone's fist?"

"How are you today, Claudia?" Javi asked, holding the door open for her. His question derailed Claudia's inquisitive and distrustful nature, no doubt just as he intended.

She hugged her books to her chest, smothering Stewie, and gazed at Javi with stars in her eyes. Apparently, I wasn't the only one who had a crush on Javi Castillo. "I'm great," she said with a little too much enthusiasm.

As soon as we crossed the threshold, the stench of rotting wood and farts filled my nostrils. Ah, how I'd missed the smell of education! The three of us walked into the hallway, which was already packed with students rushing back and forth. When they saw Javi with us, most of them paused as if they couldn't believe their eyes. How could Javi not notice? If he did, he certainly didn't care. He waved and smiled at everyone as we walked through the sea of disbelief.

"Claudia, would you do me a favor?" Javi asked once we made it to the foot of the stairs that would take me up to my locker.

She practically beamed. "Of course."

"I've got to run and see coach before class. Would you mind escorting my new friend, Tru, to class?"

What the hell? Even though the gesture was appreciated, I didn't need a babysitter. I'd gotten through many days all by myself before meeting Javi. Why would today be any different?

But before I opened my mouth to say something I'd regret, I remembered Mr. Castillo's words from last night. Sometimes a man did need to lean on others. Javi was just trying to be a good friend. After all, he hadn't pushed me for details about the fight yesterday even though he could have. He was just making sure that I'd be trouble-free today.

Still, I couldn't shake the need to resist at least a little bit. "I don't think that's really necessary."

Javi switched his gaze from me to Claudia, who nodded in agreement. "I can do that," she said. "We don't want Tru falling off his bike anymore, do we?"

Javi laughed while I stared blankly at them both.

Claudia hooked her arm in mine and tugged me up the stairs. "Let's get going," she said. "And I want you to tell me about the quote and the photo."

As I ascended the stairs with Claudia, I glanced over my shoulder to see Javi salute me a good-bye before being swept away by a wave of friends who had been waiting for me and Claudia to depart.

SHORTLY AFTER arriving to first period, Claudia marched up to Mr. Rodriguez to announce I'd be sitting next to her from now on. Since there was an open seat to her right, Mr. Rodriguez nodded.

"You didn't have to do that," I said as I moved my stuff to my new seat, but I wasn't very convincing. It was nice to feel as if I had the beginning of a safety net in this school.

"Yeah, well, we aren't dating or anything," she said, trying to be her usual indifferent self. "So don't get any ideas."

I chuckled. "I'll consider myself warned."

"Besides, anyone who can get a quote and pic from Javi Castillo is an investment I intend to keep my eye on."

The noisy entrance of some of our classmates drew my attention to the classroom door. I held my breath. Within the next few minutes, Rance Parker and his twisted scowl would enter and drain all light from my world.

"He'll be late," Claudia said. "He always is."

I turned to face her. "Rance?"

Claudia's face scrunched in disgust. "Oh, God no! I'm talking about Javi," she said. "Not Rancid Puker. I loathe that idiot more than I do misogynists and bigotry. Of course, with Rancid, that's just being redundant."

I laughed so loudly, I drew Mr. Rodriguez's silent disapproval. Rancid Puker? That was perhaps the funniest name I'd ever heard in my life. "Yeah, well, I'm not a big fan either. And the feeling's mutual."

"I thought so," she said with a nod. "Rance is responsible for your face, isn't he?"

Crap! I should have been more careful. Now that I'd been asked a point-blank question, I couldn't lie. "Just don't tell Javi."

"What? Why not?"

"They're best friends."

She stared at me as if I was stupid. "What does that have to do with anything?"

"I just don't want Javi to know. Okay?" The desperation in my voice was apparent. Hopefully, it would be enough to convince Claudia to keep my secret.

The bell rang, announcing class had begun. Two seconds later Javi scrambled into the classroom, his charming half grin plastered on his face.

Mr. Rodriguez shook his head in exasperation and nodded for Javi to take his seat. Javi did but not before saying, "Hey, Tru," in front of the whole class.

My cheeks once again burned as I returned his greeting, and my cock jumped up to say hello too. The entire class did a repeat of their expressions yesterday. They stared at me with mouths agape.

"He's not an idiot, you know," Claudia whispered from her seat. "He'll figure it out."

"Maybe he will," I answered. "But I won't tell him. And I hope you won't either."

She sighed in resignation. "Fine, I won't say anything."

"Thank you."

"But I still think it's stupid," she said.

I could live with that. What I couldn't live with was Javi exiting my life as quickly as he had entered it. It wasn't a chance I was willing to take.

"Where's Mr. Parker?" Mr. Rodriguez asked as he took roll.

"He's in ISS," Rance's girlfriend, Lucy, announced. She narrowed her rich green eyes, which were obviously the result of tinted contacts, at me from where she sat a few rows over. She knew what had happened yesterday, and if Rance had been given in-school suspension for hitting me, then Lucy no doubt held me responsible for it.

But what worried me the most right now was whether or not Javi had seen the blame in her eyes. If he had, then he might put two and two together.

But Javi was as astonished as everyone else. Even the back row Jock Brigade. "What the hell happened?" he asked.

"Please watch your language in my classroom, Mr. Castillo," Mr. Rodriguez said.

"Why don't you ask your friend?" Lucy commented before slowly looking away from me.

"I will," Javi replied. Javi's broad shoulders slumped. Knowing a friend was in trouble evidently greatly affected him. So much so that he missed Lucy's sarcasm.

She hadn't been referring to Rance. She'd been talking about me.

MY DAY without Rance went on without a hitch. I was still ignored by everyone except Javi and Claudia. Although he and I only had first period together, he made it a point to stop and chat with me between classes, which made me feel special. It also deepened my already growing affection for him.

It was a precarious situation. As an awkward outcast, I appreciated how Javi's attention made me less of a pariah. But as a gay boy who'd never had the attention of any other boy before, much less the popular, hot athlete, well, I worried I would be unable to control, much less hide, my emotions.

That, more than Rance tossing me around the locker room like a chew toy, might destroy our newfound friendship.

Whenever Javi turned his lopsided grin my way, or he nudged me after teasing me about proper bike riding, my heart thudded in my chest and beads of sweat broke across my flesh. As for what happened inside my jeans, that was why God made thick history books. Although from the grimace on George Washington's face, which graced the cover of my textbook, he was getting tired of being poked in the eye.

Thankfully, Claudia usually arrived to save me from myself. Like Rance, she was in the majority of my classes, and we walked to each one together. She even ate lunch with me, which was a first. I'd grown so accustomed to gobbling down my food in solitary silence, I'd almost forgotten how to speak.

Around Claudia, though, that didn't matter. She preferred to do the talking rather than the listening, which suited me fine.

We were in sixth period journalism, working on the layout for the Friday edition of the paper, when she switched to an uncomfortable subject.

"So, tell me about you."

I'd rather drink a gallon of bleach than discuss my life. Claudia's persistent gaze, however, indicated she wouldn't be put off. And neither would Stewie. The cartoon character on her shirt regarded me with disdain, as if the next words out of his mouth might be, "Speak, you imbecile. Or die!" I'd either answer her questions, or she and Stewie would find some bleach and empty its contents down my throat for me.

"I'm not really very interesting," I answered, waiting to see if Stewie would leap out of the fabric. "Just your standard high school student exiled to the land of misfit toys."

"Love the Rudolph reference," she said with a click of her tongue. Whenever Claudia really liked something, she made that unusual sound. "But we're not talking about our favorite childhood Christmas specials. We're talking about you."

"I think the adventures of Rudolph and Hermey are far more exciting."

"Is that because you've never fit in?"

She was really going to make me do this, wasn't she? Her raised eyebrow resembled half an arch on a McDonald's sign. "Nope. Never," I finally answered.

"You're not the only one," she added. "When I was a kid, all the other girls obsessed over unicorns and rainbows. Witches, magic, and vampires fascinated me. Probably because my grandmother was a *curandera* in Mexico."

"Really?" I asked. I'd heard about traditional Mexican faith healers, who were revered in the Hispanic culture, but I'd never met anyone who knew one.

She nodded. "She taught me a whole bunch of stuff while she was alive. Like how to ward off the evil eye."

"How do you do that?" I asked, hoping to divert Claudia's attention away from me and onto her grandmother. If I could distract her for another thirty minutes, I'd escape the Claudia Zamora inquisition she was about to launch.

Claudia opened her mouth to answer but said nothing. She drew her lips together in a slant that mimicked Stewie's expression on her shirt. "Nice try," she said. "But I'm far too clever to fall for that."

Well, crap. "I don't know what you mean."

"Like hell you don't," she said before punching my arm.

"Hey, that hurt!" I complained, making a bigger deal of the pain than there was. I grasped my shoulder and scrunched up my face as if I'd eaten a whole bag of lemons.

"Oh, my God," she said in utter exasperation. "You're such a drama queen." Her eyes grew saucer-wide, and she covered her mouth with her hand.

"I'm so sorry," she said.

"Why?"

"For calling you a queen," she said. "That's probably one of the reasons you don't fit in, right? Because you're gay?"

Was it *that* obvious? But since she'd asked me directly, I had nowhere else to go but with the truth. "How'd you know?"

She shrugged as she brushed the black and purple strands from her fair skin. "I have a cousin who's gay. He's a junior in college. He and I have always been super close. More like brother and sister really. And you sort of remind me of him."

"Which I'm assuming is a good thing."

"It's a great thing," she said, beaming. The love she had for her cousin couldn't have been more evident if she'd been holding up a gay pride sign. "Which is probably why I liked you almost instantly. That doesn't happen very often. I usually hate most people because, well, most people suck donkey dick."

I chuckled. I couldn't argue with that. "That they do."

"Do you get bullied about it a lot?" she asked. Her tone had softened to a sympathetic whisper.

"Yeah. And it's not like I tell people. The only ones who know are my mom and grandparents. But it seems like people look at me and immediately see a fairy."

"I don't like derogatory names," she said. "A woman isn't a bitch. A black man isn't the N-word, and gay people are *not* fairies."

What planet had Claudia Zamora come from? Most people insisted on labeling others. "Sorry about that. I didn't mean to offend."

"You shouldn't worry about offending me," she said bluntly. "You should be offended by the name. By calling yourself a fairy, you take on the negative power everyone else gives that word. You should love yourself more than that. That's all."

I nodded. Claudia was right. I did need to love myself. It was difficult to do that, though, when so many people hated you for just being you. "I'll work on that."

"You'd better," she said with another jab to my arm. This time I didn't pretend to be hurt. I took it like a man.

"So is that why you came to Burbank? Because you'd been getting bullied?"

I sighed. "Being bullied" didn't adequately explain what I'd suffered through five high schools and three junior highs. "Yeah. This is my sixth school."

"Fuck!" She gritted her teeth. "That's rough."

"It hasn't been easy," I agreed. "Especially for my mom. It breaks her heart every time she sees me banged up. It's like they're kicking her in the stomach, and every time I see that sadness, I feel like I've failed her. That I should somehow be stronger and beat up the guys who use me for a punching bag. But I'm no match for them. I'm not big or strong. I'm just me."

"Well, I think who you are is pretty damn great so far."

No one besides my family had ever told me that before. "But you don't really know me," I said. "I could be some jerk or a gay who hates breeders."

She gazed deeply into my eyes, searching deep within my soul. When she found what she was looking for, she shook her head. "Nope. You're just as I thought you were."

"And what am I?"

"You're a good guy with a big heart. I can see that as plainly as the scabs on your face. I don't think there's one spiteful bone in your body or that you could hate anyone. Not even Rancid Puker, the worthless fuck."

Although I hated to agree with her, she was right about the last part. I didn't hate Rance, or any of the other bullies who'd made my life hell. I pitied them. To inflict that much pain on someone spoke more about their internal suffering. "Well, some might say that makes me a spineless coward. To quote my stepfather, 'A man stands his ground. He speaks his mind. He doesn't give a fuck about anyone else.'"

Claudia gritted her teeth again. She only did that when she didn't like what she was hearing. "He sounds like an asshole."

"You're being far too kind."

A smile briefly lit up her face. "I don't know if anyone's ever told me that before."

The computer beeped. The photos had finally started to upload on the slow-ass machine. In a few moments, we would see the photos I'd snapped of Javi and me.

"Is your mom still married to your stepdad?" she asked once they were done.

I shook my head. "He's dead. Drove his car into an approaching semi."

"Holy shit!" She crossed herself and said a silent prayer. "Why didn't you tell me I was speaking ill of the dead?"

"I think God will forgive you because I'm pretty sure he's not up there anyway." Not many people knew the details of my life with Bart Cox, so I surprised myself by providing them without being asked. I revealed everything: how Bart used to hit my mother and me when he was drunk, how he'd worked at some accounting firm and embezzled money. He'd even lost most of the more than two hundred grand my mother had received in death benefits from the city when my dad, a police officer, was killed in the line of duty. Then, to get their money back, Bart's company went after all of his assets, and since my mother was married to him, that included everything they'd owned together. My mother was left with nothing besides Bart's debts that she had to work like crazy to pay off. The only possessions we still had were the few items she'd owned when she was married to my real dad, and we had to pinch every penny we had in order to squeak by every month.

"Holy shit!" she exclaimed again when I was done. "And most everyone in this school thinks *they* have it rough."

"We all have it rough. It's just a different kind of rough for everyone."

Claudia stared at me in silence. For probably the first time in her life, someone had made her speechless. That didn't last long. "I've never met anyone like you, Truman Cobbler."

"Likewise," I said with a click of my tongue.

She wrinkled her nose. "Don't make that noise," she said. "It's weird."

I almost burst out laughing. She clearly didn't realize she did the same thing.

I was just about to let Claudia in on the joke, when her confused expression changed to complete shock. If her mouth had hung any lower, she'd be a character in *Family Guy*.

"What's going on?" I asked.

"Holy fuck!" she practically screamed.

I tried to shush her into silence, but she continued cursing and staring over my shoulder. I rushed to the door of the computer lab, where we were working by ourselves, to listen for Mr. Avila's footsteps. If he'd heard her cursing, she'd be in trouble.

"I should have known," she said. "It makes sense. No wonder I liked him so much."

"What are you talking about?" I asked after sticking my head through the doorway. Mr. Avila was not stomping toward us. He sat in his office listening to music while the rest of the staff worked to meet their deadlines.

"I'm such a big dumbass, but I can see it so clearly now."

"Will you tell me what's going on?" I asked as I made my way back to where she was having a meltdown.

"Just look at the pictures," she said gesturing to the images I'd taken that morning.

They were pretty good shots for selfies. In each one, Javi's arm hung around my neck, and seeing the photos brought me back to earlier that morning. I still remembered the warm weight of Javi's arm, and the tingling sensations the contact had caused across my body. It had been as if hundreds of feathers were stroking my skin at exactly the same time. I hadn't wanted the moment to end.

My smile was still all teeth, and I did look like a horse. That would probably never change, but from the angle I'd taken the shots, my nose and ears looked almost normal.

"Do you see it?" she asked, obviously greatly concerned.

"See what?" I looked from one photo to the next. The only thing different was Javi's expression. A shy, hopeful smile had replaced his trademark grin in one of the five.

"So he's not grinning like he does all the time," I answered. "So what?"

"Oh, my God!" she said. She practically pulled her purple-tinged hair out by the roots. "He's not looking at the camera. He's looking at you."

"Take a chill pill, why don't you. It's not like we don't have others." I pointed to the other photos on the screen. In them, Javi looked squarely at the camera with his standard mischievous grin. "We can use one of those. Unless you want to do a reshoot without me in the shot. I can certainly understand that. I didn't want to be in the picture, but Javi insisted."

Claudia took several deep breaths to calm down. Apparently, I wasn't seeing what she was.

"Men *are* oblivious."

"So what am I missing?"

"Javi likes you."

What was so shocking about that? Of course he liked me. Why else would he have said hi to me yesterday or done any of the others things he'd done? "And you find this so shocking you practically turn into a foul-mouthed sailor?"

"You don't understand," she said. "Look at the picture. *Really* look at the picture."

So I did, and I saw everything I did before. Except this time I noticed Javi's eyes. The ones that had locked onto my soul the first time our gazes connected. He looked down upon me with a tender affection I'd only seen once before. In a picture of my parents where my father was looking at my mother.

Suddenly the meaning of the word "like" took on a whole different meaning. But it couldn't be true. Claudia had read more into the expression than there was. Javi didn't like me in *that* way. He wasn't even gay.

Javi probably liked me as much as his lucky gym socks and not one bit more.

EVEN THOUGH Claudia had wanted to discuss the matter further, I saw no reason to. I'd made up my mind she was either delusional or crazy. Telling her so had gone about as well as grabbing a hornet's nest and shaking it like a tambourine.

She'd buzzed in anger before zooming out of the lab, and I hadn't seen her since. Although I hadn't liked upsetting her, I'd stuck to my guns. It was ridiculous to think someone as popular and attractive as Javi would in any way be interested in a pipsqueak outcast like me.

Besides, Javi could pick any girl from the packs of admirers who constantly swarmed about him. And with the way he flirted with them, Javi couldn't be any more of a red-blooded American boy if he tried.

"Will you call me after the game this weekend?" a girl asked Javi.

I turned away from the bike rack, where I'd promised I'd wait for him after school so we could ride home together, and glanced up the front stairs. At the top, Javi was propped against the door, his backpack slung over his left shoulder, as his latest crush leaned into him.

Her name was Leticia, and she sat next to me in economics. Nobody called her Leticia, though. Everyone called her Letty because, according to rumor, Letty let pretty much any boy do whatever he wanted to her.

She was attractive in that slutty, low-class way that appealed to most guys. She wore blouses at least two sizes too small to emphasize her full, round boobs and had gotten in trouble at least twice that week for showing too much cleavage. Far too much makeup clung to her eyelids, cheeks, and lips, and whenever she bent over, which was far more frequently than necessary, her ass crack peeked out to say hello.

If Letty had her way, more than just her butt cleavage would be making their acquaintance with Javi. She was practically molesting him right there on the front steps. She offered up her boobs while flipping her raven hair from side to side. I couldn't help but notice how Javi resembled a rabbit caught in a trap. His eyes frantically darted from side to side as if he was looking for an escape route.

I decided to give him one. "Hurry up, Javi," I called, "or we're gonna be late."

The panic in Javi's eyes floated away when he saw me waiting for him. A grateful smile replaced the wide-eyed panic. "I'll be right there," he called.

I nodded in pretend annoyance as Letty glared at me. If she'd had a knife, I'd be filleted and skewered.

Javi gave Letty a hug, which she leaned her entire body into. I wanted to shove her down the stairs, before he stepped out of it and bounded down the steps.

"You're a lifesaver," he whispered as he made short work of his bike lock. What was that about? Most teenage boys would have tripped over themselves for a chance with such an obviously easy score. But I didn't have time to contemplate because a few seconds later, we were speeding away from school and Letty, who kept yelling for Javi to call her.

For the first few blocks, we rode in silence. Javi breathed deeply and smiled as the wind buffeted his skin and blew through his hair. He resembled a child first learning how to ride more than a high school senior who should probably be driving home in a convertible. Most kids our age would hate being forced to pedal to and from school. Not Javi. His innocent smile indicated how much he was enjoying this.

"No practice today?" I asked when he suddenly noticed me staring at him like Letty had earlier.

He snickered. "Nope. Coach gives us one afternoon off each week. But that's only before the season starts. Then it's practice every damn day. But until then, I intend to take advantage of my freedom."

"What are you gonna do?" I asked after we cut through a particularly busy intersection.

A lopsided grin replaced the innocent smile. "Follow me," he said before veering onto a side street and pumping his bike as fast as his muscled legs would go.

I had to strain to keep up with him. Had Javi forgotten I wasn't a toned athlete like him? After what felt like a mile at top speed, he stopped pedaling and coasted. My lungs had never been more grateful. I was wheezing, and the stitch in my side reminded me of an appendicitis attack I'd had in the third grade.

"Where are you taking me?" I asked through ragged breaths.

Javi answered with a nod of his head.

A few yards in front of us stretched a park about seven neighborhood blocks long. Its rich, lush grass carpeted the entire expanse, and huge, leafy trees reached high into the sky. We rode past a playground where little kids ran through a wooden play jungle or took rides on swings powered by their parents. Directly across from the laughing children were three empty tennis courts, but beyond those two areas, there was nothing but a clear path of green against the concrete backdrop that was inner city San Antonio.

"Wow!"

Javi nodded. "I think so too." He aimed his bike for the biggest elm tree, directly in the center of the park, and dismounted. I joined him, and we let our bikes fall to the grass before sprawling out underneath the branches of the tree. The cool blades brushed against my skin, made warm from the feverish bike ride, and a refreshing breeze whipped around the tree and us.

"It's so peaceful here."

"Yes," Javi said from my right. I had my eyes closed, taking the sweet air into my lungs. "I like to hang out here on my days off practice. Or sometimes just to get away. It's my escape from the real world."

My eyes fluttered open. Was it because he was gay and hiding it like Claudia suspected? Or was I reading more into his words because of Claudia's misguided perception?

Even though I trusted my gut over Claudia's suspicions, I had to ask. "What do you need to escape from?"

"Responsibilities. Expectations." He paused, as if there was something more he wanted to say but found the words too difficult to voice. "Whatever happens to be stressing me out," he finally added.

I sat up and leaned my back against the tree. "And what's stressing you out?"

"What doesn't stress me out?" he asked in reply.

"You're being very vague," I said. "If you don't want to talk about it, I understand. Sometimes I do that too. Talking about things makes them too real."

"Is that why you've never told me about the fight? Or who beat you up?"

Not really. But since it was a partial truth, I'd go with that for now. "Yeah."

"I'd really like to know," Javi said. He kept his eyes closed, thank God. If he'd opened them, I'd have told him everything, and I didn't want that. I'd seen how concerned he was about Rance being in ISS that morning. How could he put his new friend in the middle of such a conflict? It was better to keep what happened between Rance and me from him for now.

"It's not important anymore," I said. "Especially when it's easier to overlook things and move on."

Javi opened his eyes and stared at me. Why did I see hope reflected in his gaze? "And does that work?"

Not really. No matter how many times I tried to avoid a problem, there usually arrived a time when I had to deal with it. Sweeping crap under the rug only lasted so long before you couldn't help but see the huge lump underneath. "I guess not," I finally said.

"Didn't think so" was all he replied before shutting his eyes once again.

His bright features darkened as sadness overcame him. He lay there, trying to float away from the concerns of the world that held him fast to the ground. Javi was so starkly different from the carefree boy I'd met yesterday that I didn't quite understand what had happened in just a few short hours. It was almost as if the Javi everyone else knew, the one who walked around with the lopsided grin that charmed the world, didn't truly exist.

The real Javi was far less confident and walking along a thorny path in the dark.

"Wanna talk about it?" I asked, already knowing the answer.

He sighed. When he opened his eyes, the devil-may-care grin that snaked across his lips was all the answer I needed. "It's just baseball," he said as he sat up. It was obviously only a partial truth. His inability to look me in the eye reminded me of my dear old stepdad. That man could weave a tale most people would buy, but his eyes had been his tell. Javi, it appeared, suffered from the same tick.

"What do you mean?" I asked, deciding it was better to play along than call my new friend a liar.

"I've got tons of pressure to take us to state. If the team can get us there again, a college scout might notice me. And if he does, I've got a free ride to college. Which is something I really want to do. I don't want to be stuck here forever," he said, sweeping his arms around him. Javi was not referring to the beautiful park he'd brought me to. He wanted out of the barrio and to get away from the poverty that clung to its inhabitants like tar.

"That is a lot of pressure," I agreed. "But I'm sure your parents will support anything you end up doing."

Javi glanced at me askance before snuffing. "My parents are the worst!"

Who was he kidding? "You're parents are the best," I said, feeling the need to stick up for two people who had been nothing but nice to me.

"Oh, they are great, but they're the worst at piling on the pressure." He cleared his throat and said in a thick Spanish accent, "You've got to win, mijo. You've got to show them how good you are so they will pay for your school." He was apparently trying to mimic his mother. He cleared his voice again and spoke in his father's deep voice. "You'll be the first Castillo to make something of himself. The first to get out of the neighborhood. And the first to move us all into his mansion when he's a famous athlete."

After he finished mimicking words that clearly haunted him, Javi let loose a lungful of air. What was I supposed to say to that? Javi had a lot riding on his shoulders. No wonder he was stressed out. But what bothered me the most was this didn't seem to be everything that troubled my friend.

"And now Rance is being a dick weed," Javi mumbled.

Was this the true cause of Javi's distress? "What do you mean?"

"Well, you know he's in ISS?" Of course, I knew. I was most likely the reason. I nodded, and he continued. "Well, I tried talking to him after school today. To see what the hell he did to get in trouble this time because Rance is *always* in trouble! It's been that way since I met him in fourth grade."

Since fourth grade? How could I compete with that kind of history?

"And you know what that fucker did?" Javi asked. This time he locked eyes with me. Whatever Javi was about to reveal was the complete truth.

"What?"

"He told me to fuck off and then walked away."

I didn't know what I was expecting, but it certainly wasn't that. "Do you know why?"

Javi shook his head. "Nope, but I'm getting tired of him being such an asshole all the time. He wasn't like that when we were kids. Sure, he got into trouble. But it was little stuff like talking in class all the time or not doing his homework. But ever since he came back from camp last summer, he's been an unbearable prick to just about everyone. Including me."

"What happened at camp?"

"I don't know." Worry crept into his eyes. "I asked him when he got back and was acting all moody and shit, but he played it off. Said he was just tired of being stuck with a bunch of whiny fags for the summer who were crying about their mommies and daddies."

That sounded like the Rance who'd practically torn me apart in the locker room yesterday. "And you didn't believe him?"

"Nope. But he's got a big chip on his shoulder now, and I've gotten tired of dealing with it. And with him." When he looked at me, the light in his eyes returned. As if I was something he'd spent the last few months searching for. "That's why I'm glad I met you."

I almost fell over. "What do you mean?"

"I'm not sure really," he said with a chuckle. "But when I saw you standing there in precalc, I just knew I had to be your friend."

Now that I couldn't believe. Javi seemed to be the most popular guy in school. Not only had Claudia told me how beloved he was by the student body, but I'd seen it firsthand over the course of the last two days. Why would Javi need to be *my* friend? "Don't be pulling my leg," I said. "You've got tons of friends already."

"I do," he said with a nod. "And I count myself lucky. I really do. But fate brings people into your life for a reason. At least that's what I believe."

I'd never believed in that old saying. New people only brought fresh pain. At least that had always been my experience. Still, hearing those words come from Javi gave me faith.

Perhaps, for once, my life had taken a turn for the better.

JAVI AND I sat in the park for hours, enjoying the sunny afternoon and then the cool evening breeze. And in that time, I'd learned a little bit more about Javi Castillo.

When Javi ran for sophomore class president and had to make a speech in front of the entire tenth grade, he'd been so nervous he'd thrown up on stage and all over Ms. Garcia. It took me at least fifteen minutes to stop laughing. I couldn't get the image of Javi blowing chunks all over Ms. Garcia's fake boobs out of my head. Of course, in true Javi fashion, he'd been elected president anyway. He probably could have gotten on stage and farted in the microphone, and still won by a landslide.

Besides being class president at one time, Javi was also a member of the National Honor Society, the drama club, the student council, where he currently served as vice president, and was a school ambassador, which meant he'd been selected by the administration as what an ideal high school student represented. According to Javi, he'd been chosen as an ambassador because it had always been easy for him to make friends. He didn't fall into the social cliques everyone else did.

He preferred being friends with everyone. He didn't care if someone was considered a nerd or unpopular by everyone else. As long as people were kind to him, he'd always do his best to return the favor.

It was hard for me to believe someone like that really existed in the world, but as Javi whistled to the birds in the trees, it was hard to deny the truth when it sat right in front of you.

"Your turn," Javi said as he conversed with a robin perched upon its nest.

I stared up at the bird that chirped back in response. "I can't whistle like you."

Javi picked up a small pebble and threw it at me.

"Hey!" I said as I searched the grass for a retaliatory stone.

"I meant for you to tell me about yourself," Javi said.

My gut wrenched. First Claudia and now Javi. Would this madness never end? "What you see is what you get," I said after I'd selected a stone and tossed it at Javi. He easily ducked and the small rock sailed over his left shoulder.

"All I see right now is someone with piss poor aim."

I gestured to myself with a flourish of hands. "Then you know all about me already."

Javi snatched another pebble from the grass and chunked it at me. It hit me on my shoulder before I had a chance to blink. "Damn it!" I pored through the blades of grass, searching for another projectile. "How do you do that?"

Javi rolled his eyes. "I'm the pitcher for the baseball team," he said matter-of-factly. "A good arm is kind of a requirement."

When I found another small rock, I hurled it as quickly as Javi had, but it went wide and high. Javi watched it fly over his head.

"Damn, you suck at this!" he said with a chuckle. He pegged me again on the other shoulder so quickly I hadn't even seen him select a new weapon. What was weird was that even though rocks were hitting me, the impact never hurt. It was as if Javi instinctively knew at what force to throw the stone to both hit his target and to not cause any pain.

I found two pebbles, but this time I took my time. I held Javi in my sights as I prepared to hurl them at the same time. The cocky little shit sat there grinning at me. He clearly didn't expect me to hit my mark.

I reared back and let them fly, expecting Javi to deflect or dodge them at the last moment. Instead, he sat still as one sailed to his left and the other struck him square in the forehead. He immediately fell backward in the grass.

"Oh, shit!" I scrambled over to where he was sprawled a few yards away. His eyes were closed, but his tongue dangled from the corner of his mouth. He was playing dead. "Asswipe," I said as I gently shoved his shoulder. When I made contact, the electric spark I'd felt yesterday after Javi had shaken my hand once again shot through me in one quick jolt.

Javi opened his eyes and stared up at me. "You should have seen the look on your face when you actually hit me." He laughed as if it was the funniest thing he'd ever seen. I replied by giving him a raspberry. "You were both happy and scared shitless. Talk about priceless."

As he lay there lost in a laughing fit, I couldn't help but notice the tiny red mark the rock had left on his forehead. "Are you sure you're okay?" I asked, and then without thinking, I brushed my fingertips across his tanned, smooth forehead, tracing the edges of the indentation. Javi's flesh was soft, warm, and inviting. I could touch him all day long.

Javi cleared his throat. When I met his eyes, I suddenly realized I'd been caressing him. Shit! How long had I been touching him? Based on the uncomfortable expression on Javi's face, it had been way too long. I immediately withdrew my hand and backed up on my knees. "Sorry," I said, turning my gaze to the ground. How could I look at him ever again? No doubt Javi would get up, hop on his bike, and ride out of my life for good.

"No worries," Javi said as he sat up.

I couldn't believe my ears. I glanced up and was surprised to see his usual slanted grin instead of his face puckered in revulsion. "I was just—"

Javi waved my words away like nothing had happened. "Now that you've hit me, though, you've got to tell me about yourself."

I groaned.

"Come on," he urged. He winced in pretend pain as he rubbed his forehead. "I think I deserve something for being hit in the head with a rock."

After letting out a deep sigh, I retold the sad tale I'd shared with Claudia earlier that day.

"Damn," he said, when I finished speaking. "Your life's been one big crap storm."

"Tell me about it," I said with a nod.

He sat there for a moment in quiet contemplation before a grin broke his stoic expression.

"What's the smile for?"

"I'm just in awe of you," he said.

Well, that was completely unexpected. Usually after telling my story, people stared at me as if I was some dog they'd found beaten to near death on the side of the road. "Why?" I finally asked once the breath returned to my body.

"I've seen lots of kids who've had hard lives." He surveyed the neighborhood as if our surroundings supported his statement. "And I've seen what it's done to them. They turn to drugs or alcohol to escape a parent who whales on them every day. They get arrested for petty thefts because their families don't own shit, or they walk around with a pissed-off look on their faces, just itching for a fight. But you," he said as his smile broadened, "you don't have any of that hardness. It's like all the bad stuff has been unable to change who you are. I think that's pretty neat."

Since I'd grown more accustomed to teasing than compliments, I didn't know how to respond. I sat there with a dopey grin on my face and my cheeks aflame with embarrassment.

"I have to ask you something," Javi said as he lay back in the grass.

I'd lost the ability to form words, so I simply nodded.

"Where'd the name Truman come from?"

This was a story I usually hated telling above all else, so when my usual dread didn't descend, I was surprised. "It's a silly story," I said. "And it's one that usually ends with people pretending to bring up their lunch."

Javi held up his fingers in the Boy Scout salute. "No retching. I promise."

I told him the origin of my name. "My parents were high school sweethearts, and my mom's told me that when she saw my dad walking down the halls in his ROTC uniform, she knew she'd be with him for the rest of her life. She said everyone else in the school vanished and it was like my dad was walking straight for her. And the funny thing about that was, he was. He apparently saw her and made a beeline to ask her out before anyone else did."

At that point in the story, most listeners typically checked out, believing the tale too sweet to be consumed. Javi sat forward, eagerly wanting more. "Go on," he said after a few seconds of silence.

"Well, my parents got married a few months out of high school. Mom worked in an office downtown, and Dad joined the police academy. Shortly after my dad graduated and started patrolling, they found out they were going to have me. When I was born, they said I was their true little man."

Javi grinned. "Ah, so 'true little man' became Truman."

I touched my finger to my nose, letting Javi know he was spot on. But I didn't tell Javi the rest of the story. I wasn't ready to drop any clues about my middle name. The "L" in Truman L. Cobbler would stay hidden from as many people as possible. It was just too much.

"I don't understand the fuss," Javi said. "It's a sweet story about your parents. You should be proud of it."

I knew that, but it was difficult to be proud of something I'd been teased about for as long as I could remember.

"We should probably start heading home," Javi said as he stood up. The sun had disappeared, and the sky had grown dark. "My mother is probably sending out search parties looking for me."

I envied Javi being able to go home to a mother's warm embrace. My mother worked so much, we only saw each other before school. The notion of going home to an empty apartment suddenly made the wonderful tale I'd shared a sad reminder of what I never had the chance to experience—a loving family.

"Want to come for dinner?" Javi asked as he swung his leg over his bike.

"Hell, yeah," I answered immediately. If I'd been any more excited, I'd have squealed like a little girl. How embarrassing! "As long as you don't think your parents will mind."

Javi laughed. "Are you serious? My mother lives for feeding people. Her motto is 'the more, the merrier.'"

So I hopped on my bike and followed Javi to his house, where his mother greeted me with open arms and a kiss on my forehead. We sat down to dinner after Mr. Castillo got home from work, and we each took turns talking about our day. Afterward, I rode back to my empty apartment, but the memories of the food and conversation filled both my stomach and my heart.

For the second night of my life, I drifted off to sleep without fear or loneliness crouching at the edge of my bed.

Chapter 4

THE NEXT couple of months were the best of my life. Javi and I rode our bikes to school every day, and while he had practice in the afternoon, I did my homework in the library or worked in the journalism room until he was done. Then we'd ride home together, sometimes stopping in the park or at the local drugstore to buy some candy and a Coke before riding to Javi's house.

Mr. and Mrs. Castillo never made me feel as if I was an imposition. Every time they saw me, I was greeted with hugs and kisses by Mrs. Castillo and a pat on the back by Mr. Castillo. They eagerly embraced me as well as my friendship with their son.

Mr. Castillo even said he'd never seen Javi smile so much. Mrs. Castillo agreed, saying I wasn't a troublemaker like Rance. Even though she twisted her face when she mentioned Rance's name, Javi, like the true friend he was, came to Rance's defense. He cited problems at home as the cause for Rance's shitty attitude and some internal conflict he refused to share, but his parents either didn't buy it or didn't care. They simply shrugged off Javi's comments.

It took a few days, but Claudia eventually forgave me for saying she was crazy for thinking Javi liked me, even though she still tried to convince me Javi's interest in me was more than just friendship. Whenever she poked my side and pointed at his wide grin as he approached us, or cited the fact that we constantly hung out after school together, I shook my head. Javi and I were friends, and that was all we would be.

And it didn't upset me at all.

Sure, I was still crazy attracted to him and jerked off daily in the shower while thinking about his devilish smile. Or the way we sometimes brushed against each other. Or that time he'd worn his baseball uniform. It would be foolish to deny how Javi set my heart and groin on fire.

But that was my damage to deal with. What mattered most was having Javi in my life however he was meant to be.

"What's up, Tru?"

I turned in the direction of the unfamiliar voice. It was Selina Perez from my English class. She hung with the popular crew. Other less popular kids had taken to greeting me in the halls the past few weeks, which had been pretty damn strange, but now that someone like Selina was acknowledging me, I didn't know how to act. She smiled and waved at me as she approached with a group of her gal pals, who also greeted me. They wore almost the same style of denim, low rise and bejeweled along the rear pockets, and the same shade of pink blouse. The only real difference was that Selina's hair hung loose and long, while the other girls had their hair in ponytails.

"See you later, Tru," they said in unison.

Had someone else named Tru transferred to this school? I glanced over my shoulder to check. Instead of finding a strange boy I'd never seen before, I locked eyes with Ruben Lopez, who sat across from me in physics and was rummaging through his locker. Although he wasn't one of the cool kids, he wasn't one of the outcasts either. He nodded hello.

What the hell was going on? I nodded back and then mumbled a reply to Selina, who smiled before leading her pack down the hall to class.

"Hey, Tru," someone else said. This time it was Destiny Villarreal from precalc. She bounded toward me in her cheerleader outfit. "Did you finish all the homework for Mr. Rodriguez?"

"Um, yeah," I stuttered. "Why?"

"Because I've not gotten a single good grade in his class all week. This imaginary number shit is kicking my ass."

"It's tough," I agreed, not knowing what else to say.

"Well, I see you sometimes studying in the library after school. If I need help with whatever hell he has for us next week, can I stop by after cheer practice?"

Had I awoken in the *Twilight Zone* this morning? "Uh, sure."

"Thanks," she answered with a smile before walking away. "See you in class."

"Uh-huh," I said as her ponytailed head bobbed down the hall.

"There you are, dumbass."

It was Claudia, but I feared if I turned around, she'd be wearing a rainbow shirt with a unicorn prancing across the front. Everyone else had gone crazy. Why not her too?

"Oh, don't pretend you don't hear me," she grumbled from behind me. At least she still sounded like the Claudia I'd seen at school yesterday. When I slowly turned to her, no glittering sparkles or flying unicorns pranced across her black T-shirt. It was a zombie, reaching out for his next victim. The white block print next to the rotting corpse face said, "All my friends are undead." I was glad some things didn't change, like the scowl on Claudia's face.

"Thank God," I said in relief. "You're still you."

"Who else would I be?" she asked, staring at me through narrowed eyes. "Did you fall off your bike into Rance's fist again?"

She grinned broadly at me while I stuck out my tongue. I had initially worried about the fallout once Rance was released from his in-school holding pen, but since returning, he'd made every effort to keep our paths from crossing. His eyes still shot daggers at me, and I had no doubt if we met in a dark alley, I'd never make it out alive, but Coach Moore had threatened to kick him off the team if he was caught fighting on campus one more time.

That had been incentive enough for Rance to back off a bit.

But it was more than just Rance. Even the Jock Brigade hadn't been giving me trouble. They hadn't suddenly become BFFs or anything. It was like some unseen cease-fire had been magically declared. Maybe it was because of Javi, or maybe it was because Rance wasn't there to egg them on. Whatever it was, I was glad for the reprieve.

But now that people I passed in the hall were actually acknowledging me, I found the sudden recognition far too bizarre.

"Well, look who's Mr. Popular all of a sudden," Claudia said. She walked on my right toward precalc with a smug look on her face. Did she know something I didn't?

"What's going on?" I asked as I smiled at another "Hey, Tru" that floated down the hall. This time it was Enrique Fuentes, the senior class president, from history class.

"Are you kidding me right now?" she asked.

I glanced at Claudia, who practically huffed in derision.

"If you know what's going on, I wish you'd tell me."

She blew a strand of purplish-black hair out of her eyes as she reached into the big, clunky black bag she carried with her everywhere. "You're like the worst journalist ever!" she said when she pulled out the school paper.

I still had no clue. I'd seen the paper. I did work for *The Harvest* now, so it wasn't like I hadn't already seen the mockup. "What's the paper got to do with anything?"

When Claudia handed it to me, I glanced down at the picture I'd taken of Javi and me my first week of school. Claudia had decided not to use it for the article she ran back then. That had been a story on the new team returning to state. Now that we were spotlighting individual players with each new issue, she used one of the shots of me and Javi, where he looked at the camera instead of at me.

But in this shot, Javi's arm was draped around my shoulder, and silly smiles were plastered on our faces. The story I'd written about Javi had made the front page. Was that all it took to get noticed around here?

"This still doesn't make sense." I folded up the paper and tucked it under my arm. "So what if I wrote the lead story?"

Claudia sighed loudly. Her disappointment in me clearly knew no bounds. "It's not the article, you dumbass. It's the photo."

"What about it?" I asked as I unfolded the newspaper for another glance. There didn't seem to be any reason others would find the picture so special. I sure as hell did. In fact, I'd hung in my bedroom the one where Javi was staring at me. Why did anyone else care?

"That photo," she said, as she poked our faces on the paper, "basically announces to the entire school that you two are friends. And when you're practically best buds with the most popular guy in school, well, others tend to take notice."

Best buds? Is that what everyone now thought, and was that why I was no longer the pariah?

When we entered precalc, my classmates, who were already in their seats, didn't grimace and turn away. Some smiled begrudgingly while others went out of their way to say hello as I passed.

I was thankful I made it to my seat without passing out. This sudden change was freaking me out. I had experience with scorn and derision. I could deal with that. But to suddenly be someone after a long stretch of being no one set my head spinning.

IT WAS one of the craziest days I'd ever had at school. In each class, students who'd been ignoring me since day one were asking me questions about homework or my weekend as if we'd gone to middle school together. Even at lunch, Claudia and I had to contend with people asking to join us at the bench in the quad that had been exclusively ours the past few months.

Lunch had turned into musical chairs with new people constantly filling up the vacant spots. I'd never been more exhausted in my life.

Claudia hadn't been pleased with the sudden introduction of new people. As a fellow outcast, she detested most of the classmates who talked to us. Probably because they were primarily conversing with me and excluding her.

"That was such a good article you wrote," Alison Gutierrez said. She was one of the really popular girls, who counted Rance's girlfriend, Lucy, as one of her best friends. And like most of the popular girls, Alison wore too much makeup to try and look older and blonde highlights in her hair. It was as much a uniform as a cheer skirt or a baseball jersey.

Alison purposely fanned open the paper in front of Claudia's face. Only my reassuring hand on hers kept Claudia from tearing it from Alison's grasp and leaping across the table. "You really got me excited about baseball season. When does it start again?"

I gently moved the paper out of Claudia's way before responding. "I don't remember. I'm not good at dates, but Claudia here has everything memorized." I refused to play high school politics. Claudia was my friend, and I wasn't going to exclude her from any conversation. The slight flicker of the hate-fueled inferno that burned in her gaze revealed Claudia appreciated the gesture, but she was only a few seconds away from turning into the girl in Stephen King's *Firestarter*. "Do you remember?" I asked, hoping to delay the body count.

"March 2," Claudia said through gritted teeth.

"That sucks," Stephanie Gonzales said, jutting out her lower lip. Not as popular or as thin as Alison or Lucy, Stephanie was a lackey who did as she was told. That was why she was allowed to hang with the cool crowd. She had yet to be given permission to be a cool girl clone. Stephanie's makeup was more moderate, and her dark hair was highlight free. "That's too long to wait."

"Well, baseball *is* a spring game," Claudia said in a tone that bit deeper than the hungry zombie on her shirt.

"Tell me something I don't know," Alison replied. Her red lips gathered into a smirk.

"How much time do you have?" Claudia asked.

Stephanie glanced down at her watch. "Not too long. Lunch ends in about ten minutes."

Alison glared at Stephanie, who clearly had no idea what she'd just done. Claudia, however, howled in laughter.

"What's so funny?" someone asked behind us. I didn't need to turn around to know who it was. Only one person on this planet was capable of making me feel like a helium-filled balloon.

"Javi!" Stephanie said. She grinned broadly like an idiot. She was obviously yet another girl who longed to sample Javi's offerings. I couldn't help but feel somewhat territorial. As if Javi belonged only to me and I should gouge out her eyes with the plastic spoon she ate her yogurt with.

"Let's take a selfie!" Alison said as she stood. She crossed to Javi and wrapped her arms around his waist as she held her phone above them at a slight angle. She puckered her lips into a duck bill. Why was this look so popular with girls my age? It made them look silly, not sexy and sophisticated. "Facebook!" Alison announced as she headed back to her seat to upload the pic.

Javi squeezed in between Claudia and me on the bench. When his thigh rested against mine, I about rocketed to the moon.

"What are you doing here?" I asked. Javi ate during second lunch and was supposed to be in his English class right now.

"Bathroom break," he replied. His trademark grin hitched up his lips.

"I think you took a wrong turn somewhere," I said, nudging him. He leaned into me and laughed, and instead of pulling away, the entire right side of his body remained in contact with mine. Forget the moon, I was on my way out of the solar system.

"So what's with Claudia?" he asked eyeing her suspiciously. She was still in the middle of her hyena routine, and Alison, who'd finished posting the picture to all her social media sites, had death in her eyes.

"Nothing," Alison replied dryly.

Her response made Claudia almost laugh herself off the bench.

"You're weird, you know that?" Javi asked before chuckling at Claudia.

"You have no idea," Alison added with a nod. "Claudia Zamora is a freaky devil-worshipping, emo loser with more scars on her wrists than friends."

My hackles rose. I'd never been one to stand up to others, mostly because I was usually the one being made fun of. But Alison's comment about my friend turned the rocket I'd been flying on thanks to Javi's warm touch into a missile.

And that missile headed straight for Alison Gutierrez.

"If Claudia really worshipped the devil," I told Alison, "she'd be bowing before you, wouldn't she?"

Stephanie gasped in horror, and Claudia's laughter died almost instantaneously. Alison's only reply was to cross her hands on the wooden tabletop and glare at me with arched eyebrows.

Javi's sudden chuckling caught all our attention. "That was priceless," he said as he wrapped his arm around my neck. He hadn't done that since I'd taken the now famous photo. "Tru has some good comebacks and always cracks me up."

What the hell was he talking about?

"It was pretty good," Stephanie added with a nod. Her shock had been replaced by amusement.

Alison didn't buy it. The slant of her eyebrows revealed she had no trouble discerning between a true insult and a playful jab. But Javi's protective presence kept her poison at bay. "I'll give you that one, Tru," she said with a hesitant smile. "But everyone only gets one."

I understood the warning. If I crossed Alison again in any way, she'd find some way to cut me off at the knees. Being friends with Javi apparently only went so far.

"What are you up to this weekend?" Javi asked. He no doubt desired a subject change.

"What else but party at Heather's tomorrow night?" Stephanie answered. Heather Barnes was one of the richer students at Burbank. Her parents had a two-story house with a pool. I'd overheard Heather talking about her big house in economics class earlier in the week.

He nodded as if he'd forgotten about the gathering. "What time does it start?"

"Ten o'clock," Alison answered. "You coming?"

Javi turned to me. "Are we?"

I not only became speechless but turned deaf too. After all, I couldn't have heard Javi correctly. There was no way he was inviting me to a party filled with jocks and popular kids.

"You should come," Alison said with a nod. This time she was looking at me. Not Javi. "Everyone will be there."

Why did it suddenly feel as if someone had walked all over my grave? I couldn't stop shaking.

"What do you say?" he asked. He switched his gaze from me to Claudia and then back to me again. "We should all go."

"I don't think so," Claudia answered with a snort. "Not my scene."

Alison's quick sideways glance at Claudia seemed to be her way of saying, "no shit."

"Come on, Tru!" Javi pleaded. He wrapped his arm around my neck and drew me closer against him. His lips hovered mere inches from mine. His hot breath fanned across my ear and neck as he whispered, "It'll be fun. I promise."

There was no way I could turn down that offer. "Okay."

Claudia warily glanced at me over Javi's shoulder. She no doubt believed I was an idiot. And as I stared into Alison's beaming face, I couldn't help but feel she might be right.

AFTER SCHOOL ended for the week, Javi and I made our customary stop under the elm tree in the park and then rode our bikes over to his house. His mother was at the store picking up groceries, so Javi threw his book bag on the couch, grabbed his pitcher's mitt and baseball, which always sat on the sofa table, and led me outside to the backyard.

"I'm not any good at this," I complained as I followed him out the back door and fumbled the spare mitt off the kitchen table where I'd left it yesterday.

He didn't bother responding. No matter how many times I protested a rousing game of catch, which usually ended up with Javi chasing the stray balls I threw and me not catching whatever he hurled at me, he refused to hear anything other than "let's play ball."

"Ready?" He stood about twenty feet deep into the backyard. Did I have any other choice?

"I'm not so sure about this party anymore," I said, hoping a serious discussion might derail Javi's one-track, baseball-loving mind.

He scrunched up his face as he tossed the ball in the air and caught it in his glove. "Heather's party? Why?"

"I won't know anyone there."

He scoffed. "You'll know me. Who else is there to know?" He flashed his smile at me. Normally that would get me to do anything, but after the way Alison had grinned at me when lunch ended, I had serious doubts.

My gut told me Heather's party was a disaster waiting to happen.

"I don't think I'd fit in."

"Oh, please," he said. "From what I've heard and seen, you've been making new friends left and right."

Yeah, right. They weren't friends. Everyone who'd talked to me today had only done that because of my picture with Javi in the paper. They were trying to impress the hot, popular baseball star with the fact that they were cozying up to his freakish new friend.

After all, Javi stood at the top of the popular pyramid, and everyone knew he didn't do cliques. If he liked someone, they followed suit. It was the name of the high school game.

"I'm not ready," I said as I hesitantly put on the baseball glove.

"What does that mean? It's not like I'm asking you to go bungee jumping."

That was exactly what he was asking me to do. Except I doubted the safety harness would keep me from crashing into the jagged rocks below. "I've never had friends. Or been invited to parties. I don't know how to act or what to do."

"That's easy," he said, waving my concerns away. Sometimes that got pretty annoying. Just because he didn't see the problem didn't mean there wasn't one. "Just be yourself. I like you for who you are. Even if you can't ride a bike or catch a ball worth a damn. You have to give others the same chance. After all, how do you expect to make friends if you don't get out there and meet people?"

Now he sounded like my mother. She told me the same thing every time she dropped me off at a new school. How often had that worked? Like never.

"So you're going, and that's final." He gave me one firm nod to indicate the discussion was over. Most people might interpret his resolve as cockiness, but there was no nastiness in his intentions. He believed going to the party was a good thing, and I had enjoyed all the time we'd spent together this week.

Perhaps he was right. Maybe I was overthinking things and letting my fear lead me around by the nose. It was a difficult emotion to release when it had kept me relatively safe for so many years.

"Are you ready to play now?" he asked. If he were a racehorse, he'd be itching to get out of the gate.

When I nodded, Javi smiled and tossed the first pitch, which bounced off my mitt and rolled away from me.

"Keep your eyes on the ball," he instructed. "From the time it leaves my hand till it reaches you."

I was getting annoyed. What did he think I was doing? "Yeah, yeah," I said, standing with the ball in my hand. "You sound like a broken record."

Javi ignored my whining. "Follow the ball into the glove and create a pocket," he said, demonstrating once again how to properly catch the ball. "Then bring your other hand to the glove to keep the ball in place."

I answered with a wild throw that went to his far left. Instead of mumbling about my ineptitude, Javi smiled and chased after it. "We'll get you there yet," he said with complete faith.

Of course, he had self-confidence in his abilities. Besides baseball, he enjoyed most sports and watched pretty much every televised event except boxing. I had never watched a single one. "I don't like this," I announced for the umpteenth time. Javi wasn't the only broken record around here.

"Why not?" he asked.

"I'm not good at sports," I said as I gestured to what we were doing. He tossed the ball at me again, this time underhand. I tried to mimic Javi's actions, but the ball hit the edge of the glove and fell away. "And since I've never learned how to play, I used to always get teased in gym class. When you get basketballs thrown in your face or tackled by your own team in football, you really start hating everything involved with sports."

Javi nodded. "I guess I can see that. I've always played because my parents love sports. Watching them together is a family event with popcorn, hot dogs, barbeque, and soda. My mom is our personal concession stand."

The faraway look in Javi's eyes told me he'd been transported to fond memories. I had no such events to recall. The only sports recollections I had were of Bart telling me to shut the fuck up because the game was on. "That sounds fun," I said. "And delicious."

He laughed at my comment as I threw the ball again. This time it stopped short. Javi attempted to catch it, but it met the dirt before his glove could get under it. "It is." He snatched the ball from the ground. I could tell by the twinkle in his eyes he'd just gotten an idea. "You should totally go with my parents to our preseason game in a few weeks. They'll show you what it means to be a fan. Plus, you'll get to see me play."

The notion of Javi running around in tight baseball pants instantly filled my thoughts and caused a boner to crowd the confines of my briefs. I had to crouch like a catcher to readjust myself and hide my excitement. "That might be fun," I said. But I wasn't sold on the idea, no matter how hot he might look in his uniform. I really didn't enjoy spending weekends with classmates like Alison and Stephanie, who typically went to every game.

"Might?" he asked. He couldn't have been any more offended if I'd slapped him. He spanned the distance that separated us and glowered playfully down at me. "You doubt how fun it would be to see me play?" His lopsided grin grew into a full taunt.

"Oh, shut it," I said before scooping up some dirt and throwing it at him. I was amazed I actually hit my mark. That was a first.

"You did *not* just do that," Javi said, wiping dirt from his eyes.

I puffed up my small chest with pride. "I sure did."

"Do that again, and you'll be sorrier than when you face-planted off your bike."

The slant to his lips was his way of double-dog daring me.

So I did.

Before I knew it, Javi sprang from where he stood and crashed into me. I landed on my back with a thud as Javi grabbed my wrists. He pinned my arms to my side and hovered over me, his handsome face mere inches from mine. On the air between us wafted an intoxicating mixture of sweat and the sandalwood cologne he wore every day. After a few seconds, his lips parted in a big grin.

"What are you gonna do now?" he asked. His legs straddled my chest while his butt rested on my stomach. His body over me, on top of me, sent electric currents shooting across my flesh. It was as if Javi was the lightning, and I was the lightning rod. I had never been so alive.

If he hadn't been holding me down, I'd have reached up and brought him all the way to me until his warm mocha cheeks rested against my pale flesh, until the musk of his body filled my lungs, and until his skin brushed my trembling, hungry lips.

Every part of me had been awakened and needed more.

Then I realized the danger.

His rear end sat just a few inches from the raging erection in my jeans. If he turned around or adjusted his position even the slightest, he'd brush up against my hard-on, and that would most likely be the last I'd ever see of Javi Castillo.

"Get off!" I complained as I writhed under Javi's grasp. I arched my back, trying to buck him off. Javi held fast. He leaned closer to me, his hot breath pluming across my skin. I had to bite my lip hard, hoping the pain might keep my dick from popping out of the waistband.

"Not on your life," Javi teased.

When he sat back on my groin, his eyes grew wide, and he released my hands.

"I'm sorry," I said as I scrambled out from underneath him. If I could have willed myself to die, I would have expired on the spot. I couldn't look at Javi as he kneeled on the ground, open-mouthed. Practically having a cock shoved up your butt could do that to a guy.

Especially if he was a straight jock like Javi.

I tore the glove from my hand and sprinted to the back door. I had to get out of here. I couldn't watch the friendship I'd come to cherish self-destruct because I couldn't control my hormones.

I'd ruined the best thing that had ever happened to me, and I'd never forgive myself.

When I flung open the back door to the kitchen, I was surprised to see Mrs. Castillo standing there. She'd been gazing out into the backyard and jumped when I suddenly entered. "I'm sorry, Mrs. Castillo," I said as I rushed past her. "I've got to get home."

She said nothing. Her gaze never left the window.

"I'VE RUINED everything!" I said as I crashed onto my bed in my closet-sized bedroom. I buried my head in the pillow, trying to suffocate myself in order to end my suffering.

How the hell could I have been so stupid? I'd known from the very beginning I needed to control myself around Javi, but I'd gotten too comfortable. I'd let the ease of our friendship tear down my natural defenses, and instead of being on guard all the time, I'd allowed my lust to get the best of me.

And now I'd lost my best friend.

"I'm such a fuckup!"

"Are you done?" Claudia asked. She sat on the edge of my twin bed. After I'd gotten home, I'd called her in a panic. She'd been unable to interpret my ranting over the phone, so she'd driven over to see what was going on.

"No," I said, my voice muffled by the pillow. I punched the mattress twice before screaming at the top of my lungs.

"How about now?" she asked. Although I couldn't see her, I pictured her staring at me with that usual arch to her eyebrows. She always did that when anyone tested the limits of her patience.

I looked at her. Instead of the perturbed expression that usually twisted her features, she stared at me with an almost motherly affection. As if she wished she could chase all my demons away. "Maybe," I replied, turning on my side.

"So why don't you tell me what's going on?" she asked. "When you left school, you and Javi looked like you were kings of the world. Laughing while you rode away on your bikes."

"You saw that?"

She patted my leg. "That's the way you two look every day after school. Like kids off to the candy store."

That was about the way I felt. Being with Javi was sweeter than all the chocolate at Willy Wonka's factory. It gave me a natural high I'd never experienced before.

"So I assume your current state has something to do with him?" She sat cross-legged at the foot of my bed, no doubt preparing herself for a long story. "Did you have a fight? Or did you finally tell him about Rancid beating you up on the first day of school?"

"It was nothing like that," I said. I sat up and mimicked her posture, looking her straight in the eye. If I was going to recount the embarrassing details, I couldn't hide from them. I had to tell them like a man.

When I was done, Claudia sat in silence. She closed her eyes as she typically did when she was trying to solve a math problem or imagining how a layout for the paper should be fixed. Usually when she was done, she had an answer.

Was it too silly for me to hope she could fix my problem as easily as she had others?

"Okay," she said, once she opened her eyes. "I really don't think you're as screwed as you think you are."

I opened my mouth to protest, but she held up her hand. She wasn't done, and she wasn't about to be interrupted. I nodded and zipped my lips.

"Let's start with what we know about Javi. He's not someone who rejects others for stupid reasons." She eyed me when my lips almost unzipped. When I placed a hand over my mouth, she continued. "Yes, you popped a woody, which was pretty stupid, but you're a boy. You guys can't control your cocks to save your life. Javi, as a boy, realizes this. He's not going to reject you for a biological reaction that was beyond your control. I've known him for a long time. Since grade school. And he's pretty much the same sweet boy who helped me cover up the fact that I peed in the sandbox in second grade."

I snickered at the image of Claudia sitting in sand-soaked urine. Her glare informed me I'd better hush, or I'd have bigger problems than Javi on my hands.

"So, we know that he doesn't abandon his friends or judge them harshly," she continued. "Hell, look at Rancid, for God's sake! He's been friends with that shit stain for longer than I care to remember. If anyone deserves to get bounced from his life, it's Rance. But that's not Javi. He sees the best in people. Don't you think so?"

How could I argue with that? He'd befriended me within seconds of meeting me. "You're right," I said. "He's a good guy."

"A great guy," Claudia added with a vigorous nod. "And a guy who's as into you as you are into him."

I groaned. Not this again. "How many times do I have to tell you? Javi's not gay, and he's not interested in me."

"Oh, he's gay," Claudia said. She stood and walked over to inspect the picture of us I'd pinned to my wall. Javi's luscious, dark chocolate eyes stared down at me with tender affection. I sometimes felt bad beating off to the photo every night. It was so sweet and innocent, and I violated it nightly, using the image and the memories it evoked to bring me to mind-blowing release. "He just doesn't know it yet."

"Are you kidding me? That's the most ridiculous thing I've ever heard."

"Not everyone's like you, Tru. No matter how screwed up you may think your life is, you actually have your head on pretty straight. You know who you are. That's pretty big for kids our age. Most of us are trying to figure out where we stand in the world and where we want to go. But you have most of those answers already."

Claudia oversimplified me a bit. We'd discussed life after graduation, and while Claudia didn't know what she wanted to do when she grew up, I had always wanted to follow in my father's footsteps. I wanted to be a cop, to protect the city as he had. And give my life for it, if need be. But I'd come to grips with the fact I'd likely never pass the physical. So I'd decided to become a lawyer. I might not get to catch the bad guys, but I could put them away. And I'd defend the little guys from the big, bad wolves in the world. "What does any of that have to do with Javi?"

"He's been searching for something for quite some time," she said as she studied the picture of us. "Sure, he has tons of friends. But he's never really gotten close with any of them. He embraces all of us, but he also keeps us all at arm's length. I think that's why so many people are drawn to him. They want to be the first to get past that invisible barrier, but most of us just smack against it. Over and over again." She turned from the picture, her flesh made pale by her long black hair. "I don't know if you've noticed it or not, but that silly grin of his is the same no matter what he's doing. Playing baseball, talking to a teacher, or just sitting with friends. It's the same damn smile for every person and every occasion."

Now *that* I had noticed.

"You're the first person I've seen get a different reaction. Something greater than the grin he presents to the rest of the world. It's like when he looks at you, he's looking at what he's been searching for. And, to be honest, I don't think he's realized he's found it."

She sat on my bed, waiting for me to respond. But what she'd just told me made me speechless. Could she be right?

It was a question I pondered long after Claudia left and well into the night before exhaustion took control, and I drifted off to sleep, where I dreamed of being in Javi's arms.

Chapter 5

SATURDAY, THE early-morning light reached into my room and embraced me. I tried to shake it off, to burrow within the warm comfort of my blankets. I'd been dreaming of Javi, and the two of us were lying on the bed in his room, watching TV. I rested my head on his smooth, muscular chest, listening to the even rhythm of his heartbeat, while his strong arms held me close.

The light aroma of musk and cedar that made up Javi's scent filled the air, and I buried my nose in his shirt and inhaled deeply. I wanted nothing more than to have his scent on my body and in my lungs every moment of every day.

He hooked his thumb and forefingers under my chin and moved my gaze up to his. The full smile on his lips couldn't outshine his big, radiant brown eyes. Whenever he looked at me that way, I couldn't help but feel as if I was the most important person in the world.

He craned forward, inching his lips closer to mine as he pulled me closer, drawing me deeper into his embrace. I clutched his shirt, digging my fingers into the fabric.

The moment I'd waited for had finally arrived. Our first kiss.

As the distance between us grew shorter and shorter, his hot breath spread across my blistery cheeks. I reached up with my left hand, wrapping my arm around his neck to bring our lips to where they desperately longed to be.

But before we could kiss, the sun's light intruded upon my fantasy, slipping through the cracks in the homemade curtains and shining on my face until it pulled me out of Javi's embrace and left me alone on my empty bed.

Fuck!

I shut my eyes tight, fighting to return to where I belonged. But no matter how hard I tried to force my consciousness back to the haven it had just left, it refused to budge.

I was here, and I wasn't going back.

But that didn't mean I couldn't do other things.

I kicked the blankets off and tugged the underwear from my body. My hard cock slapped against my smooth stomach. Beads of clear precum spilled from the slit and slid down the red swollen head. I collected the liquid on my fingertips and coated the head of my cock and shaft with the slick fluid.

I fluttered my fingers along the length of my dick, imagining it was Javi's hands that were causing my cock to twitch. When I reached the base, I gripped it hard and slid all the way up to the head, where I teased more precum from the weeping slit before gliding down to the base once again.

I continued this motion and then switched my gaze from my hardness to the picture of Javi and me. I pumped my cock into my hand as I recalled the warmth of his touch, and the hint of soap and aftershave that radiated from his freshly bathed skin.

In my mind, I trailed my tongue across his lightly tanned cheeks, over the small freckle to the left of his strong chin, and up to the lips I longed to savor.

His tongue darted inside my mouth. Its warm wetness invading as he shoved me backward on my bed. He ravaged my lips while he tore the clothes from my body. Once I was naked, his fingers enclosed my cock, jacking me closer to the edge I wasn't ready to fall from.

Sensing my release, he let my cock fall from his strong grasp, nibbling a fiery path to my full balls. He sucked one, then the other into his mouth before raising my legs up and over my head. I gasped as his tongue found my center, licking crazy circles around the rim. It pushed past the opening, parting my flesh and swirling inside me before withdrawing again.

For a few seconds he'd leave my twitching hole to suck my cock down his throat, bobbing on it while gazing up at me with those beautiful black-brown eyes. He wiggled those big, bushy eyebrows at me, knowing how crazy he was making me before releasing my cock and once again tonguing my ass.

I clutched the bed, thrashing onto his tongue. I wouldn't be satisfied until every inch of him rested inside me. Javi knew what I wanted. He gripped my hips and forced me harder and faster onto his tongue, which swirled and twisted inside me.

"Oh, Javi," I mumbled.

He suddenly stopped. He wiped the spit from his lips and positioned himself between my open legs. Sometime between sucking me off and eating me out, he'd taken off his clothes. I whimpered at the sight of his naked body over mine.

His smooth, flawless, light brown skin resembled creamy peanut butter, and I followed every curve of flesh and dip of muscle down to his hard cock. It rested amid a thatch of black hair that fanned down to his upper thighs and dusted a small trail to his belly button.

I'd never seen anything more beautiful.

He nodded at me, wanting to know if I was ready. I gripped my cock at the base and grinned in reply. When he slid effortless inside me, I held my breath. My body had never been filled so full before, and I cherished the sensation. His cock pushed in and out of my ass as I palmed my cock.

I was close to coming already. Javi was too.

His eyes turned glassy, and his mouth hung open in silent pleasure.

I ground my hips onto his cock and fisted my shaft furiously. Within moments, he screamed as his cock pulsed inside me. When I shot my load across my chest, I almost passed out.

"Tru, is everything okay in there?" my mother asked with a knock at my unlocked bedroom door. "I'm hearing some strange noises."

Holy shit! I took my fingers out of my ass, grabbed my sheets with my cum-slick hands, and quickly ducked under the covers. "Yeah," I answered, trying my best to hide the mortified tremor in my breathy voice. "Just a bad dream."

"Okay," she said. Her footsteps proceeded hesitantly down the hall. "I'll make you breakfast when you're ready."

I didn't answer. I was completely out of breath, not only from the terrifying prospect of my mother walking in while I was violating myself but also from the mind-blowing orgasm that had just racked me.

I'd jerked off to various fantasies about Javi before today, but this was the first time I'd ever entertained the idea of him fucking me. Or stuck my fingers up my ass.

It seemed the conversation with Claudia yesterday had had some rippling effects. Not only had I started to think she might be right, but now I was imagining not just giving my heart to Javi, but my body as well.

AFTER I showered and got dressed, I walked into the kitchenette, where my mother had already prepared what she dubbed her Saturday Special: scrambled eggs and two slices of fried Spam sandwiched between two heavily buttered pieces of toast. On the plate next to the two breakfast sandwiches were four pieces of crispy bacon. A tall glass of orange juice stood off to the right.

I loved Saturday. It was the one day each week we were allowed to splurge on food. With money being so tight because of that turd Bart, we normally ate much smaller portions. Mom only bought groceries once a month, so we had to make them last.

"Smells great," I told her as I sat down.

Mom smiled at me from the kitchen counter, where she was assembling her sandwich. Instead of already being suited up in her IHOP uniform, preparing to tackle the double shift she usually picked up each weekend, she wore gray slacks and a white button-down blouse. I'd never seen that outfit before. Where was she going? "Not working today?" I asked.

"Actually, I am," she replied with a smug smile. Her eyes radiated with a hope I hadn't seen in a long time. And it showed in more than just her clothes or her smile. It could be seen in the way she wore her hair.

I'd long believed my mother's hair was her best physical trait, the symbol of her prettiness and femininity. But for as long as I could recall, she either had it gathered in a ponytail for her waitressing jobs or tucked underneath one of my dad's baseball caps she liked to wear around the apartment. Both made her look far too masculine for a woman with her slim shape and delicate features.

But today, her long brown hair had been freed from its prison. It cascaded down her small shoulders in a gentle wave of golden brown. She was stunning.

"You look beautiful," I told her as I crunched bacon.

She crossed over to me, plate in hand, and kissed the top of my head. "And you are a sweetheart."

I nodded as she sat to my left. "Can't help it. I was born that way. Now, would you mind telling me where you're going?"

Her face lit up. She had big news. "I got a new job. I'm going to be working weekends at a doctor's office downtown that's also a twenty-four-hour minor emergency clinic," she said. "It's nothing fancy. Just part-time secretarial work. Filing. Answering phones."

"That's great," I said after taking the first delicious bite of my sandwich. I was in salt and butter heaven. "Sure beats being on your feet for sixteen hours."

"That's for sure. And serving rude customers who don't tip well or men who think it's okay to get grabby."

I looked up from my sandwich. This was the first I'd heard of such inappropriate behavior. I choked down the bite I had just taken before asking, "Who's grabbing you?"

"Don't worry about it," she said with a shake of her head. She then took a big bite of her breakfast, clearly using the food in her mouth to avoid answering my question.

"I'm not pleased," I admitted with a scowl. "No one should be touching you."

She nodded as she swallowed. "But the good thing about this office job is that it has the potential to turn into full-time work. With benefits. Then I can say good-bye to waitressing for good. And I can work normal nine-to-five hours. We could actually spend time at home together, and the weekends would just be for us. No double shifts and no late hours." She practically bubbled with excitement. "What do you think?"

"I think any job where my mother isn't grabbed is a plus."

She rolled her eyes and swatted at me. "There is a down side, though," she admitted with a sigh. "Until this office job becomes full time, I have to prove myself on the weekends. That means no double shifts at the restaurants."

And that meant less money coming in. The weekends produced most of the tips Mom used to keep us afloat. Things were lean already. Now they'd be outright meager. But I'd do whatever I needed to give Mom the support she always gave me. "Whatever you need, Mom," I said. "I'll do it. I can even get a job like I've always wanted. Okay?"

The scowl on her face gave me my answer. She'd been adamant I not work. It was her job to provide for me, and it was mine to get good grades. Education, according to Mom, was my only way out of the life she'd led. Although she never regretted marrying my father so young, she did lament not going to college. If she had, she would be better able to provide for me now. "We've had this discussion already," she said. "And I won't have it again."

I nodded. It was useless to argue. When Grace Cobbler made up her mind, there was no changing it. "Fine." I finished one sandwich and started on the other. As I bit into the bread, though, the expression on her face changed. It shifted from excitement about her new job to motherly concern. I'd seen it enough to read it amid the worry lines on her forehead. "What's on your mind?"

"You know me too well," she admitted with a smile and a sigh. "I've been thinking about something, and I've wanted to talk to you about it for a while now. I just haven't known how to bring it up without making you upset."

Conversations that started out that way rarely went well. But if talking about it eased my mother's mind, I was game. "Do it like a Band-Aid," I said. Mom chuckled. That had been one of Dad's favorite sayings.

"It's about your new friend Javi."

I stopped midchew. What bad could she possibly have to say about him? "I don't understand," I said after I swallowed.

She thought about her words as she bit another piece from her sandwich. Whatever she had to say had to be big. Otherwise she'd just voice what was on her mind. Right now, she was treating me with kid gloves. "I'm worried about your relationship with him." She put her sandwich on her plate and grabbed my hands. This was her standard gesture when she wanted me to really consider her words. "I see how you react when he shows up in the morning. And you've been spending a lot of time together."

"And?"

"You like him," she said with a smile. "I can tell. It's all over your face every time you look at him or speak his name. You light up and can't stop talking."

I still didn't understand where she was going. She already knew I was gay. "Okay, so what's the problem?"

"I just don't want to see your heart get broken. Or anything else for that matter."

Had she found out what happened yesterday? "Javi won't hurt me," I said. Whether he continued to be my friend or not remained to be seen, but no matter where he and I went from here, I'd never have anything to fear from Javi Castillo.

"I'm not saying he would," she said with a smile. "But you know better than most how mean kids can be. You already get teased enough because people think you're gay. What's going to happen if they see how big a crush you have on Javi? What would they do to you then?" Her eyes turned wet just thinking of the possibilities.

I rose from my chair and hugged her. It was difficult to be the parent of a child others constantly ridiculed and beat up on. It made her feel helpless. I had to do what I could to give her hope. "I'm gonna be fine, Mom," I said as I held her tightly. "Don't worry about me."

"I do," she sniffled into my shirt. "You have a picture of the two of you in your room. I've seen it. I know he means a lot to you, and I certainly understand why. He's a good-looking kid, who's been more than decent to you. But I want you to be careful, Tru." She looked at me and gripped my forearms. "Please promise me that."

What else could I do? I couldn't tell her what happened between us yesterday. She'd only worry more. So I gave her what she needed. "I promise."

I felt awful. I hadn't told her the truth, and I'd just gotten away with a lie for the first time in my life.

Claudia had given me hope Javi might return my feelings, and after what happened in my room earlier, I'd already made up my mind to find out whether or not she was right. That wasn't exactly being careful.

I was putting everything on the line, but Javi Castillo was worth it and so much more.

AFTER MOM left for work, I called Javi's house three times that morning and twice in the afternoon. Each time his mother answered and told me he wasn't home. An unusual tension caused Mrs. Castillo's voice to quaver each time. Was she lying? Had Javi given her instructions to tell me he wasn't home?

By three o'clock, I couldn't take it anymore. If our friendship was over, I had to hear it straight from Javi. So I rode my bike to his house.

When I knocked on the door, Mr. Castillo answered. His tanned face broadened into a big smile as he swung the door open. At least someone in the house was happy to see me. "Tru!" he said as he stepped aside to let me in. "I was surprised you didn't stay for dinner last night. What happened?"

How was I supposed to answer that? I couldn't very well tell him the truth. No matter how kind Mr. Castillo was, learning his son sat had on my boner would likely reduce his kind smile to a disgusted sneer. "I had tons of homework to get finished if I wanted to go to the party tonight." The lie flew out of my mouth before I knew what I was going to say. It seemed that once you'd lied successfully, each one after that proved much easier to tell.

"Oh, yes," he said with a nod. "Heather's party. Javi went on and on about it last night. It was all he talked about."

Probably because he didn't want the conversation to turn to why I wasn't there. "That's the one," I said. I gave him an innocent smile. God, I was getting good at putting on a false front. "Is Javi home? I wanted to talk about the party tonight."

He shook his head. "He hopped on his bike earlier this morning, and I haven't seen him since," he said. So he hadn't been home when I called. That eased my worries somewhat.

But what was Javi avoiding? What happened yesterday or whatever feelings Claudia believed he may have for me?

"You want to wait for him?" Mr. Castillo asked. "I was just about to turn on the game. You can sit and watch with me."

No. I couldn't ambush Javi in his own home. That would accomplish nothing. It was better if we talked someplace else. "That's okay," I said as I turned toward the front door. "I've got some more homework to do before tonight. I'll just catch up with him later."

"Suit yourself. It gonna be a good game. The Cowboys versus the Chargers." His face scrunched up. "I hate the Chargers."

I shook my head and exited the house. "You enjoy," I said before riding away.

I wasn't going home. I was going to find Javi, and I had a pretty good idea where he'd gone.

AFTER A fifteen-minute bike ride, I arrived at the park. The first time Javi brought me to North Park, he admitted he came here whenever he needed to escape, when his problems or his life stressed him out. What could be more stressful to a boy, who may or may not be questioning his sexuality, than to suddenly find his ass resting atop his friend's boner?

The comforting shade of his favorite tree and the tweets of his feathery friends gave him the center he needed to cope. Even if the air had grown colder as south Texas approached its version of winter, he'd be there. I just knew it.

When I zoomed past the playground and the tennis courts, a smile spread across my face. Javi was hunched underneath the protective arms of our elm tree.

Well, technically, it was *Javi's* tree. But after all the time we'd shared there, I couldn't help but claim a small patch of grass under the majestic green canopy.

As I drew closer, I fought my rising panic. A thin sheen of sweat coated my palms, which often slipped from the handlebars, and a crushing weight pushed against my chest. It was as if some invisible bear had wrapped its arms around me and squeezed tight.

But I refused to give in. Fear wasn't going to win.

I had no clue what was going to happen between Javi and me, but I was done going through life with my head down and my tail tucked between my legs. For too long, I'd had nothing to fight for, but I did now.

Whether Javi returned my affections or not didn't matter.

What mattered the most was being with him. In whatever relationship we managed to carve out after yesterday.

That was definitely worth fighting for. So I bounded the curb and wheeled across the grass, stopping a few feet away from the tree. The clanking of my bike chain and the skidding of my tires announced my arrival, but he didn't look my way. He kept his attention focused on the bird above and the whistle on his lips.

I dropped my bike and joined him under the tree, propping my back right next to his against the trunk.

I listened as he let fly a string of ten consecutive cheery notes that rose and fell in pitch but were delivered in a steady rhythm. He paused a few seconds before repeating the entire sequence again. A robin flew down and hopped on the dry grass before us. It turned its head sideways, giving us the once over, before repeating the exact same call Javi had just produced.

For about a minute, the two of them carried on a secret conversation. Were they talking about me? It sure seemed that way, especially when the robin glanced at me for a few seconds before once again singing to Javi.

The robin chirped one final shortened response before taking to the sky and flying away.

"I knew you'd find me," Javi said once the bird had disappeared from sight.

I nodded. "Wasn't too hard to figure out where you might be."

"Not for you," he said as he plucked a wide blade of grass and wrapped it around his finger. "You're the only one who knows about this place."

"I'm honored." My nerves were getting the best of me. My feet refused to stop their uneasy twitching, so I drew my legs to my chest and wrapped my arms around them. Although it wasn't terribly cold, a chill cut through my bones.

"So I guess you're gay, huh?" It wasn't really a question since Javi no doubt already knew the answer. It was his way of starting the conversation we had to have.

"Yeah," I answered.

Javi began rolling the grass he plucked into a ball. "And I guess you're what? Attracted to me?"

Did he really need me to say it? Hadn't my boner already established that? I let loose a long sigh. Once I admitted it, there'd be no taking it back. "I think you know the answer to that."

He nodded. "I guess I just need to hear you say it."

"Why?" I looked at him for the first time. He was wearing faded blue jeans, and a long sleeve red and white jersey. Funnily enough, written across the chest in black letters was "Just Relax. I've got it all under control."

Hopefully, that was true, but I just couldn't tell. Since I'd met Javi, reading him had been relatively easy. His eyes reflected what was going on inside him. But when I gazed into the deep, dark chocolaty pools I still longed to wade into, I had trouble making out what I saw.

The light that perennially twinkled from within like starlight had dimmed as if some unseen turmoil churned the waters deep below.

"Don't really know why," he admitted with a shrug before averting his eyes.

"All right, then. Yes, I am attracted to you." He opened his mouth to respond, but before he said whatever he was going to say, I had to clarify. "I don't want you to think I've only been hanging out with you because of how I feel. There's been no ulterior motive. I haven't been hoping to get you alone so I could jump your bones or anything. And I'm not on some recruiting drive to increase the ranks of gay boys in this area, just so you know. You've been a good friend, and you were there for me when I really needed someone. And you didn't do it out of pity, or because anyone asked you to befriend the new loser at school. You were nice to me because that's the kind of guy you are. And I appreciate that more than I can ever tell you. So, if I've ruined our friendship or made it so you aren't comfortable around me, I'm so sorry for that. I'd never do anything to hurt you. I hope you can believe that."

"I do," he said, and I believed him. "I just have some questions I'd like to ask you."

"Okay." I moved so I no longer sat next to him. I repositioned myself so we gazed at each other eye-to-eye as we'd always done. If he was comfortable enough to talk about it, I deserved to make him feel as if anything he asked would be answered truthfully and without reservation. "Go for it."

"How long have you known?" he asked.

"That I was attracted to you or that I was gay?"

His lopsided grin teased across his lips. "Well, I assume you were attracted to me the moment you met me," he said. The spark in his eye relit, forcing the inner storm to briefly retreat.

"You're such an ass," I said with a roll of my eyes.

"Which I'm sure you think is pretty hot too," he added with a proud jut of his chin.

And just like that, the Javi I'd come to know had returned from whatever darkness had threatened to sweep him away.

I stared blankly at him. "Do you want me to answer your question or not?"

He tapped his chin in thought. "Sure," he finally said with a nod. "We can address the hotness that is my ass later."

I held up the first three fingers of my right hand in a "W."

"Don't 'whatever' me," he said with a grin. "The hotness of my ass is a well-documented fact."

That was the truth, but I wasn't about to admit it. We had just settled back into the ease of our previous relationship prior to the great boner fiasco. I wasn't about to ruin that now. "In answer to your question," I began. "I think I've always known deep down I was attracted to other boys. I guess it's the same way you or other straight guys know you're attracted to other girls. It's just a part of you. It's not really something you question."

"Have you ever been with another guy?"

"I've never had a boyfriend, if that's what you're asking," I said. "I have kissed a boy before, but that was in the second grade."

Javi's eyes grew wide. "Second grade? What a fucking slut!" he said with a laugh. "In second grade, I was clueless about sex."

"I didn't have sex in second grade," I replied. "I said I kissed a boy in the second grade."

"How does something like that happen?"

"How does anything like that ever happen?" I questioned. "It's not like those kinds of things are planned."

"Not true," he said. He sat forward, leaning into the space between us. It was as if this story was meant for my ears alone. "I kissed my first girl in sixth grade. Her name was Dina, and she was in seventh. Dina would follow me everywhere. I knew she liked me. I just wasn't quite sure if I liked her or not. It wasn't like she was gross or anything. Well, she was a little annoying. But she was a girl. I was a boy. And I thought, well, let's see how this goes. So one day after school, I took her out to the music building, which was basically a portable building out back, and I pushed her against the wall and kissed her."

"And?"

He shrugged. "It wasn't bad. It felt kinda weird, having someone else's spit on my lips. And then she slipped me the tongue. I had no fucking clue what that was. I thought I'd swallowed her tooth or something." I busted out laughing. I could picture Javi backing away and trying to fish Dina's tooth out of his mouth. He didn't find my reaction quite so humorous. "It wasn't funny. I was seriously grossed out. I made her smile real big to make sure she still had all her teeth."

"Oh, my God!" I howled. "That's priceless."

"Yeah, well, I'm glad you think so." He grimaced. "After that, she wanted to make out all the time, but I avoided her. I wasn't able to kiss a girl again until the following year."

I wiped the tears from my eyes. "That's the best story I've ever heard. Do I have your permission to put it in the paper?"

Javi fake sneered at me. "Do that, and I'll string you up the flagpole."

"It might just be worth it," I said with a big grin.

He nudged his foot against mine and said, "Now tell me about your first kiss."

After that story, my reluctance to share fell away. Javi knew exactly how to put me at ease. "His name was Carl, and we were at recess in the gym one rainy day. We were playing vampire with the girls."

"Vampire?" He wiggled his eyebrows suggestively.

"It's this stupid game one of the girls made up to have the boys chase them around. Think of it like tag but with pretend biting of the neck." When he nodded in understanding, I continued. "So, anyway, we were chasing the girls, and we cornered one of them—I think her name was Gloria—under the bleachers. Somehow, she fit through this tiny crack and got out, which left Carl and me under the bleachers together. A strange look flashed across his eyes, and I just knew that for whatever reason, he wanted to start chasing me now. So I ran out and headed to the boy's restroom."

"What is it with gay guys and public restrooms?" he asked.

"It's in the manual," I deadpanned. Javi snorted and motioned for me to continue. "Carl followed me into the restroom, and this weird game of cat and mouse began. He chased me into the corner and leaned into me. My body tingled. You know the way it does when you're getting on a rollercoaster for the first time? It's something you want to really do but you're terrified of at the same time."

Javi nodded before he swallowed hard.

"Well, that was the way I felt, and I didn't want it to end. So I ran out of the restroom, and Carl chased me around the gym. We did a lap around the building before heading back to the restroom. We did that like four times before I finally ran farther into the restroom. The look in Carl's eyes changed. Like it was time for the chase to end. So he strutted over to me, put his hands on either side of the wall where I was leaning, and went in for the kiss."

"And?" Javi asked, leaning even closer as if my story was the most riveting he'd ever heard.

"And we kissed," I said. "It was a pretty good kiss. Like I'd finally been given the answer to some problem I never knew I had. I don't know how long we were there, but we somehow wound up on the floor with Carl on top of me."

"See," he said, once again nudging my foot with his. "Slut!"

I shook my head in exasperation and continued, "But then some of the boys from our class ran in."

"Oh, fuck!" Javi said, sitting straight up. "What happened?"

"I don't really remember, to be honest." It was the truth. The rest of second grade was a blur. "I only remember Carl leaving our school a few weeks later. Shortly after that was when the teasing and bullying began."

"Shit," he said as he rubbed my knee. As soon as he touched my bare skin, I tensed, and my cock sprang to life. If Javi wanted me to stop sporting wood around him, he'd have to learn to stop touching me. "That sucks, man. I'm sorry."

He withdrew, and I said, "It is what it is."

"And you've never had a boyfriend?"

I laughed, and he squinted at me. He no doubt had no clue what I found so funny. "No one came within ten feet of me after that. I've been pretty much alone ever since. And when you have to move every few months because you keep getting your ass knocked around, it's tough to build relationships. Most people don't really want to be friends with the faggot loser."

Javi took exception to my comment. His face twisted into a frown. "Don't talk like that," he said. "You're not a faggot or a loser. Don't let anyone ever make you feel that way."

"Claudia's told me basically the same thing."

"So Claudia knows?" he asked. This bit of information intrigued him for some reason.

"Yeah, she pretty much guessed it the moment she saw me." I wasn't about to let him in on who else Claudia thought might like to kiss boys.

"I'm glad she's cool with it." He leaned back on his hands in the grass. "It's important for someone who's been as alone as you obviously have been to have friends."

Even though I hoped I knew the answer already, I still had to ask. Like Javi had said earlier, there were some things we just needed to hear. "And what about us? Are we friends?"

Javi snorted as if I was the stupidest person he'd ever met. "Of course we are," he said. His half grin grew to a full smile.

"I'm glad," I said. "I was worried that when—" I stopped, not wanting to say the words and have him relive the incident. "Well, you know. That you might not want anything to do with me."

Javi stared off into the sky for a few moments as he searched the clouds and the sunny, yet cool day for the appropriate response. "I won't lie," he said. "It took me by surprise."

I could only imagine. But he seemed to be handling everything wonderfully now. What had changed? Or had he just needed time to process?

Chapter 6

BY THE time ten o'clock rolled around, I'd become a nervous wreck. I'd never gone to a party in my life. I didn't know how to dress for one or what to do when I got there. Luckily, I'd convinced Claudia to help me get dressed. If she hadn't agreed, I don't know what I would have done.

"Are you sure I look all right?" I studied myself in the full-length mirror in my mother's bedroom.

Both my mother and Claudia sighed. I'd already asked them both like ten times.

"You look great," my mother said. I could still see the apprehension in her eyes. Shortly after she'd gotten home from her new job, I asked her if I could go. She had immediately said no. Thankfully, Javi, who'd been there when I asked, promised he'd stay by my side every minute. Only then had she begrudgingly relented.

She still wasn't pleased about Heather's party. Worry lines crinkled her forehead. She feared I might run into trouble with some bully intent on hurting me outside school. And I couldn't exactly tell her she had nothing to fret about.

It concerned me too.

But Javi was my friend, and he'd asked me to go. After what happened yesterday and then our discussion in the park today, I couldn't tell him no.

"I just don't know," I said as I studied my outfit in the mirror.

"Oh, my God!" Claudia said in frustration. "I razored holes in your jeans to make them more stylish. Not to mention I loaned you my favorite black tee."

She didn't need to remind me I was wearing a girl's T-shirt. I hated that it fit my petite body so perfectly. At least it didn't have zombies or emo Stewie on it. It was a plain black shirt. Even if it hadn't been, what choice did I have? My clothes came from resale shops and were at least five years out of fashion. Most were baggy and worn thin. If I showed up to a party in my usual outfits, I'd be torn to pieces on my appearance alone. And I couldn't have that happen. Not when I was trying to impress Javi and some of his friends.

"We just need to fix your hair," Claudia said. She grabbed me by the wrist and led me to the bathroom. When had she laid out all these products? Tubes of hair gel and pomade littered the sink. A ginormous can of hairspray sat on the lip of the bathtub. Spraying that thing likely opened up a hole in the ozone layer capable of making the entire human race extinct. She'd even brought a hair dryer and a flat iron. Just what the hell did she plan to do to me?

"Is all this really necessary?" I asked.

She stared blankly at me in the mirror. "Tru, I love you to pieces, but for a gay boy, you have absolutely zero sense of style and your inability to sculpt your hair to perfection leaves me rather speechless."

I couldn't argue with her. Since my days usually consisted of just trying to survive, I never cared much for my appearance. Whatever I wore usually got covered in mud or blood. Sometimes both. And it wasn't like we could afford nice clothes anyway. I had to make do with the little I had. As for my hair, well, why spend time on it? I'd likely get my entire head shoved into a toilet anyway.

But the wild mess of tangled straw belonged on an eight-year-old, not on someone who'd soon be eighteen.

"All right," I said. "Make me over."

"I STILL can't believe I let the two of you talk me into this," Claudia griped as she drove us to Heather's house. She'd had no intention of going to the party. She'd intended on dressing me up like a life-sized

Ken doll and then heading home. Javi had asked her to take me. He planned on meeting us there after he finished with some baseball function he had to attend, some dinner with the Booster Club.

And naturally, since Javi had asked her, she agreed to do it.

But now I was paying the price. She hadn't quit complaining about hanging out with the "popular pricks" since we'd driven away from my place. After a few blocks, though, I'd stopped listening.

I couldn't stop staring at myself in the vanity mirror of Claudia's mother's Ford Escape.

My hair usually hung about my face like a shag carpet, but she'd manage to tame the unruly locks. Instead of a disorganized mess, a side part cut diagonally across my scalp from the center of my head all the way to my right temple. The hair on the right side of the part had been combed down and fanned over my big-ass ears and then gelled into place. She'd brushed wisps of hair forward about three inches above my cheekbone.

The hair on the left side of the part took more time. She had plugged in both the hair dryer and the flat iron and styled the hair forward so it hung over my forehead with stray strands hanging in front of my eyes.

"You need to stop staring at yourself, or I'm gonna have to slap you."

I turned my gaze from my reflection to Claudia's amused eyes. Her tone might have been abrasive, but the joy in her eyes gave her away. She appreciated how much I liked the miracle she had worked. "I just can't get over how different I look."

She snorted. "Tell me about it. I never noticed how blue your eyes are. But your blond hair dangling in front of your face draws attention to your eyes." She switched her attention back to the road. "You look great."

"Only because of you."

"That's right," she added with a chuff.

Claudia didn't look so bad herself. She usually wore her dark hair straight and parted in the middle like Morticia from *The Addams Family*. Tonight, though, she'd parted it to the left before straightening it. Then, she'd blown it wild so it had an intentional flyaway look. It was as if she'd spent part of the day in a convertible driving along the beach.

She still wore her signature color, but a black scoop-neck blouse with sequins had replaced her oversized emo tees. A pretty decent body hid under all that fabric. And stylish black denim clung to her lower half. "You're pretty smoking yourself," I said.

"Thanks." Her red lips parted into a surprisingly un-Claudia-like grin.

"Why don't you always dress this way?"

"Why don't you always dress *that* way?"

Fair enough. "I've never known how to dress, and I've never really cared."

"And now?" she asked, taking her eyes momentarily off the road.

I chuckled as I gazed at my reflection in the mirror. "Well, I might care a little bit more now. But you obviously know how to spruce up. Why don't you do it more often?"

She frowned. "Jesus, Tru. Are you saying I usually look like a piece of shit or something?"

"Not at all." I had to find the parachute, or I'd go splat in five seconds flat. "I think you look great however you dress. I was just wondering why you don't glam yourself up more. I get teased for how I look and how I dress. But there's not much I can do about it. My clothes are second- or thirdhand at best because that's all my mom can afford. As for my hair, well, I certainly never knew how to do what you just did. I'm still not entirely sure I can duplicate it, but I'm gonna try. But if you know how to make yourself look as smoking hot as you do now, it makes me believe you work hard to not fit in. That you dress the part of the outcast intentionally. And I just want to know why."

"You think I look smoking hot?" she asked. She glanced at herself in the rearview mirror and grinned.

I glared at her. "Is that all you heard me say?"

"Pretty much," she said with a nod.

"You need to answer me, or I'm gonna have to slap you," I said, repeating her threat.

"Well, well," she said. Why did she sound so impressed? "Give the gay boy a makeover, and all of a sudden he finds his balls."

I didn't dignify her comment with a reply. Instead, I turned my nose up in the air in righteous indignation.

"All right, no need to throw a bitch fit," she said in complete exasperation. "I look at it this way, Tru. Why do I want to fit in with shallow little shits like Heather, Lucy, or Alison? They're so busy following each other and the latest trends they couldn't identify their own asshole if they were squatting over a mirror and staring at it. They rely on others to tell them how to be, what to think, and how to look. I don't live that way. And I sure as hell don't want to be confused with people who do. So, yeah, I know how to dress up. I do it a lot. When I'm going out with my cousins or friends from out of town. But at school? Hell, no. I don't want friends who only like me for the way I look. I want true friends, who love me no matter what. The vain bitches don't give me a second glance. They walk past me as if I'm nothing. And that's okay. But the true friends, the people who are worth my time, see who I really am. Those people are my friends. And for them I'd do almost anything." She turned to look at me. "Like dress in this getup and go to a party with a bunch of popular pricks."

"I love you, Claudia Zamora."

"Oh, God," she said after a quick exhalation. "Now you're gonna get all sappy on me. I don't do sappy."

"Whether you do sappy or not, I love you. And now I know you love me too."

"If you don't shut up, I'm gonna kick you out of this car."

"You love me," I sang at the top of my voice and continued to sing those same three words.

She laughed. "You're such a dumbass."

"Maybe," I said. "But I'm your dumbass."

"On that point, I won't argue." She stopped the car in front of a two-story white stucco house where music blared out the open front door. Parked cars lined the street, and dozens of kids from school ambled up the sidewalk. Others talked and drank from red Solo cups on the porch or the second-story balcony.

The uncurtained windows revealed a packed living room with more of my classmates, and each one of them held a red cup. They swayed to music that sounded like nothing but bass, and every now and then a roar of laughter escaped the flashing interior. Somewhere inside, a strobe light turned the house into a dance club.

"You still want to go through with this?" Claudia asked.

I nodded. Terror had stolen my words.

She parked the car along a side street and shut off the engine. "Then let's do this," she said as she grabbed my hand.

IF CLAUDIA hadn't been holding my hand as we walked inside Heather's house, I likely would have run out the front door screaming. The lights inside were off and strobe lights had been positioned throughout the living room; they cast creepy white flashes across the interior landscape.

Was this a party or a haunted house?

To make matters worse, the strange lighting made it virtually impossible to identify who stood a few a feet from the front door. Those standing in the cone of light cast from the hall lighting were clearly having a good time. A group ate what looked like brisket and mashed potatoes from huge foil serving dishes. They were intent on devouring every morsel, and the sweet smoky scent that lingered in the air told me their hunger was pot induced.

Past the stoners and along the adjacent wall stood couples that were far more intent on devouring each other than the food, alcohol, or drugs that surrounded them. How many babies would be conceived here tonight?

What unsettled my nerves the most though was the blaring music. It was as if every single person inside had a hearing problem.

I was edgy enough without all the overstimulation, especially considering the odd stares Claudia and I drew from those closest to us. The potheads stopped eating long enough to gawk, and even some of the soon-to-be parents interrupted their tonsil jockeying to take a gander.

"High school," Claudia whispered into my ear. "It's the time of our lives."

"Yeah, right," I mumbled in reply.

"You made it!" Alison's overly excited voice screamed from somewhere in the dark. Before I could locate her, Alison stood in front of us with Stephanie in tow. Alison wore a red strapless dress and had on far too much makeup.

Stephanie had on a far more conservative outfit that fit her fuller figure. She wore tan jeans and a white blouse with beige polka dots scattered along the front. A light blue denim jacket with the sleeves rolled up to her elbows hung open, exposing just enough of the shirt and her frame to give the illusion of a trim body.

She beat Alison hands down as the prettier of the two.

"Selfie!" she screamed. Suddenly, Alison was at my side, her arm around my shoulders, and her phone held high. Before I could smile, she took the photo after she cocked her head to the right and turned her lips into a duck's bill. From the huge smile on her face, she was pleased with how she looked in the shot. A few seconds later, the picture was uploaded to Facebook.

When she was done, she gazed at me. Her dilated pupils and inability to stand up straight told me she was drunk. "I'm so glad you decided to come." She grabbed me and delivered a hug that was mostly her falling into me and me propping her up.

I clutched Claudia for support. If I hadn't, Alison's constant swaying would have brought us to the floor. "Me too." Apparently, I was on a lying streak.

When Alison finally released me from her embrace, she gave me the once over. "And look at you. What a difference the right clothes and styling make. I barely recognized you."

"Thanks," I said, doing my best to ignore the backhanded compliment. "It's all Claudia's doing."

She turned her attention to Claudia and arched her eyebrow. It was difficult to tell whose appearance shocked her more. Mine or Claudia's.

"That's okay," Claudia said. "I don't need a hug."

The two girls stared blankly at each other in silence. If this had been the Wild West, they'd be walking out of the saloon preparing for their showdown at the not O.K. Corral.

"Are the two of you, like, together?" Stephanie asked. She pointed to our joined hands.

After following Stephanie's pointing finger, Alison screamed, "Oh my fucking God! I never in a million years would have seen *that* coming."

"And you still haven't," Claudia said as she withdrew her hand from mine. "Tru and I are just friends."

Alison nodded. "Now *that* I believe," she said before draining the rest of the drink. Her phone suddenly dinged, and Alison opened it and giggled. "Jeremy just liked the picture," she told us. She turned to Stephanie. "He's been ignoring me all night, that bastard."

"I know." Stephanie nodded.

"And did you see that slut he came here with? The one with the hoochie momma skirt that barely covers her crab-infested cooter?"

Stephanie nodded again. Claudia and I locked eyes. Were we a part of this conversation or could we go?

"That girl is so ratched," Alison said as she grabbed my hand. We were evidently stuck here for a few moments longer. "If he thinks liking my selfie is going to make up for bringing that skank here, he's got another thing coming, right?"

"Right," I replied. What else was I supposed to say?

She smiled at no one in particular. "Maybe I should take another selfie."

Before Alison had a chance to strike her pose, a group of guys entering behind us drew her attention and elicited ear-piercing screams. She handed her glass to Stephanie and then jumped into the waiting arms of some of the Jock Brigade from precalc.

I moved to the other side of Claudia, hoping her body and the shadows in the room blocked me from their view. They weren't exactly my biggest fans, and I didn't want to start any trouble, especially since I hadn't found Javi yet.

"She's pretty lively when she's drunk," Stephanie said with a nod to Alison.

"I hadn't noticed," Claudia replied as Alison was passed from one jock to the next. Each one kissed her lips and grabbed her ass. Who had Alison called a skank again?

"There's drinks out back in the coolers or in the kitchen fridge," Stephanie told us as Alison was manhandled by two studs at the same time.

"Um, don't you think you should go get her?" Claudia asked. One of the guys stuck his face in Alison's cleavage while she stumbled backward.

"Only if she goes horizontal," Stephanie replied. "Those are the rules."

Claudia nodded as if she understood completely. "Classy."

"Is Javi here?" I asked Stephanie. I'd had enough of the Drunk Alison Show.

Stephanie nodded. "He was talking to Heather in the kitchen last time I saw him."

"We'll never find him standing in one spot," Claudia said as she grabbed my hand and led me away from Stephanie and through the flashing interior. We passed houseguests making out far more seriously than those in the living room. Back here in the dark, hands were shoved down pants and up blouses. One girl I didn't recognize ran by topless, chased by a guy I hoped was her boyfriend.

"*Real* classy," Claudia commented.

Once we made it past the living room and the annoying strobe lights, we entered an appropriately lit hallway, where a line of drunken revelers waited to use the bathroom on the opposite end. While they waited to empty their bladders, they took shots from a tray that was being carted around by our inebriated class president, Enrique Fuentes.

"I can't feel my legs, bitches!" he shouted at us as he handed Claudia and me a shot each. He then proceeded past us on unsteady legs.

Claudia took the drink and swallowed it in one gulp.

"Claudia!" I couldn't believe she'd just done that. She was driving.

"Relax," she said as she tossed the empty shot glass on the carpet. "My tolerance is pretty high, and if I'm gonna stay here one minute longer, I'm gonna need to be socially lubricated." She eyed my drink and then me. "You drinking that?"

I rolled my eyes and handed it to her. After tossing it back, she grimaced. "That'll do for now."

After a wrong turn into an occupied study, where a couple had begun the path to parenthood, we found the kitchen. Heather Barnes stood with three other girls, pouring a pink-colored drink from the blender into their cups. Javi was nowhere in sight.

Before we'd left my house, Claudia had given me the skinny on Heather. She was the product of divorced parents, who assuaged their guilt over their failed marriage by letting their daughter do whatever she wanted, which made her pretty popular at school. If people needed a place to party, they came here.

That meant she literally held most of the students by the balls. If someone pissed her off, they spent the rest of the year on the outside looking in.

Heather looked over her shoulder at us, and instead of sneering like I expected, she smiled. "Wow! The two of you look great," she said as she waved us over. The bell sleeve of her white lace dress fluttered back and forth. She brushed honey blonde hair from her eyes and held out her arms. "You've got to try this."

We crossed the kitchen to where she stood with two full glasses of whatever concoction she'd just made.

"I really shouldn't," Claudia protested before taking the drink.

Thank God I had my driver's license, because it appeared I'd be driving us home. "Come on, Tru," Heather said. She tossed back her long locks and grinned. "It's to die for."

Peer pressure sucked balls.

I grabbed the drink from Heather's hand, and she waited for me to take a sip. I glanced at Claudia, who had already drunk a fourth of the contents in her glass. We'd be having a discussion later about drinking responsibly. "I'm not much of a drinker," I admitted.

They smiled and waved my admission away. "You've got to start somewhere," Heather said with a wink. "I started after my dad moved out."

I hesitantly brought the cup to my lips and took a sip. Fire scorched my throat, and I immediately started coughing. Heather and the girls giggled while Claudia rolled her eyes. "Stick to soda," Claudia told me as she snatched the glass from my hand. "Everclear isn't for you."

I had no clue what that was, but Claudia couldn't have been more right. It had tasted like pure rubbing alcohol. Why would anyone want to drink that?

"I'm so happy you're here tonight," Heather said as she rubbed my shoulder. "I was glad Alison invited you."

"Really?" I asked with far more disbelief in my voice than I had intended.

She laughed. "Of course. I haven't really gotten a chance to talk to you since you came to BHS, and then when I saw that picture of you and Javi in the paper, well, I knew I just had to get to know you. Any friend of Javi's is a friend of mine." Her girlfriends nodded.

"Do you know where he is?"

Heather nodded. "He's out back by the pool," she said with a motion to the door on the opposite end of the room.

"Thanks," I said before crossing toward the door.

"Tru, wait." Claudia caught up to me as I reached for the door.

"What is it?"

"I'm supposed to stay by your side, but I need to pee."

"You should've thought about that before you started drinking so much," I told her.

"And maybe you should stop trying to be my mother," she said with stitched eyebrows.

She was right. I was being silly. But being here without Javi made me nervous. "Go get in line," I said. "I'm just gonna check and see if Javi's back here. If I don't find him, I'll come inside and join you."

She twisted her lips in thought. She didn't like the idea, but she apparently had to pee really badly. "Fine," she said. "I'll give you five minutes."

I turned around and exited the kitchen door.

FINDING JAVI wasn't going to be easy. The backyard proved even more crowded than inside. People cluttered the lawn and clogged up the swimming pool, which had been turned into a froth of choppy white waves as people splashed about.

Laughter echoed throughout the night even louder than the steady downbeat of the music blaring inside. The cops would likely be raiding this place soon. And since Claudia was already a tad tipsy, I hoped once I located Javi, we could get away from here before the minors in possession citations were handed out.

I wove in and out of the pods of people that had gathered in circles. Those who recognized me as Javi's friend said hello. I returned the greeting with a smile and a nod before continuing on. Most people, though, glared at me before looking away.

By the time I'd made a lap around the entire backyard, I still hadn't found Javi. A quick glance at my watch told me my five minutes were up. If I didn't head back to Claudia soon, she'd bust out of the house with a searchlight.

I aimed for the back door when I noticed a side yard. I hadn't seen it at first because the night shadows had created a dark pocket around that part of the yard. It was a small area about twenty feet in width between the house and the wooden fence.

It was as good a place as any for Javi to be.

I cut back through the maze of drunkenness, emerging a few feet from the side yard. Shortly after rounding the corner, I stopped in my tracks.

Javi was here, but he wasn't alone. Rance was with him.

Luckily, they were facing the street and hadn't seen me. I quietly inched away. Though Rance had been giving me a wide berth at school, I couldn't count on the same treatment outside the protective school walls. It was just simpler, and safer, to avoid him all together.

Once I stood unseen at the corner of the house, I sighed in relief and leaned against the stucco.

"I just don't understand." Javi's voice drifted on the air.

"What the fuck is there to understand?" Rance asked. His tone had a harsh, angry edge to it.

"You barely talk to me anymore, and when you do, you're an asshole. I'd like to know why. For fuck's sake, man, we've been friends since we were kids. I've known you longer than anyone else."

Rance sniffed. "And here I'd thought you'd forgotten."

"What the hell's that supposed to mean?"

"Don't sweat it, Javi," Rance said. His big feet crunched across the grass.

I was about to bolt when Javi spoke, stopping Rance from leaving. "I *am* gonna sweat it," he replied. "Until you give me a good reason for what's going on. You've been different these past few months. Like you've been avoiding me or something. I tried to give you space, figuring you had some shit with your parents to work through. The last you told me was they were getting a divorce. Is that was this is about?"

"My parents are fine," Rance said. "My dad sleeps on the couch, and my mom cries herself to sleep every night. Everything's back to normal."

"Shit, man. I didn't know it was that bad."

"How could you? You don't come over anymore. Or invite me to your house." I could hear the pouty child in his voice. "I miss your mom's cooking."

"Dude, you're always welcome. You know that."

"I don't," Rance said. "Not anymore."

"I don't understand. What's changed?"

"You." The sulky kid gave way to a pissed-off teenager.

Javi's audible gasp revealed he hadn't been expecting that answer. I had been. The source of Rance's beef with Javi had to be his friendship with me.

"How have I changed?"

"You mean besides the ugly new pet you've got following you around school?"

"Who are you talking about?" Javi asked. I appreciated the confused tone in his voice. He had no clue who Rance was referring to. That meant he didn't see me the way so many others did. "Are you talking about Tru?"

Rance snorted. "Do you have any other Donkey-from-*Shrek* lookalike motherfuckers trotting behind you these days?"

"Tru's a nice guy," Javi said. This time his timbre changed. He immediately went on the defense. "What the hell do you have against him?"

"Absolutely nothing," Rance responded. "He's not worth my time."

"That's a pretty sucky thing to say."

Rance laughed. "I don't collect strays the way you do, man. I stick with people who are worthy of being around me. I don't waste my time with losers. Much less dump my friends for guys the world shits out of its ass."

Dump? That was an interesting choice of words.

"Don't go blaming this on Tru, Rance. You checked out on our friendship long before he came to Burbank. We both know that. And I wish you'd tell me why."

Suddenly, unseen hands shoved me forward, and I sprawled onto the grass.

"Tru?" Javi asked. He ran over and helped me up. We turned to see who'd pushed me. Rance's girlfriend, Lucy, stood with hands on her hips and a hateful glare in her eyes. "What the fuck, Lucy?"

"Don't 'what the fuck?' me," she said. With her long dark hair and blood red lipstick, she resembled a witch. "This little fuckhole was eavesdropping."

Rance and Javi both turned to me. Javi appeared stunned. An impish smile danced across Rance's lips.

"I'm sorry," I said. "I shouldn't have done that."

"No," Javi said. "You shouldn't have."

Lucy crossed to her boyfriend and pressed against him. "Why don't you break his jaw next time?" she asked. "Maybe that'll teach him a lesson."

Javi spun to face them while Rance glowered down at Lucy.

"Shit, Lucy. Thanks a lot," Rance said.

"What?" she asked, clearly oblivious to what she'd just revealed.

"What did you just say?" Javi asked her. "Next time break his jaw?"

She refused to meet Javi's eyes. Instead, she glanced up at Rance, who crossed his arms and glared at her too. She was about to get it from all sides.

"When was the first time?" Javi asked. He crossed the lawn to them and switched his gaze from Lucy to Rance. "Want to tell me, Rance? When the fuck was the first time?"

Javi's angry words drew the attention of some of the party guests like Oscar Gomez, an ugly, scowling member of the Jock Brigade Rance had been spending more of his time with. Selina Perez and Ruben Lopez, who had been among the first to greet me in the halls after seeing my picture with Javi in the school paper, inched closer to witness the events with a macabre curiosity. Some people even exited the pool to avoid missing the action. Destiny Villarreal, who'd asked for my help in math class, was one such rubbernecker. In only her bra and panties, she crossed the lawn.

Last to arrive was Claudia. She cut through the onlookers, surveyed all of us, and said, "What the fuck is going on?"

"Oh, look," Rance said with a nod to Claudia. "Another of your loser friends."

Javi practically snarled. "It was you, wasn't it?" he asked. "You're the one who beat up Tru on his first day. That was why you were in ISS, wasn't it?"

Rance lowered his arms and took a step toward Javi. Javi wasn't a small guy like me, but he was nowhere near Rance's height or bulk. At least four inches and about fifty pounds separated the two. "And what are you going to do about it?"

Suddenly, I was standing between Javi and Rance. It wasn't exactly the wisest place to be, but I couldn't let Javi get into a fight with his best friend. No matter the circumstances, Javi would likely regret being such a hothead later. "It's no big deal," I said. "We should get out of here. Claudia will drive us home."

I nodded to Claudia, who joined me at Javi's side. "Yeah," she said as she tossed a grimace at Rance and Lucy. "This party blows worse than Lucy."

Lucy lunged, but Rance stopped her with one meaty paw.

"I think it's time for you to go," Rance said to Javi.

Javi didn't reply. He turned around and cut through the gathered crowd.

"WHY THE fuck didn't you tell me?" Javi yelled as Claudia drove us back to my place. I'd never seen him this upset. I couldn't tell if his anger was solely directed at me or at what he'd learned about Rance. "And you," he said to Claudia, who sat next to him in the front seat. "I bet you knew, didn't you? Why did you keep it from me too? You know how I feel about bullies."

"Don't be yelling at me," Claudia said through gritted teeth. She took her eyes off the road to shoot Javi a long, piercing stare. By the time she returned her gaze to the road, Javi had taken several deep breaths. "Besides, it wasn't my story to tell. I promised Tru."

Javi turned to look at me. "But why?" he asked. "Didn't you trust me? I thought we were friends, especially since...." He stopped, not sure whether it was okay for him to bring up the fact I was gay.

"I didn't want to hurt you," I said. "I knew how much Rance meant to you, and I didn't want to put you in a situation where you felt like you had to choose."

"That's not good enough, Tru." He had calmed down a lot, but the anger in his voice still cut through me like a switchblade. "Friends aren't supposed to keep things from each other. And I thought that's what we were. When you told me you were gay—"

"Wait," Claudia said. She peered at me in the rearview mirror. "You told him?"

I nodded.

"And when were you planning on sharing that little tidbit with me?"

Talk about jumping from the frying pan into the fire. "I was going to tell you," I said to Claudia's reflection. "I wasn't going to keep it from you."

"Can we deal with one secret of Tru's at a time?" Javi asked. He sat sideways in his seat, trying to get a good look at me. "Why keep this from me?"

I had no choice but to tell him. No matter how pathetic it made me sound. "I was scared you'd stop talking to me," I finally admitted. "You and Rance have been friends for, like, ever. And you were the first person who was nice to me. Who became my friend. I didn't want to lose that. I figured once you knew, there'd really be no choice. That you'd just choose the guy who'd always been your friend and leave the loser I am all by myself again."

"Stop the car," Javi told Claudia.

"What?" she asked. "I'm driving in the middle of the road here."

"Stop the fucking car!"

Claudia slammed on the breaks. When Javi opened his door, I couldn't watch him exit the vehicle. What I feared was about to come true. Javi was walking away.

"Move the fuck over," Javi said after opening the rear door.

"Huh?"

"I said move the fuck over."

I undid my seat belt and scooted over as Javi climbed in next to me and shut the door.

"Can I go again, Your Majesty?"

"Please do," Javi replied to Claudia. He rubbed my shoulder like he had the day I fell off my bike. The warm comfort of his touch almost brought me to tears. "Look at me," he said.

I glanced up into Javi's smiling face. He stared at me as if I was the weirdest and most wonderful thing he'd ever looked upon. "I don't abandon my friends, Tru. And it hurts my feelings that you think I'm the kind of person who would. I don't care what people think or what they say. Not even Rance. Does it suck that he can be the biggest douchebag in the world? Yes. Does that stop me from wanting to be his friend?" He paused. "Well, maybe a little. But it's not something I just turn off. Not for you. Not for Rance. I'm a big boy who makes his own decisions, and you and Rance are going to have to trust in my friendship. And trust I'll make the decisions that will keep us friends."

He wrapped his arm around my shoulders and drew me close. I wanted to bury my head in the crook of his neck and rest my hands on his chest, but I didn't. I closed my eyes and leaned into his touch and inhaled Javi's sweet scent. Both always seemed to make everything better.

"And what's with this new look?" he asked while gazing down at me. "A new hairdo and clothes."

"Claudia helped me get ready for the party," I told him. "I didn't want to embarrass you with my usual self."

Javi chuffed. He ran his fingers through my perfect do and messed it up. He flicked my chin and then my nose. "I like your usual self," he said. "Don't change a thing."

I didn't know how to respond. It was perhaps the nicest thing anyone had ever said to me. I was about to say that when I caught Claudia staring at us through the rearview mirror. When our eyes locked, she turned back to the road.

She obviously thought Javi's words sweet as well. She wore the biggest smile I'd ever seen on her.

Chapter 7

OVER THE next few weeks, Javi proved true to his word. We continued biking to and from school together and hanging out under our tree or at one of our houses. I also went with his parents to see him play his preseason games, and Javi was right. His parents definitely taught me the ways of the true fan.

They hooted and hollered for Javi and ate a buttload of snacks Mrs. Castillo prepared for each game. It didn't take me long to jump up and down like an idiot along with them. Most people in the stands stared crosswise at us, as if we were crazy. The Castillos only beamed in satisfaction that I'd grown to love watching Javi play as much as they did.

Of course, the games hadn't mesmerized me. It was watching Javi standing on the pitcher's mound in his tight white baseball pants that clung to his lower half like a second skin. They highlighted his firm butt nicely, and the front? Good Lord. I practically creamed my underwear the first time I saw the bulge Javi sported.

"What did you think of the game?" Javi asked as we headed back to his parents' car. They walked a few feet ahead of us, chanting "Go Bulldogs!" since we'd won yet another game.

"I liked it," I said, trying my best not to stare at the front of his uniform. I made sure my eyes scanned the ground instead.

"That's it?" he asked, walking into me. I took several side steps to avoid falling over. Javi laughed before rejoining me at my side. He was so close, our arms practically touched as we walked. He'd been doing that for a while now. I tried not to read too much into it. Javi was just a touchy-feely kind of guy.

"What do you want me to say?"

"I want you to say that the game was phenomenal, and I'm the greatest thing since sliced bread."

I stared blankly at him as his dark eyes glowed in amusement. "I'm not stroking your ego. You can stroke yourself."

Javi busted out laughing while I blushed at what I'd inadvertently said.

"I do that every night," he said with an eyebrow wiggle. "I am a growing boy, after all."

Naturally, when I got home that evening I beat off to the image of Javi in his bed. I came so hard, I almost blacked out. But even after I came, my cock refused to go down. It took three jerk-off sessions before my body finally relented and let me go to sleep.

I had done my best to curb my attraction for my best friend, but it was proving harder and harder, pun absolutely intended, to ignore. Javi had gotten so comfortable in our friendship, he must have forgotten I was gay or that he'd once sat on my hard-on. When we were together, his arm hung around my neck or our legs brushed together.

If I didn't know better, I'd think Javi found reasons to touch me.

But I chalked it up to Javi's divided attention and him trying to reassure me that nothing had changed.

He'd been trying to patch things up with Rance by spending more time with the guy who'd been his best friend. Rance, who'd broken up with Lucy shortly after the party, ate up the attention. He still didn't like that Javi remained my friend, but he seemed determined to put on a show that it didn't bother him.

Even though it obviously did.

Rance still hated me. That much was obvious every time he saw me. For Javi, he played nice. But I wasn't fooled. Rancid was just biding his time. For what, I had no clue. But I'd learned enough over the years to trust my gut.

"I'm hanging out with Rance tonight," Javi told me as we rode home from the park. It was Friday night, and we typically ate dinner with his parents and then watched movies till it was time for me to head home. From his downcast eyes, I could tell he felt bad. "He's having a tough time with Lucy," he said, trying to explain why he was breaking from our routine.

It had been almost a month since their split. "I still don't understand why they broke up."

"I'm not sure I understand it either," he admitted. "I don't think Rance does either, to tell you the truth. All he's told me was that it was time. He just didn't feel the same way about her anymore." We rode for a few minutes in silence before he said, "I think there's someone else."

"Who?"

He shrugged. "He hasn't said."

"What are you two gonna do tonight?" I asked. I tried my best to hide the sadness behind the question. I loved being with Javi. Not being with him made me crazy. I moped around the apartment, sighing, counting down the minutes until I saw him again. I'd been driving my mother and Claudia crazy.

"I don't know," he finally said. "I think we might play some Grand Theft Auto."

Rance would love a game that included beating prostitutes and running down cops. "Sounds like fun."

"Yeah," he said. "I'm gonna spend the night over there too. And then we're going with some of the guys to Oscar's father's property out in Somerset. We're gonna do some target shooting, eat barbeque, you know, shit like that."

I didn't like the way this was going. From the sounds of things, I wouldn't see Javi until school on Monday.

"But I was thinking," he said as we turned onto my street. "How about I come over tomorrow night after I get back from Oscar's, and we have a movie marathon?"

I perked up right away. "That sounds great!" I said. I was so pleased, I almost lost control of my bike, weaving back and forth before regaining control.

Javi laughed. "You're going to need to get better at that, or you're gonna find yourself flying over another rock."

I flipped him off before hopping the curb and skidding to a stop on the small lawn in front of my apartment. "I can ride just fine."

He didn't look convinced. "I'll take your word for it." He winked before pushing away and riding off. "See you tomorrow."

"Okay," I shouted back as he sped away.

I'd be counting down the minutes.

EVEN THOUGH Javi and I spent almost twenty-four hours apart, he called me twice to check in. He wanted to touch base and make sure I was doing okay and having some fun. I thought the gesture exceptionally sweet. All I'd done was homework, and he made me promise to have it finished by the time he arrived. He wanted my full attention.

When he walked in, it was like Javi hadn't seen me in months. He drew me into a big hug and squeezed. I had to make sure our groins didn't touch. Otherwise, Javi would once again feel my boner against him. He'd been cool about it once. I didn't want to chance a second go around, no matter how much my cock strained to reach him.

After he reluctantly released me from his embrace, we made popcorn and watched horror flicks.

My mother, who was definitely *not* a fan of people being dismembered on the television screen, retired to her bedroom to read. She planned on heading into the twenty-four-hour clinic where she worked to get started on a few projects her new boss had mentioned. She clearly wanted to make a good impression.

"More blood," Javi chanted as he shoved a handful of popcorn in his mouth. He sat next to me on the small couch that took up practically the entire floor space of the anorexic living room. The pitiful surroundings never bothered him, and neither did he mind when our legs sometimes brushed together while we sat on the cramped couch.

The gentle tickling of his dark leg hair against my smooth skin certainly got a reaction out of me. But I did my best to keep my erection from tearing through my shorts. Javi was my friend. My cock had to learn that eventually, right?

It throbbed once as if saying, "Bitch, please."

"Are you deaf or something?" Javi asked as he fished his hand into the giant popcorn bowl on his lap. "I said more blood!"

Dawn of the Dead had just finished, and before that we'd seen *Night of the Living Dead*. Since we had a theme going, why stop now? "How about *Planet Terror*?"

Javi's eyes lit up. "I love that movie! When Rose McGowan's character loses her leg and straps that rifle to her stump to kill zombies, man! That is *badass!*"

I agreed and fumbled to open the DVD case.

"Hurry up and put it in!"

I snickered at Javi's comment and grinned over at him. "I bet you say that to all the gay boys." Recently, our banter had gotten a bit risqué. But with the way I sometimes heard the jocks talking about tits and such, sexual humor among guy friends seemed par for the course.

Javi groaned and tossed a handful of popcorn at me. "Nasty boy!"

"Yes, well, you're the one who's so convinced I'm a slut. Seeing as how I kissed a boy in second grade." I placed my hands on either side of my cheeks and pretended to scream in horror.

Javi chuckled. "That's Tru," and then he broke into hysterics over his pun. I scooped up some of the popcorn that littered the area around me and hurled them. Most didn't even get close, but one managed to land back in the bowl. Javi's nod told me he was impressed. "You're getting better. Now you just need to master that form with actual balls."

At that point, we both lost it and fell into fitful laughter. We got so loud, my mother came out to see what was going on.

"Are you two okay?" she asked. She pulled her blue terrycloth robe about her and eyed us suspiciously. She believed us to be up to no good.

"Yes, Mom," I said between gasps. "Javi just said something stupidly funny."

"And what was it?" she asked.

Javi's cheeks burned red. "I'd rather not say, Mrs. Cobbler," he said after a snort and a snicker.

Mom glanced at the digital clock that sat on the small table beside the couch. "It's really late."

When Javi saw the time, he nodded. "You're right. I should probably head home."

"You don't have to," I said. "We can stay up late watching movies, and then you can crash here. It's not safe to bike home this late at night in this neighborhood. Right, Mom?"

What could she say? It was true. The Projects didn't exactly have the safest reputation in town. Drive-bys were as common as having a SWAT team suddenly barge into your neighbor's place. It would be irresponsible of us to send Javi home now.

"I'll be fine," Javi said as he placed the popcorn bowl on the table. "I'm a big boy." He validated the statement by flexing his bicep and flashing a cheesy smile.

I gawked at my mother. This was the point where, as the adult, she spoke with the voice of reason and responsibility. Why did she just stand there scrutinizing us? "Mom?"

She finally sighed and nodded. "Tru's right, Javi. It's not safe for you out there. If I had a car, I'd drive you home. Why don't you call your parents and see if it's okay that you stay the night?"

"I don't want to be a bother."

She shook her head. "A friend of Tru's is never a bother."

He smiled. "Okay, then. Let me just use your phone. My cell died this morning, and I forgot my charger."

"You know where it is," she said with a nod to the kitchen area behind her. "While you call them, Tru and I will get sheets for you."

Javi headed for the phone, and when he was out of sight, my mother pointed at me and jerked her head toward my bedroom. She wanted me to follow her. I did as she silently commanded. When my mother appeared this determined, it was best not to argue.

When we entered my bedroom, she closed the door behind us.

"What's up?"

She gazed at me as if I were a silly little boy who'd just been caught with his hands in the cookie jar. "You can seriously ask me that right now?"

"I don't understand," I said, which was the God's honest truth.

"You've just asked the boy you have a crush on to spend the night."

Oh, was that the source of her concern? "Mom, it's okay. Really it is. Javi knows I'm gay, and he doesn't care."

"That doesn't make me feel better." Worry lines once again tracked across her forehead.

"Mom, Javi's not gay. He's just a boy who's a friend."

She still wasn't convinced. "If you were a girl, I would never allow a boy you liked to spend the night in the same house as you. You realize that, right?"

"You realize I can't get pregnant, right?" I'd hoped she'd see the humor in my joke. Boy, was I wrong! She crossed her arms, and her eyes turned into thin slits. I'd done it now.

"I don't find that funny at all. Gay or straight, the same rules apply. I'm your mother, and I don't want you to have sex before you're out of high school, much less before you turn eighteen. You're not mature enough to handle such an intimate physical commitment as that, and I'm certainly not going to provide the bedroom for your first time. This is my house, and you will respect my rules." She lowered her voice to a deadly serious parental whisper, which was always a thousand times worse than yelling. "Do you understand me?"

"Yes, ma'am," I uttered immediately.

"Javi has my permission to stay tonight because I'm as guilty as the two of you for not keeping a watchful eye on the time. I can't chance sending him out this late, but this won't happen again. In the future, I expect Javi to go home at a decent hour, and if you are at his house, for you to come home at a respectable time."

I nodded. Although I understood her concerns, I found them silly. Nothing was ever going to happen between us.

"My dad said it was fine for me to stay," Javi called down the hall.

"Good," my mom called back. "Just finishing up in here. We'll be right out."

"Nothing's gonna happen, Mom," I said. "I swear."

She shook her head and smiled at me. "I know you truly believe that," she said as she drew me into a hug. "But you're both teenage boys, and your hormones are bouncing around uncontrollably inside you. It's my job to set up the rules and the boundaries that keep you in line. You may not like me for it, but you don't have to. That's part of the job too."

"I don't like you," I told her as I kissed her cheek. "I love you, and even if you have nothing to worry about, which you don't, I promise to respect your wishes."

She nodded. My mother knew me well enough to know once I made a promise, I didn't go back on it. "Good. Now let's get everything ready."

As we took the sheets out of the closet and made a pallet on the floor, where I would sleep, I still had trouble understanding the source of my mother's worry.

SHORTLY AFTER Rose McGowan barely escaped her fight with the zombies, Javi and I headed to my room. I fell upon the pallet on the floor. It wasn't the most comfortable place I'd ever rested my head for the night. My sleeping arrangements basically consisted of four bedspreads piled on top of each other, a sheet, and a pillow, but having Javi on the bed next to me more than made up for the sore neck and back I'd likely have in the morning.

Javi's sleeping over meant the world to me. It told me he had no problem with my being gay or with the knowledge that I had a crush on him. It was no big deal.

"I'll be glad to sleep on the floor," Javi said as he sat on the edge of my bed.

I spread out along the pallet and stretched. "You're the guest, so the bed's yours," I said as I stifled a yawn. Who knew watching zombie movies for six hours could be so exhausting?

"You sure?" he asked. "I don't mind. My family goes camping all the time, so I'm used to roughing it."

"Take the bed," I insisted before ripping off my socks and wiggling my toes.

Javi nodded and pulled his T-shirt off. As the fabric slid slowly upward, I gazed upon his smooth, bare flesh for the first time. My breath caught in my throat. His creamy skin was just as I pictured it. Light mocha in color with a small trail of hair rising out of his shorts and up to the most perfectly shaped belly button I'd ever seen. The muscles of his long, lean torso stretched and flexed as he removed the shirt, and he used the fabric to wipe the beads of sweat that had sprung up across his broad chest and down his taut stomach.

"It's hot in here," he said. "And way too hot for winter. Mother Nature needs to make up her mind what she wants in south Texas. Mind if I switch on the ceiling fan?"

I could only nod. If I attempted to speak, I'd likely only manage gibberish.

He discarded his shirt at the foot of the bed before rising to pull the fan's chain. A sudden rush of wind buffeted Javi, sending the loose strands of hair that fell across his forehead fluttering. He raised his arms to stretch, revealing the small tufts of hair nestled within his pits. I suddenly had the strange desire to run my tongue along the dips of the flesh and devour the scent and taste that his underarms produced.

That was a new longing for me, and if I could have gotten up, I'd have rushed off to the bathroom to jerk off. But there was no way standing was possible. My cock was about ten seconds away from boring through the fabric that kept it confined. I had to pull the sheets over me in order to conceal my boner. Javi had been up close and personal with it one time too often already.

"What's this?" he asked, walking to the wall opposite the bed. His backside proved just as impressive as the front. His tight, perky butt flexed underneath his shorts as he walked away, and his broad, chiseled shoulders seemed to go on for miles.

If I died now, I'd go with a smile on my face.

"What's what?" I asked.

We rarely came into my bedroom because we spent most of our time at his place. It was nicer and bigger than my closet-sized room with only my bed, a small desk, and a chest of drawers my grandmother had given us.

He was standing in front of the picture of us I'd taken, the one where Javi stared at me, not the camera. Holy shit! I'd completely forgotten about it in all the excitement. What the hell was he thinking right now?

"Um, it's just one of the photos I took for the paper." I tried my best not to sound nervous, but the tremor in my voice gave me away.

"I like it," he said as he turned. "Think you can get me a copy?"

Was that it? That photo practically screamed how much I liked him and probably revealed that I'd spent most evenings since then beating off to it. "Uh, sure," I said.

"Thanks," he said as he headed for the bed. When he reached the foot of the pallet, he stopped and studied me with an arch of one bushy eyebrow. "Aren't you going to get dressed for bed?" I must have looked quite foolish lying fully clothed under the covers.

"Oh yeah," I said pretending to be so tired I didn't know what I was doing. I yanked my shirt off and tossed it into the corner. I immediately drew the covers back over my naked chest. "All done."

"You can sleep in shorts?" he asked. He unbuttoned his shorts and undid the zipper. Good God! Did he not realize how he was torturing me? "There's no way I'd ever get to sleep," he said as he shoved his shorts off his hips. They floated to the floor.

I gulped.

With his shirt off, Javi had been a dream come true. Now in only his underwear, he'd become a waking wet dream. A dusting of dark hair covered his legs and ran up his muscular thighs before disappearing along the edges of his blue briefs. Within the underwear rested a heavy bulge that made my mouth water and my breathing turn into ragged pants. If I had touched my throbbing dick, I would have shot my load.

"I prefer shorts." I finally managed to force the words from my lips.

He padded over to the bed after switching off the ceiling fan light. "I'm just the opposite," he said as he settled in above me in the darkness, but soft moonlight fell between the slats of the blinds. I sat up, and since he didn't pull the sheets back to climb underneath, I glimpsed Javi's mostly naked body on top of my bed. He lay on his stomach on top of the covers. "I usually don't sleep with anything on."

I opened my mouth to tell him not to let me stop him, but I remembered my mother's warning. My lips immediately sealed shut.

His voice drifted to me in the semidarkness. "Tru?"

"Yeah," I said, lying back down.

"I'm glad you came into my life."

I smiled as my eyes grew heavy. "Me too."

A few seconds later, Javi's low, even breathing filled the room. The rhythmic tone made my drooping eyes even heavier, and as I drifted off to sleep, Javi's arm suddenly fell from the bed, and his hand landed on my shoulder.

I fell into the most peaceful sleep of my life.

Chapter 8

THE SHATTERING of a glass caused my eyes to flutter open.

Soft moonlight no longer spilled into the room. The harsh morning sun now poured through the slats. The shadows of the night had been chased to the corners, and the golden rays revealed Javi's hand still rested on my shoulder.

I sighed. Had I ever been this happy? That was an easy no.

One quick glance up revealed Javi still slept soundly, so I moved my cheek over to his hand and brushed my face against his fingers. They twitched in response, fanning across my flesh, and I imagined Javi willingly caressing me instead of simply involuntarily reacting to the sudden increase in pressure on his hand.

Glass crunched in the kitchen. "Shit!" my mother softly cursed.

Javi stirred in response to the new sound. He withdrew from me, and he turned over on his side and faced the wall.

Instead of getting up and crawling into bed next to him, which was what I most wanted to do, I stood and quietly left the bedroom. I closed the door softly behind me before heading to see what the ruckus was about.

"Good morning," I said, when I saw my mother with broom in hand. Today, she wore black slacks and a gray blouse, and the only other pair of shoes she owned, black high heels with scuff marks across the front. She swept a pile of glass into a dustpan in quick jerky motions. "What's the matter?"

"I'm not pleased, Tru," she said. She emptied the broken glass into the trashcan. "Not pleased at all."

"Why? What happened?"

She glanced sideways at me, as if I knew what had set her off.

"I'm clueless here," I said. "I promise."

Those two words released some of the bluster from her sails, but the wind of pissy still blew strongly enough to force us upon a rocky shore. "I saw you," she said, as if that made her anger evident.

"You saw me what?" I asked. "I've been asleep this whole time. I swear. Whatever you think I've done, I haven't."

"You mean I was just seeing things when I poked my head in your room and saw Javi's hand on your shoulder?"

Ah, now I understood. "Oh, that," I said, hoping my casual tone might further abate the roaring storm.

Obviously, I was unsuccessful. She placed her hands on her hips and stared me down. "Yes, *that.*"

"Mom, nothing happened. When I heard the glass break, I opened my eyes, and I saw Javi's hand on me." Of course, I neglected to tell her it had been there when I went to sleep. It seemed I no longer had problems with misdirection at all. "Then I got up and came in here. That's it."

She studied me intently, searching my expression for the truth.

"It doesn't matter if his hand fell on me while he slept. That means as much as Claudia falling asleep in my lap after watching a movie. Nothing would ever come of it. Claudia doesn't see me that way. I sure as heck don't see *her* that way, and Javi's *not* gay." Although after spending the night with Javi's hand on my shoulder, the hopeful butterflies in my belly fluttered their tiny wings.

I was prepared for my mother to see the logic of my words. Her snort took me by surprise. "Honey, I don't know if this will burst your bubble or just feed your hope, but boys who are *truly* into girls, don't spend the night in their underwear with their hand on another boy."

I couldn't refute that logic. However, there was a point she refused to see, and one that kept my tummy butterflies from taking flight. "Unless his arm just happened to fall off the bed. You know, the way you sometimes dangle your leg off the edge while you sleep."

"Right, but if I brushed up against something, I'd realize it. I would wake up, see what was touching me, and then move away."

Before I could respond, Javi shuffled into the kitchen bare-chested. Thankfully, he'd pulled on his shorts. "Good morning," he said as he ran a hand through his unkempt hair. He stifled a yawn and then sat at the small kitchen table, completely oblivious to the tension in the air. "I'll be leaving in a bit. I just need to finish waking up first."

"Take your time," I said while my mother eyed me. She clearly preferred for Javi to leave before she did.

"Am I interrupting?" Javi asked, suddenly dawning to the situation. "Maybe I should leave now."

"You don't have to," I replied. I loved my mother and defying her in this manner wasn't something I typically did. But Javi was my friend. The first friend I'd made in years. Certainly she had to understand that.

"Are you sure?" he asked my mom.

I don't know if it was the completely innocent expression that lit up his face or the desperate pleading she saw in my eyes, but she took a deep breath before saying, "It's fine. No rush at all."

Javi's dazzling smile replaced the look of concern. "Great!" He turned to me and said, "I thought maybe we'd do something today. Like go see a movie or something."

I scrunched up my face. "I'm all movied out." Plus, I lacked the funds for the ticket. Seeing a movie these days required a small personal loan. But when a slight pout tugged downward on Javi's gorgeous lips, I couldn't say no to a day together. "How about we do something else? Like go to the zoo or something?" With my student ID, I could get in cheap, and I loved the zoo. I went there often, and it would be nice to share it with Javi. Plus, it looked to be another oddly warm December day.

He grinned. "I haven't been to the zoo in years. That could be fun."

"Is that okay with you, Mom?"

She nodded, clearly resigning herself to the fact that her son no longer simply obeyed. She'd grown accustomed to my complete compliance, but I wasn't the same Tru anymore. Not since I'd met Javi. There were things I had to do for me. Besides, I had already promised her nothing inappropriate would happen, and chances of that were next to nil anyway. Why she didn't accept that continued to confuse me.

"Great!" Javi said as he stood. "I'll just go home, shower, and change. With any luck, I'll get to borrow my dad's car. Otherwise we have to take the bus."

After Javi departed the room, my mother reached for her purse and pulled out a twenty-dollar bill. "I know it's not much," she said as she handed it to me. "But you deserve to have some fun."

I took the money as if I'd been handed a kingdom. "Thanks, Mom."

She brushed her fingers through my tangled hair and gazed deeply into my eyes. "I'm truly grateful for Javi," she said. "You've needed someone in your life for so long, and I'm glad you finally found that. I truly am. But I'm still your mother, and I worry. It's my job to protect you and keep you safe."

"Javi's not going to hurt me, Mom. He's my friend."

She glanced over my shoulder to my bedroom where Javi whistled the same birdcall he'd sung in the park at most every visit. Worry crouched like a tiger at the edges of her eyes.

A COUPLE of hours later, we paid our discounted admission to the San Antonio Zoo and immediately headed over to the lemur exhibit, which started off the animal showcase. From there, we observed the American black bears wrestle, the gibbons play chase high in their enclosure, and the jaguar pace nervously around a tree.

"I'd forgotten how much I loved this place," Javi said as we left the jaguar and continued on. "I used to beg my parents to bring me every summer, but that was years ago. I think the last time I was here, I was ten."

"My mother used to always bring me too," I said as we viewed the Komodo dragon. I rested my hand on the rail in front of the thick glass separating us from certain doom, and he joined me, wrapping his fingers onto the rail about an inch from mine. The heat from his body rushed against me in pulsing waves. I entertained the idea of leaning into his touch, of brushing my pinky finger against his thumb and joining our hands in secret.

But I lacked the nerve, even though an itch in the back of my brain told me that was what he wanted me to do. I dismissed it as wishful thinking. Claudia's suspicions about Javi's feelings, which she had spouted almost daily the past few weeks, had wormed their way inside my thoughts, and the concern in my mother's voice once again rang in my ears.

I pulled away, crossing to the next exhibit, where I once again leaned against the rail and Javi took his place at my side, his fingers even closer than before.

"When was the last time you were here?" Javi asked.

"Last week actually."

He peered down at me. Confusion stitched his eyebrows together. "While I was at our away game?"

I nodded.

"Then why'd you want to come here again?"

I shrugged as I pulled away, and Javi moved beside me again. Why did this little dance remind me of playing vampire with Carl in second grade? "You'll think it's sad and pathetic," I said as we arrived where the reticulated python currently digested something the size of a small cat.

"I bet I won't," Javi replied.

This time, I didn't put my hands on the rail. I crossed them over my chest to see how Javi would respond. He mimicked my stance in front of the python's area, and his elbow brushed against my upper arm. "Well, before you and Claudia, I didn't really have any friends, and my mom's always working. So I came here a lot to be around people who weren't going to chase me or try to beat me up." I nodded to the python. "These guys have been my only friends for years."

Javi's stance grew rigid. "I don't like to think of someone beating you up. Especially now that I know Rance was one of them. It's not right." He glanced at me, his eyes hooded in affection. Why did I get the feeling he wanted to pull me close, pull out a sword, and behead all my past tormentors?

"I couldn't agree more, but what can I do?" I led him to the big cat grotto. The lions stretched out in the thinning sunlight. Clouds had crept across the sky, and the animals sniffed the air. Two of the lionesses stood up and headed into the den. No doubt, they sensed an approaching storm. "High school is like an animal pack. There are the alphas who run the show, and the betas who get bitch-slapped for daring to sneak a bite of food off the carcass. You're one of the alphas. Everyone at school loves you. As for me, I'm new to the pack. I don't have a place in the normal order of things, and even some of the betas think it's okay to piss on me when I walk by. I guess that knocks me all the way down to an omega, the absolute last in the pecking order."

"Is that really the way you feel?" His eyes reflected disbelief.

I nodded. "For pretty much as long as I can remember."

"That's got to change."

"What do you plan on doing?" I asked. "Alter high school social politics that have been in place for generations? It's the nature of the beast, and I've learned how to survive."

"Life shouldn't be about just survival," he said as we approached the howler monkeys. They screamed at us as if they were in complete agreement. "It's about being happy and experiencing all life has to offer."

I glanced at Javi, who stood before the spider monkey area. A smile was upon his lips as two of the males groomed each other, picking fleas from each other's fur and popping them in their mouths for an afternoon snack.

"And what about you?" I asked. "Are you happy?"

He turned to me, flashing his half grin. "Do I look miserable?"

I studied his expression. On the surface, he seemed to be the Javi I'd known for the past few months, but somewhere deep lived a Javi no one got the chance to see. The Javi that smiled differently at me. The one who slept with his hand on my shoulder or found some excuse to touch me. That Javi clawed up from the deep well where he'd been held captive, but every time he scaled to the top, someone or something shoved him all the way back down to the shadowy bottom.

I'd first noticed it that day in the park, when some unseen barrier had fallen as we talked. Over the last few weeks, the bricks in the wall had crumbled, leaving gaping holes.

"I don't think you're as happy as you'd have everyone believe," I answered.

Javi's eyes grew wide. "What are you talking about?"

"I've got a lot of experience with acting, Javi. I've done it most of my life. Trying to get other kids to believe the way they treat me doesn't bother me. That I can dust myself off after someone pushes me into a locker or does some other shitty thing to me. So I know what pretend looks like, and sometimes when you smile, there's a certain hollowness there. As if you're trying to cover up something you don't want others to see."

Javi snuffed. He put more distance between us than had been all day. I'd clearly pissed him off. "And what do you think I'm hiding?"

The clouds snuffed out the sunlight, and a light breeze kicked up around us. Rain wafted in the air. In the distance, thunder rolled across the heavens. A cold front was headed our way.

"I'm not certain," I said. "But there've been some theories."

"What the hell does that mean?" he asked as lightning flashed. Families around us darted for cover as the first raindrops fell. "That sounds like gossip and bullshit that people are always spouting."

"Don't get angry," I said, even though it was too late. Javi's chest heaved.

"How could I not be angry when you've basically told me people are talking about me? And since Claudia is the only one who's given you the time of day, I assume it's her that's been shooting off her big mouth."

"Low blow, man," I said.

Javi caught my meaning. He'd basically called me a loser without saying the words. "This sucks, Tru," he said. Rain now fell steadily. Javi's hair matted to his face, and a huge drop hung from the tip of his angled nose. I had to wipe the water from my eyes in order to see clearly. "We were having such a good day until now. Why'd you have to get all serious and shit and get up in my business? I didn't hound you about crap you didn't want to talk about. I've never brought up that fight between you and Rance because you basically asked me not to. I wanted to, but I respected your privacy. Hell, when I almost impaled myself on your cock, I didn't treat it as a big deal. And you accuse me of keeping secrets, of not being honest. Of being fake."

"Whoa!" I said, trying to rein in Javi's anger, which seemed to grow with the storm. Rain now fell in sheets, and thunder crashed overhead. A chill blew all around us. Still, we stood there in the deluge that threatened to sweep us away. "I never said any of those things. I said you didn't always seem as happy as you'd have other people believe. You're the one who mentioned secrets. What secrets are you keeping?"

Javi ran his fingers through his sodden hair. He teetered on the edge, and I could either pull him back to the safety of denial or force him to face what he might be trying to ignore.

Only the truth, no matter how hard, would calm the storm.

"Just tell me, Javi," I said as I closed the distance he'd created between us. "Are you gay?"

Javi's eyes grew colder than the rain that fell upon our heads. "Fuck you, Tru." He turned and ran into the curtains of rain that covered the zoo.

FOR THE next hour, I searched the zoo in the pouring rain. I visited each exhibit twice and shivered through all the shops that lined the trails. I couldn't find him anywhere. When I circled back around to the lemur exhibit, which was across from the entrance, I realized he might have left me here to fend for myself.

I darted through the exit and ran all the way to where we'd parked the car. When I spotted his father's blue Lincoln, I sighed in relief. I'd simply been run away from, not entirely abandoned.

That gave me a small measure of hope. Perhaps I hadn't completely destroyed our friendship. Although when I'd asked Javi if he was gay, as Claudia and my mother already suspected, he'd been almost unable to contain his anger. If I'd said those words to Rance, I'd likely be lion food right now.

Javi either was extremely pissed about being mistaken as a gay boy or his denial was rooted so deeply in his soul that digging around had caused him to practically self-destruct.

Whatever the cause, I had to find him and try to patch things up.

I surveyed the expanse of Brackenbridge Park, where the zoo was situated, but the sheets of rain that continued to pour from the sky prevented me from seeing any farther than a few dozen feet. If Javi had left the zoo for the safety of the park, which was entirely something he would do, I'd have difficulty finding him in the almost three hundred sprawling acres.

I had to put my brain to use. I'd visited the park almost every weekend for the past few years. It was as familiar to me as the back of my hand. Where could someone go to be alone and escape the rain?

The train station, which housed the small tourist attraction that took visitors around the park's perimeter, was the first obvious answer. It had an overhang that protected from the elements, but people waiting to hop on the train after the rain stopped would have likely crowded the area.

The Sunken Gardens seemed another possibility. The Japanese-inspired tea garden hosted a theater for outdoor musical performances, as well as pagodas that could provide shelter. But that was at least half a mile away. Javi would likely choose some place closer.

The picnic pavilion suddenly sprang to mind. It sat on the outer perimeter of the zoo and was only a few hundred feet from where I stood. Most people no longer picnicked there since it lay off the beaten path.

I sprinted through the rain, sloshing through puddles and sliding through mud. By the time I got there, I was soaked clear to the bone, and my teeth chattered from the cold rain. But after I climbed the steps that led up to the red-shingled structure, my heart skipped a beat when I saw Javi sitting on the ground in the center.

I splashed over to where he sat with his knees drawn to his chest and took my place by his side.

"How do you always find me?" he asked.

I shrugged. "I'm smart and persistent."

"And what if I asked you to leave me alone? Would you do it?"

"If that's what you wanted, I would."

He must have believed me. He stared straight ahead and said nothing further. If anyone was going to start this conversation, it was going to be me. The strength and confidence Javi usually carted around had been cast off. He resembled glass about to be shattered.

"I'm sorry," I said. "I shouldn't have said what I did. It was stupid, and I take it back."

Javi wiped his cheek. Whether it was a tear or a drop of rain that fell from his still wet hair, I couldn't tell. It really didn't matter. Javi had been right. He hadn't pushed me when I wasn't ready to talk. He'd given me my space and offered only friendship. I hadn't returned the favor, and I would make up for that for the rest of my life.

"Tell me what to do to make it better. I'll do anything. Just don't shut me out."

The pain in Javi's eyes broke my heart. Whatever I had stirred within him had torn him apart. I had to put the pieces back together, cobble Javi back into the boy he was before I came crashing into his life. Nothing was more important than that.

Javi might hate me from now until the end of time after this. Could I blame him? I had reduced him to this. Still, the thought of Javi remaining cold and distant cut through my heart like a blade, and the contents in my stomach slowly rose in my throat.

"Please, Javi," I said, voice cracking as pain and regret ripped open my insides. I tried to force the tears away, to blink them away, but they were too strong. They spilled onto my cheeks, and the accompanying sobs racked my body.

Javi wrapped his arm around my shoulders and drew me into him. The reassurance of his weight against mine, his warmth spreading across me, offered more comfort than I'd ever received in my life. It was strong, all-encompassing. If I gave myself over to it, it might support me better than my legs and my will.

It was better than any fantasy I'd cooked up or any of the dreams that had played while I slept. It was real. It was here. It was right.

Javi pulled me even deeper into him until my cheek rested against his chin, and he encircled me with his arms. I hugged him back, leaning harder against him, pushing myself farther into his touch, which sizzled my flesh and practically dried my clothes on my body. Javi's aroma of musk and wet cedar filled my nostrils, and I inhaled greedily.

He caressed my back with long tender strokes as the sobs turned to sniffles before disappearing entirely.

"I'm really sorry," I mumbled.

"Shh," he whispered. He rested his forehead against my wet head before brushing his lips across my temples. I gasped as his hot breath trailed across my flesh and down my cheek. At the curve of my neck, he gingerly, almost timidly, kissed my soft, moist skin.

"Javi?" I asked, my voice low and heavy. I'd meant to ask if this was what he wanted. More than anything, he had to be sure.

But his eyes gave me my answer. Half closed in longing, his lips mounted mine. I pressed back into the sweetest and most gentle moment of my life.

AFTER WHAT seemed like an hour of Javi's lips upon mine, he pulled out of the kiss and gazed lovingly into my eyes. He pressed his forehead against mine, his breath still fanning across my flesh, and his lips stretched into a full smile, not his lopsided grin façade. "Does that answer your question?" he asked.

I laughed. "Yes, it does." I moved my arms to around his neck. I wrapped my legs around his waist while keeping our foreheads joined. As far as I was concerned, we'd stay this way forever.

"I hope you're not too mad," he said.

"I have no idea what you're talking about."

"For the way I acted earlier. And for the things I said." He sighed deeply and rubbed his nose against mine. "I was sort of a prick."

He was, but that didn't matter now. "All's forgiven."

Javi traced the outline of my jaw before hooking my chin. He brought me back to his lips, where we found each other again. His tongue slipped into my mouth, and I immediately drew it farther in.

The gentleness of our first kiss gave way to surging passion that flowed between us as my tongue invaded his mouth and his shot back into mine. Javi clutched at my back, and I raked my hands through his hair.

I'd been mistaken. *This* was how we'd stay for the rest of our lives.

Javi agreed. He moved his hands to the curve of my back. He danced his fingers along the exposed skin, dipping his fingertips beneath the waistband before drawing them back out.

I shifted my position and lowered my arms. I clutched at his chest and his muscled arms as our tongues continued their dance.

My heart raced, and my breath came out in ragged breaths. A fire I'd never experienced scorched my body until I feared I'd literally burst into flame. Only the rain, which continued to pound the roof of the pavilion, might be enough to douse the fire.

Javi reluctantly pulled away. His flushed cheeks and panting breaths revealed he'd been as on the verge of passing out as I was.

We sat there for a few moments, neither of us speaking. The rain tapped out a beat atop the roof that matched the steady rhythm of our hearts.

"So, was that better than your vampire Carl?" Javi asked. He broke into a full smile.

"You put Carl to shame," I replied. "Must be all your experience."

"Maybe," he said with a nod. "But kissing girls and kissing you are two different experiences. This beats them, hands down."

I laid my head on his shoulder and nuzzled into the crook of his neck. His heady scent clung to the air around him. I could get drunk on it all day. "And you didn't swallow any of my teeth."

Javi laughed. "No, I didn't. But I sure as hell tried."

Silence once again swept over us. Not because we were embarrassed or didn't know what to say. Being in each other's arms revealed more than words could possibly communicate, so we sat there in our mutual embrace, our hands gliding across each other with the patter of rain playing like our personal orchestra.

Even though I hated to break the easy quiet that enveloped us, I had to. "Can I ask you something?"

"Ask away."

I sat up and gazed deeply into his smiling eyes. "How long have you known you were gay?"

"I was never certain," he admitted with a long exhalation. "I mean, I knew I found some guys attractive, but I felt the same way about some girls."

"So you think you're bi, then?"

He shrugged. "I'm not really sure what I am, to be honest. I've always been more confused than anything else. I've already told you about Dina, but what I didn't tell you was that there was this eighth grader at my middle school, his name was Adam, and I remember thinking he was the cutest boy I'd ever seen. All the girls loved him. And he went out with a different girl every week. I wanted to be just like him, but I was this awkward sixth grader. One day while I was playing baseball with kids during gym class, Adam came up and asked if he could join. Naturally, we let him, and I think I watched him more than I paid attention to the game. I sure as hell made more than my fair share of mistakes because of it. And every time I did, he'd come up to me and give me advice. He wasn't an asshole about it either. He was very calm and nice, and we became friends."

Javi sighed in deep thought before continuing. "I followed him around for the rest of the year. He never made me feel like a dweeb or some stupid pesky kid. He really cared about me. At least that's the way he made me feel. He was the one who told me to go for it with Dina. He said she obviously liked me, and I should get what I could while I could. I didn't know what he meant at the time, especially since what I wanted was to kiss him, but I thought if Adam says to do it, I should probably do it. And I figured it might make me less confused."

"Did it?"

He shook his head. "I think it confused me more. The kiss wasn't all that great, but it felt good. My body reacted in ways I didn't understand. All I knew was that I got the same feelings around Adam without kissing him. And I really wanted to see if kissing him would make me feel the same way Dina did."

"And you never got the chance?"

"Nope. He moved to California midyear, and I never saw him again." He cupped my cheek in his big hand. "You're the first boy I've ever kissed."

I couldn't stop my huge grin from forming. Whenever I felt it come on, I usually hid it with my hand or tried to think of something sad that would prevent me from baring my huge horse teeth, but today I welcomed it and let it shine.

"I love your smile," Javi said. Of course hearing that made my lips stretch even broader, and I ducked back into the crook of his neck. "Aww, why are you hiding?"

"You embarrassed me," I said against Javi's warm skin.

Javi laughed. "Don't be. I think it's beautiful."

Now I practically beamed. "Stop it! You're gonna make my face crack."

Javi leaned his head against mine and drew me securely into his arms. "We can't have that. I plan on kissing that face again real soon."

"I'm good with that," I said as I pressed my mouth to his neck. After nibbling my way up to his chin, Javi shivered. But before we got lost in our passion, there was something else I just had to know. "Why me?"

His eyes, which had been half-closed in anticipation of another long, leisurely kiss, fluttered open. "Huh?"

"Why am I here with you now?"

Javi stared at me as if I'd gone mad. "Because I like you. It's as simple as that."

But to me, it wasn't that simple. If I was in Javi's arms because I was the only gay boy he'd met, I needed to know that. What I felt for Javi was certainly more than just exploration of my sexuality. And it was definitely more than experimentation. Maybe that was what had concerned my mom. She hadn't worried Javi might hurt me physically. She'd been fearful that Javi, who obviously hadn't discovered who he was yet, might break my heart on his path to finding himself.

"What's going on?" he asked. He'd noted the change in my expression. The smile that had practically split my face had retreated to a thin line.

"I really need to know why you chose me," I said. "I mean, look at you. You're the star player on the high school baseball team. The same team that might return to the state finals. Pretty much every kid and teacher loves you, and you're probably the sweetest and the hottest guy I've ever met. I'm like the complete opposite of that. I'm the weird-looking new kid with only one other friend besides you in the entire school."

"First of all," Javi said as he placed his hands on either side of my face, "you're not weird-looking. I wish you wouldn't be so hard on yourself."

"Well, when you're told you look like Donkey from *Shrek*, it's kind of hard to believe differently."

Javi chuckled and craned his neck forward to brush his lips against mine. "I happen to love Donkey from *Shrek*. He's my favorite character. And I can tell you that you look nothing like him." He traced the edges of my mouth. "The big smile you're so embarrassed about is quite stunning. There's something pure about it. And when I see it, I want to do anything to keep it on your face because it lights up your eyes and kinda wipes all the shit you've been through from your soul. As if it never existed. But even more than all that, I'm here with you now because when I saw you that first day in class, there was something about you that drew me to you. I didn't know what it was at the time, but now I think about it, it was the same pull I had toward Adam. And when I got to know you and spend more time with you, it only got stronger. It about drove me crazy. I couldn't stop thinking about you. I always wanted to be with you. And when I was with you, I wanted to touch you. But I couldn't bring myself to do it because the feelings you brought out of me so quickly terrified me. I fought them. Hard. But when I brushed against your hard cock, I realized you might feel the same way too.

"That's when a whole world of possibilities opened up. And after spending all these weeks with you, fighting what I've wanted for so long, I decided to just go with it. See where these feelings take us." He pulled me close and brushed a reassuring kiss across my temple. "And that's how you're here with me now. It wasn't a choice. It just happened."

When he finished speaking, I dove onto his lips. My fears and concerns floated away, and when our lips finally parted, the gray clouds had retreated and the rain had stopped falling. Sunlight once again streaked through the haze, and my grin had never been wider.

WE LEFT the park after the storm. The rain no longer provided us the cover we needed to be together, and though we wanted to remain in each other's arms all day, that was impossible out in public.

So we drove back to my place. My mom would be at work for another hour or so, and we needed to get into dry clothing. For the entire drive across town, the only way we could stop our teeth from chattering was to hold hands. Our touch drove the chill away.

Javi had barely put the vehicle in park before we hopped out and sprinted for the front door. Once we were inside with the door safely locked behind us, Javi took me in his arms and pressed his lips against mine.

"God, I've missed you," he said into my mouth.

I moaned in reply. I couldn't do anything else. His full body now rested against mine. We were no longer sitting in a weird crab-like fashion as we had in the pavilion. His chest rested against mine, and he reached under my shirt. He traveled his fingers across my flesh before dancing around my nipples and grinding his hard cock against my straining erection.

As I explored the wetness of his mouth with my tongue, I lifted his shirt and surfed my hands across his slightly chilled skin. Goose bumps spread across his flesh, and I charted a path up his muscled back before traveling back down to his waist. I dipped my fingers beneath the waistband of his shorts and grasped the top of his firm ass.

Javi groaned and flattened me against the front door. He thrust his hips against mine as if he were trying to rip his clothes free from just the friction of his movement. His mouth suddenly left mine, and he traced the curve of my cheek with a kiss before arriving at my neck, where he alternated between gentle nibbles and light flicks of his tongue.

Every time his teeth bit into me or his tongue swirled across my flesh, I gripped his ass harder, forcing his groin firmly against mine.

"You taste so good," he whimpered before once again molding his lips to mine.

I replied only in primal noises. Nothing else could communicate the powerful desire that held us both in its sweaty embrace. But it wasn't just lust that flowed between us. It was much more. My swelling heart and the storm of butterflies flitting in my stomach told me what was happening between me and Javi was more than two horny teenage boys making out.

We had a connection that tethered us together, and it had formed before we realized what had happened. What it was, I had no clue. Javi most likely didn't either. This was newer for him than it was for me. He'd been fighting himself and his feelings for a long time while I had simply accepted who I was a long time ago.

That was why we had to stop. We traveled unexplored territory, and we needed to do it with level heads. And right now, the two heads we were thinking with were much farther south than the ones above our shoulders.

"Javi," I whispered as I pulled away.

He pounced back onto my lips. He placed his right hand on my butt, squeezing it while he pulled me tighter against him. The fingers on his other hand fluttered across the back of my neck, sending a thousand shivering pulses coursing through me.

"Javi, please," I said. This time, I placed my hands on his chest and gently nudged him away.

His eyes opened and grew wide, and he took a step back. "What's wrong? Are you okay?"

"I'm fine," I said, too out of breath to say much else. It had taken all my strength not to hand control of my body over to my hard dick. It certainly knew what it wanted. "We just need to slow things down a bit. Don't you think?"

He placed his hands on his hips and blew out a lungful of air. After a few seconds of deep, measured breath, he nodded. "Not really, but I suppose you're right."

It made me feel better that he somewhat agreed. I grabbed his hand and led him back to the couch where we'd watched our zombie marathon last night. After we sat down, I wrapped his arm around my shoulders and leaned against him. "I hope you don't think this is too girly or anything," I said. "But I don't want to rush things. I mean, you've just now accepted you might be gay. That's a pretty big step for anyone. Adding something like sex to the equation is probably not the smartest move."

"Probably not, no," he agreed as he laced the fingers of his right hand with my left. "But it sure felt good."

I smiled up at him. "You'll get no argument from me on that."

"I'm glad," he said as he pressed his lips to my forehead. "Can I ask you something?"

"Ask away."

He snuffed before speaking. "This might sound girly, but what are we now?"

I laughed. I'd just been thinking the same thing. "I'm not sure."

Our relationship had evolved rather quickly. One minute we were friends and the next we were eating each other's faces. It seemed like the smart thing to do would be to determine the parameters. But just what were they? He was just now coming to grips with his sexuality. It seemed far too soon to be boyfriends after such a revelation. Plus, we still had the shark-infested waters of high school to navigate. How would we handle trying to be a couple at school? Sure, gay kids and people were more prevalent these days. The closet doors of society had already been flung open, but in the barrio of San Antonio, where the citizens were mostly Roman Catholic and not as free thinking as other parts of the nation, coming out as a couple would likely destroy Javi's life and rain further hell upon my head.

"Yeah, me either," he said with a sigh. "I know what I feel, though. And it's good. I don't want that to end."

"I agree."

"How about for now we be friends who care a lot for each other and who just happen to make out? And I mean like a lot." His lopsided grin inched across his face.

That sure as hell sounded like a train I was willing to board. "I like the sound of that. And we can see how things go. Just let it happen like it's done so far."

"I like that," Javi said with a nod. He opened his mouth but then immediately closed it.

"What?" I asked. "No need to get shy on me now."

"I was just wondering if you were going to tell Claudia or your mom."

I'd actually already given that some thought. The excited little boy inside me longed to run to both of them and spill everything that had happened. After all, finding someone like Javi was like a dream come true, but sometimes when dreams were shared, reality intruded. When something was new, it was usually better to leave it alone and let its roots take hold. Then, when reality inevitably shook the ground, what was once new had had time to become established enough to withstand the shocks of life. "No," I finally said. "I'm not. Right now, this is just for you and me. It's too soon to bring anyone else into it. It'll make things only more complicated."

Javi gazed down at me before leaning forward to sweep his lips against mine. "I feel the same way."

"Then it's settled," I said. "And it's time for you to go."

"What?" Javi asked, his mouth still open for more mouth-to-mouth action.

"My mother will be home within the hour," I said with a nod to the clock. "And she can't find us both soaked through, making out on the couch."

"And she won't," Javi said. "I just need one final kiss before I go. It'll help get me through what will likely be the longest night of my life." He reached for my hand and pulled me on top of him. He nestled his lips against mine before his tongue once again came alive in my mouth. Javi had about stolen all the breath from my body by the time he hesitantly broke free. After burying his nose against the exposed flesh of my neck, he inhaled deeply.

When it was time for him to go, my hands refused to let him depart. My stomach sank to the ground as I waved good-bye and stared after him as he drove away. But knowing that he and I would be together tomorrow lifted me higher than I'd ever been before. And long after my mother came home from work and I'd crawled into the bed where Javi had slept the night before, the smile on my face couldn't match the one in my heart.

Chapter 9

FOR THE next few weeks before the end of the semester, Javi and I did our best to stick to the routine we had established to keep anyone from guessing the nature of our relationship had changed. It was difficult limiting our time together to our rides to and from school and hanging out in the park or having dinner with his parents.

But when Christmas break finally came, we spent practically the entire vacation with each other. We watched movies, and we made out. We hung out with Claudia, and we made out some more. We held hands on our way to and from places whenever we got to borrow either of his parents' cars. We did our Christmas shopping together, only separating to buy each other gifts. I got Javi a baseball-stitched wallet, and I placed the picture of us inside it. When he opened it and saw the photo, he almost pulled me into a kiss. Thankfully, he remembered his parents were in the room.

He gave me a chain with a charm of St. Michael, the patron saint of protection. "To watch over you when I'm not with you," he said when we were alone in his room. He kissed the back of my neck as he clasped it around me.

For New Year's, Javi, Claudia, and I headed downtown to watch the fireworks. And as we rang in 2014 together, with the multicolored lightshow exploding overhead, we stared into each other's eyes instead of at the fireworks. For me, nothing was more beautiful than the comforting, warm blanket of Javi looking at me. He obviously felt the same, because while everyone oohed and aahed around us, Javi bravely reached out and rubbed his thumb along my cheek and over my lips. I did the same thing. It was how we kissed in the middle of San Antonio, surrounded by thousands of people.

When Javi turned eighteen a few days later, I made up a small picnic of chicken salad sandwiches and sodas, and chocolate cupcakes for his birthday cake, and took him back to the pavilion in the park, where we'd shared our first kiss. Even though Javi had to drive us there, he enjoyed the gesture, and we snuck in a few kisses too.

Both of us wanted to do more. We'd gotten close a few times since that time in the apartment, but I'd promised my mother. Javi didn't want to be part of breaking a promise I'd made. The closest we'd come to breaking that promise was masturbating together, which we were doing more and more these days. "What about when you turn eighteen?" he asked as he licked the icing from his third cupcake. "Can we do it then?"

"She wants me to wait till graduation," I reminded him.

Javi groaned. "That's so far away."

And it certainly seemed that way, especially once Christmas break ended and we went back to school. We had a tough time readjusting. We had to go back to acting as if we were just friends instead of so much more.

But we kept spring break as our goal. We'd have a whole week to ourselves, and my birthday was just a few days after. Although I hadn't told Javi, I'd seriously considered not waiting until after graduation for us to finally experience each other's touch.

Being in his arms and kissing him felt right. I could only imagine what doing all that naked would be like.

But that was a few weeks away. Right now, we had to get through the torture of being at school, unable to express how we felt. So we tried to show it in little ways.

When we stopped to talk or clasp hands, as we sometimes did in greeting, we'd sometimes linger for a second longer than was needed. When we ate dinner with his parents, Javi's legs would inevitably find mine under the table. He'd rest them against me or rub his foot up and down my shin.

Staying focused on the day to day proved almost impossible. My mind constantly rushed forward to the next time Javi and I would spend time together under our tree. Or the next time we might be alone for more than an hour at a time and rest upon each other's lips or in each other's arms instead of keeping a watchful eye on the clock for when my mother might get home.

Usually, thinking about how and when we'd spend quality time together resulted in a raging erection that refused to go down. I abandoned carrying my books in my book bag and simply left it in my locker. I took my US History book with me to every class to conceal the never-ending boner I carried around in my jeans, and George Washington couldn't have been any less amused. He had my cock pressed against him more than Javi did, which was a sad and depressing fact.

But we had to keep our relationship a secret. At least for now. That made sticking to our routine important. If we didn't, and if we didn't censor the emotions that stirred within us, the high school rumor mill might churn out gossip neither of us needed.

As it was Claudia was proving difficult to keep in the dark.

"I know there's something you're not telling me, Tru," she said while I manipulated an image in the journalism Mac lab. That sentence had become her mantra over the last couple of weeks, and she'd turned into a dog with a bone. "And I want to know what it is."

I blew her a kiss. "I've fallen in love with you and want you to be the mother of my children."

She pretended to gag. "Now you're just being gross," she said with a roll of her eyes, which had been excessively outlined with dark pencil liner. In fact, Claudia had even dyed the purple out of her hair. It was now as pitch-black as a country road at night. Her clothing remained the same. She wore a black, long-sleeve shirt with print that said, "Yeah, yeah. Yadda, yadda. Whatever."

"I think we'd make beautiful children," I said as I went back to work. "They'd have my good looks and your charming disposition."

"Sweet talking me will get you nowhere." She took the seat next to me and studied me as I continued to ignore her. "I can sense it. You're hiding something. I noticed it a while back. After you told me about Javi accidently sitting on your—" She stopped, and instead of saying the word, she wiggled her eyebrows and nodded to my groin.

"Now who's being gross?" I asked as I stuck out my tongue at her. Her blank look revealed she was not going to let the matter drop as easily as she had in the past. She smelled a story, and she intended to get the scoop. I removed my hand from the computer mouse and locked onto her gaze. "That is so last year. Besides, I already told you what happened between Javi and me after that."

She waved away my words and then pointed to the lettering on her shirt. "You guys talked about it at some park. Javi asked you questions about your past. You told him some vampire story, and you laughed the whole thing off."

"That's what happened. I swear."

She studied me with one eyebrow raised. "You choose your words carefully, you know that?"

Uh-oh. That didn't sound good. Claudia knew me too well. So far, I'd been able to get away with not lying by doing what she had accused me of. Technically, I was committing the lie of omission, but not everyone needed to know my business. I'd been able to justify not revealing everything under those terms. But if Claudia happened to ask a point-blank question, how on earth was I going to respond? "I'm telling you exactly what happened," I finally said.

"There you go again," she said, pointing at me. "I believe what you're telling me is the truth. I've gotten to know you pretty well, and you suck balls at lying."

"And there you go," I replied with a hand flourish. "Case closed."

She snickered. "Oh, hell no! The case is most definitely open. I just haven't asked the right question yet, but I will. You can bet your life on it."

I was getting annoyed. While I appreciated Claudia's interest in my life and well-being, her continuing intrusion on the matter might stir up unforeseen trouble. Claudia would certainly not tell anyone if she knew about Javi and me, but she'd definitely want to constantly talk about it if she knew. And if we happened to discuss it when unseen ears were listening, everything Javi and I had spent the last few months trying to accomplish would be destroyed. "Just let it go," I finally said. "If there's something for you to know, I'll tell you."

She eyed me again and grinned. "That's all I needed to hear." She got up and walked out of the lab with a Cheshire grin plastered across her face.

What the hell did that mean, and what was she up to now?

AFTER I finished up in the Mac lab, I waited for Claudia so we could walk to seventh period together. We had different classes, but they were only a few doors down from each other.

Mr. Avila, however, told me she had left, and when I checked her desk, she had already snagged her things.

I didn't have time to think about it, though, as the pretardy bell rang to let us know that we had less than five minutes to get to our next class. I said my good-byes to Mr. Avila and strolled down the hall toward my physics class.

As I rounded the corner and crossed the glass-enclosed breezeway that connected the north part of the building with the south, I spotted Rance strolling toward me with a small pack of the Jock Brigade. They were laughing and carrying on about some nonsense, completely oblivious to my presence among the small trickle of students that had not yet entered their classrooms.

Since he and Javi had mostly patched things up, Rance had kept his distance. That, and he still had the threat of being kicked off the team if he was caught fighting on campus again. But Javi had spent less time with him again recently, since he'd been spending it with me, and I could see the storm once again brewing in his eyes.

Every now and then it came out in muttered curses at me under his breath. Calling me a fag when I passed was a routine experience. And usually, when Rance saw me, he made sure to shoot enough daggers at me that he made his point.

He hated me, and he wanted me to die.

Somehow, Javi was completely oblivious to Rance's obvious antagonism. Granted, Rance did a halfway decent job of masking his loathing of me when Javi was in the general vicinity. It was as if he feared losing Javi's friendship more than he hated me. I didn't understand it, but I took what reprieve I could get. But for Javi to be that unaware confused the hell out of me.

How could someone so loving and caring not see that his best friend hated the guts of, well, the boy Javi loved to kiss? It seemed counterintuitive, especially since I could count on one hand how many times both Rance and I had been around Javi at the same time.

"Faggot!" Rance called as he drew closer. The word echoed down the hall, and the students around me gave me a wide berth. While being Javi's friend compelled most to be nice to me, they most certainly weren't going to spill any of their blood in my defense.

I ignored the insult as always and continued on my way to class. Although part of me wanted to tell Javi that Rance hadn't buried the hatchet at all, I couldn't do that to him. I cared about Javi too much to hurt him in any way, and if keeping him in the dark about what an asshole his best friend truly was kept Javi safe, then that was what I aimed to do.

The next thing I knew, my foot caught on something and I went crashing to the floor. My books flew out in front of me and slid halfway down the corridor. I half expected to find Rance looming over me, ready to make my face a bloody mess, but it wasn't Rance who'd tripped me. It was Rance's even dumber and uglier friend, Oscar Gomez.

He wasn't as big as Rance, whose larger frame benefited him in his role as catcher for the team. But Oscar was at least twice my size. He reached down to snatch me up, and no doubt toss me around the corridor, when Javi suddenly appeared between us. He shoved Oscar, and he fell hard on his ass, skidding backward a few feet before he eventually came to a stop.

"What the fuck, man?" Javi asked. His angry voice rebounded off the walls. He was ready to pounce again if need be, but he obviously didn't want to leave me on the ground unprotected.

I got up as quickly as possible and backed out of the way. While it was slightly embarrassing to have someone come to my rescue, I had to school the smile that wanted to crawl across my face in appreciation of how much Javi clearly cared for me.

"Who the fuck do you think you are, Javi?" Oscar asked once he got up. The rest of the Jock Brigade had cleared a path between them.

They glanced back and forth between Javi, Oscar, and Rance, obviously unsure what they were expected to do. Rance's expression held no such confusion. He was ready to intervene. "You don't get to push me and walk away."

"Well, come and get it, then," Javi challenged. "I'm not scared of your fat ass."

Oscar charged, but Rance snagged Oscar and held him back. "Chill, man," Rance whispered. "This isn't the place or the time."

"Fuck that, Rance!" Oscar cursed. "Javi needs to remember his place."

"And what's that?" Javi asked. "Knocking down people smaller than me? That's never been my place and never will."

"No, man," Oscar said. "Your place is with us. The Bulldogs. The team you've been a part of for almost four years." He nodded at me. "Not that fucking fag you've turned into your little pet."

Javi lunged toward Oscar, and the rest of the Jock Brigade responded. They surrounded Oscar and blocked Javi. A few of them even held him back from doing what Javi most obviously wanted to do—rearrange Oscar's face.

Oscar raised his hands in front of his chest, the universal sign that violence was no longer imminent. "That's what I'm talking about, Javi," Oscar said. "You come to his defense, ready to fight your teammate over some loser cocksucker the world doesn't even care about."

Javi's face twisted in rage. "You better shut him up now, Rance. Or Oscar's going to be gumming his food for the rest of his life."

Rance nodded. "Calm down, man," he told Oscar with a pat to his back.

Oscar shrugged off Rance. "You better make a choice," he said to Javi. "It's either the butt muncher or your boys. You can't have both."

Javi strained against the Jock Brigade who still held him tight. "You don't tell me what to do, fuck face."

"I'm not," Oscar said as he took his book bag from Rance. "You get to decide and live with the consequences. Show everyone you're a man and come back to us, or stay with the fag and let everyone know you suck his cock." Oscar turned to walk off as the tardy bell rang, and the rest of the Jock Brigade followed him down the hall.

Only Rance stayed behind. He stood on one side of Javi, and I was on the other. Javi surveyed the hall as the students who'd witnessed the scuffle silently waited on what he would do.

Javi headed for his book bag, which he'd tossed aside in order to come to my rescue, and yanked it from the floor. He then stormed off, but instead of following the Jock Brigade by going straight, he turned left and disappeared around the corner.

Rance glared at me. He didn't say a word, but the sly smile that slithered across his lips told me he couldn't have been happier.

THANKS TO Oscar and Rance, the rumor mill Javi and I had attempted to keep from spewing its gossip started to spin. Most of the school had heard about the fight in the hall by the time seventh period ended.

Texting and Facebook sure made gossip fly faster than the speed of light.

As I made my way to my locker, whispering voices followed me down the halls.

"Can you believe it?" someone asked as I spun the combination on my lock and opened the door.

"Not really," another voice answered.

"Why *is* Javi his friend?"

"I don't know. That's what *everyone's* been wondering for months."

I grabbed the books I needed for homework, shoved them in my backpack, and headed down the stairs. If only I could escape the low murmurs that followed me wherever I went.

"That's him, right?"

"Don't you recognize him from the picture in the paper?"

"Yeah, I wondered how that happened and what that meant. I question it even more now."

I left the staircase, my heartbeat pounding in my ears. Terror gripped my intestines and ruthlessly twisted them. Why didn't I just dash out of the halls and away from the words that pursued me like ghosts? Because reacting that way would only validate suspicions that had already begun to circulate.

"He just jumped right in there and pushed Oscar flat on his ass."

"Good. I hate that guy. He's a jerk."

Now that was one comment I agreed with.

"Tru."

But the eyes of the school had been forced open, and they were now scrutinizing our relationship instead of dismissing it as they had before. Most likely, everyone considered Javi befriending me as Javi being Javi. He was everyone's friend and an all-around good guy. Being nice was part of his reputation.

Now, his character was being called into question, and it was all because of me.

"What do you think it means?"

"I don't know, but it can't be true what they're saying. Can it?"

"Hey, Tru."

I had to find some way to fix this. There had to be something I could do to save Javi from the torment I'd lived with for years. It was nothing new to me. I'd grown accustomed to shouldering the burden, but Javi had always been liked. He had no clue what life on the outside was like. And if I could spare him that knowledge, I had to at least try.

"I've heard that they spend most afternoons together at the park."

"Really? How do you know?"

"My cousin lives along North Park, and she sees them almost every afternoon. Just sitting there and talking."

"Are you serious? Wow! That really makes you wonder. Maybe Javi is…."

I shoved the door open and exited the building before the whispering voice could finish the thought. The refreshing chaos of engines revving in the parking lot and students laughing as they left school drowned out the lingering phantasms that had followed me outside.

And I was finally able to breathe.

What I needed the most right now was Javi. Only he could make me feel better, and together we might be able to come up with a plan to do damage control.

I bounded down the stairs and toward the bike rack, where I typically waited for him after school on the days he didn't have practice. But before I made it to the bottom, I stopped in my tracks.

My bike was there, chained exactly where I had left it that morning.

Javi's bike was gone.

"Dammit, Tru," Claudia suddenly said next to me. "I've been chasing you down the damn hall. Didn't you hear me?"

I turned. Where had she come from?

"Tru, are you okay?"

"He's gone," I said as I turned my attention back to the empty slot where Javi's bike had been. And the hole in my soul Javi had filled with his presence suddenly cracked open once again.

CLAUDIA INSISTED on taking me home. Since I didn't feel like arguing, I tossed my bike in the back of her parents' SUV and ordered her to drive by North Park. Javi wasn't there.

"Tell me what happened," she said.

I said nothing. I continued to stare at our spot under the tree as misery slowly ate me alive.

For the rest of the drive, Claudia didn't speak, and I made no effort to carry on a conversation. How could I? Javi had apparently been so angry or embarrassed he had skipped and gone home.

Although I couldn't even fathom the prospect, I suspected my life was about to change in a way I wasn't going to like.

When Claudia pulled up to my apartment, I got out of the car, retrieved my bike, and headed to the front door. I couldn't make out what she was saying. Her words sounded like some alien language I'd never heard before, so I focused on chaining my bike to the front rail and unlocking the door.

"Damn it," she said as she closed the door behind us. "Will you fucking talk to me?"

I spun around. The tears I had been holding back burst free. "What do you want from me, Claudia?" My words were broken by the sobs that strangled my throat. "Javi left. He took off without so much as saying good-bye, and I don't know why. I have no fucking clue what's going on or why he's so angry with me. But he is." I collapsed on the couch, shoving my head into the pillow that still held Javi's scent from yesterday when we'd made out before my mother came home. "I don't know what to do."

Claudia sat next to me and rubbed my back. "I heard about his fight with Oscar," she said. "Did it really happen the way they said it did? Did Javi punch him for kicking you? And who had the knife? That's the part I'm *really* confused about."

I groaned. "God! Can't the rumor mongers get *anything* right?"

"Then why don't you tell me what really happened?"

I sat up and told her the truth.

"So after being asked to choose between you and the team, Javi went a different direction. And you think that means he's mad at you? You realize he stood up for you against his friends, right? That has to count for something."

"It does," I said, wiping my runny nose with the back of my hand. "I'm grateful for that. No one's ever done that for me before, but when he didn't show up after school, I knew something was wrong."

"It could mean he's busy. Or just needs to think. He had a pretty major confrontation in front of the school, Tru. And the whispers you heard today, he likely heard them too."

"I know," I answered with a nod. "But we've been following the routine for the last few months. Every day. To suddenly throw that away tells me something has changed."

Claudia sat back. The curiosity she'd hounded me with over the last few weeks no longer sparked in her eyes. She had no doubt figured it out, like most everyone else at school. "Are you going to tell me what's been going on between you two or do you want me to say it?"

"I promised Javi I wouldn't."

She nodded. "Okay, then. You can keep your promise and not tell me a thing. But let me tell you what I now realize to be fact. You and Javi have been dating ever since your weekend at the zoo. He figured out he was attracted to you, and the two of you have since decided to make a go of it, but you planned on doing it in secret. Probably because you didn't want to deal with the shit storm being together would stir up."

She waited for me to reply, but I said nothing. Her nod indicated she took my silence as agreement. "But today, when Javi saw you getting bullied, he ran to your rescue, not thinking about the ramifications shoving a teammate might have on him or you. All he saw was his need to protect you. But now that Oscar has called him out about you and told him to make a choice, you think him not walking you to class or being there for you after school is a sign he has made a choice. And it's not you."

I nodded.

She grabbed my hand and held it between both of hers. "Tru, I say this with all the affection in the world, but you need to get your head out of your ass."

I recoiled as if she'd slapped me. "What the hell does that mean?"

"It means you're being a tad selfish," she said after releasing my hand. "You're only looking at this from your perspective. Sure, what happened today sucks ass, but your world hasn't really changed, has it?"

"You mean besides Javi abandoning me at school?"

She rolled her eyes as if I was some silly child incapable of seeing my faults. "You're gay. You've known that for years, right?" When I nodded, she continued. "Javi's just figuring this stuff out, and the two of you have been doing it on your own. And I can certainly understand why. You're walking a minefield, and you don't know where to step. I get it. But today changed things a bit. Today, Javi was presented with a choice he's been foolishly trying to avoid. He can't walk both sides of the fence. That's not how life works, and that's definitely not how high school works. We operate within the social circles we fit into. Sure, Javi's been able to weave in and out of most cliques because he's not had to pick one. Everyone accepts him because he's a great person. But today, he was told for the first time in his life he can't do that. He's basically been given an ultimatum. Do you realize how confused he must be right now?"

Claudia was right. I had been selfish and shortsighted. Earlier I'd been trying to think of ways I could make Javi's life easier, but I'd forgotten all that once faced with my fears of losing Javi. This wasn't just about me or us. This was about Javi too.

"I have to find him," I said as I stood.

She smiled. "Good boy."

Someone knocked on the front door. "Can you get that?" I asked as I darted for the kitchen. "I'm going to call Javi." I didn't have a cell phone, so I couldn't call his cell or text him. I had to rely on the landline and hope he would answer when my number showed up on the caller ID.

"Sure," Claudia said.

I picked up the phone and dialed Javi's number. When it started to ring, Claudia was suddenly at my side. "What?"

She took the phone from my hand and placed it back on the receiver.

"Why'd you do that? I'm trying to call Javi."

She nodded to the door behind me. Javi stood in the living room. He ran his fingers through his dark hair and smiled. "Hey, Tru."

Tears blurred my vision as I ran straight into his arms.

JAVI AND I sat on the couch, our arms wrapped around each other, while Claudia beamed at us from the floor. "God, you two make me ill," she said.

"I guess we don't have to tell you about us now, huh?" Javi asked after he kissed my forehead.

She shrugged. "Nobody has to tell me shit. I usually figure stuff out on my own, and I'd pretty much had this pegged for a while now." She held her chin high in praise of her deductive skills. "The two of you aren't as sneaky as you think you are."

"No shit," Javi replied. He gazed down at me and said, "I'm sorry for leaving you standing there with Rance and for not waiting for you after school. I needed time to get my head on straight, and I couldn't do that around you. Being with you makes my world spin. But in a good way."

Claudia pretended to gag while I craned my head up to taste his lips. "I understand. I feel the same way."

"If the two of you are going to continue this mushy crap, please let me know so I can slit my throat now."

"Will you stop that?" I asked Claudia. "We're trying to have a moment here."

"And I'm trying to keep my lunch down here."

"All right, you two," Javi said. "I've already reached my quota for breaking up fights today."

Both Claudia and I gave him raspberries.

"So what are you two going to do?" she asked. She was right. The time for being silly was over. We needed a plan. "The whole school is wondering about the nature of your relationship."

"It's none of their business," Javi said.

She agreed. "But that's not going to stop the rumors, Javi. As long as you and Tru are doing whatever it is you're doing, people are gonna talk."

"Well, let them," he said. Anger once again brewed in his tone. "I don't give a flying fuck what people think. Or what Oscar Meyer-I-Have-A-Small-Weiner says I have to do. He doesn't own me. I own me."

"You're right again," she said. "But that doesn't exactly address the issue at hand."

"What issue is that, Claudia? Whether or not I'm a fag?"

If she had been a cat, she would have hissed. More than anyone else, she hated that word.

"That's not quite what she means," I said. "We have to decide whether we're ready to out ourselves as a couple. To tell people you and I are dating and let the chips fall where they may. Because if we're not, then we've got to figure out a way to throw people off our scent. Like, I don't know... get girlfriends or something."

"Don't look at me," she said. "I'm nobody's beard."

I smirked at her. "That's okay. I picture myself with someone with hairier legs."

"Hey, I've got hairy legs," Javi said with a big smile.

"Then you're perfect," I replied with a kiss.

"Well, that goes without saying," Javi added with an eyebrow wiggle.

"Can we please deal with the crisis at hand?" she asked in complete exasperation.

"You're right," I told her. "So, what do you want to do?"

Javi switched his gaze between Claudia and me. "Why are you both looking at me?"

"Because it's your decision, dumbass," Claudia said. "You've got the most to lose here."

When Javi rested his eyes on mine, I nodded. "She's right, and you know it."

"That's a lot of pressure," Javi said before gazing deep into my eyes. The conflict that raged within tore through him like a hurricane ravaged the coastline. The previously still waters of his life churned vigorously and threatened to capsize him. Javi held on to my hands as if he were drowning and looking for the life preserver my words could throw his way. "What do you want to do?"

"I can't make the decision for you, Javi," I replied. "I'll just follow your lead."

"I understand that," he said. "But if it was your decision, what would you do?"

I tore my gaze from his and glanced over at Claudia, who nodded. She had guessed what my answer would be, and her silent approval told me it was okay to speak my mind. "I've always just been me," I said. "I really don't know how else to be."

"So just be true to who I am and who we are together?" he asked. "Is it really that easy?"

"Don't fool yourself," she advised. "This is going to be the hardest thing you've ever done. People are not going to like it. And they'll react pretty crappy to it. Being true to yourself is never easy. It's always easier to pretend and cover up who we really are to avoid people rejecting us. But if this is what you want to do, you'll have my full support. I'll be there for both of you no matter what you decide."

He exhaled. He closed his eyes and took several deep breaths to calm his ragged breathing. When he opened them again, he stared first at Claudia and then at me. "Let's do it. Let's be true."

I almost fell over. Could this really be happening? Was Javi about to fling the door to his closet wide open and declare he was gay and dating the new kid? "Are you sure this is what you want? Because I'd completely understand if it wasn't."

"Tru's right," Claudia added. "There's no take-backs once you do it."

"I know," he said with a firm nod. "But like my dad says, a real man isn't forced into doing anything he doesn't want to do. And a real man doesn't lie to himself or to anyone else."

How could I argue with that?

He took my hand in his and turned to face me. "But if we're gonna do this, there's something we need to clear up."

"What's that?"

"I'm not going to walk through hell with you as only someone I care about. Going through something like this together means more than just making out. It means we're boyfriends, so what do you say, Tru? Will you be my boyfriend?"

"Of course," I leaped into his arms and onto his lips.

"Then, it's settled," Claudia said as she grinned at us. "But before you come out to the school, I think you need to first come out to your parents."

Holy shit! I'd completely forgotten about the Castillos, and my mother had no clue Javi and I were dating. When I turned to him, his wide-eyed panic told me he hadn't thought about any of that either.

Chapter 10

"I STILL can't believe you called me out of work for this," my mother said through gritted teeth as we walked over to Javi's house for dinner.

After talking everything over earlier, we'd decided getting our parents together for the big reveal had to happen tonight, before the shit hit the fan tomorrow. That meant calling my mom at work and getting her off the IHOP shift that wouldn't end until midnight. The only way to do that was to convince her I needed her, and it couldn't wait until the morning.

Naturally, when she'd zoomed home as fast as public transportation could carry her, she hadn't been pleased to learn she'd lost out on a shift's worth of tips to have dinner with the Castillos.

"You've been saying you wanted to meet Javi's parents for the past few months," I explained as I tried to keep up with her swift pace. It was more than just the cold of the final throes of south Texas winter that quickened her steps. When my mother was angry, she power walked.

"I know that, Tru, but we couldn't afford to lose the money I would've made tonight. You know how in debt we are because of Bart. Your father's social security benefits barely keep up with the monthly payments I have to make to pay off what that bastard still owes."

"But you're going to get that full-time job real soon," I reminded her. One of the full-time employees at Dr. Torres' office had just submitted her two-week notice, and Mom was a shoe-in as her replacement.

"Never count your unhatched chickens," she said. That had been one of grandpa's favorite sayings.

I nodded. "I realize that, but it's important for you to meet them."

She stopped before we stepped onto the sidewalk that would deposit us at the Castillo's front door. "Why is it so important for me to meet them today?" she asked. Her hands were on her hips as she studied my face. She'd been too angry earlier to contemplate the reasoning behind the dinner. Either that anger had started to fade, or she'd just realized she had never received a good explanation.

"It's just time," I said. "Don't you think so?"

"I'm not buying it, Tru," she said. She continued to scan my face. "Something's up. I can see that now. What is it?"

I started down the walk and gestured for her to follow me. "Come on, Mom. We're gonna be late, and it's cold."

She shook her head as a chilly breeze whipped around her, sending her brown hair flying in front of her eyes. After brushing the strands away, she said, "I'm not moving one step more until you tell me what I'm walking into."

I sighed as I traversed back up the walk toward her. I shoved my hands inside my new-to-me brown coat. "Please, Mom," I said. "Let's just go inside."

"If you're not going to tell me, then I'm going home." She turned around and started back the way we'd come.

I trotted after her, my hands still safely tucked inside my coat as the biting wind nipped at my nose. "Mom, please stop." She continued on as if I hadn't spoken. "Will you please just trust me? This is important." Still, she walked on. She was just like me, true to her word. If she said she was going to do something, she did it. "Fine. I'll tell you."

She proceeded a few more steps before stopping. When she turned around, she stood there in silence, waiting for me to speak.

"Javi's gay," I said. The news hadn't surprised her. She waited for the rest. "And he and I have been dating for the past few months."

Now this was news to her. Her eyes grew wide, and she opened her mouth to speak. Her voice, however, refused to cooperate.

"I'm sorry I haven't told you," I said as I walked up to her. "But it was so new, and Javi just realized how he felt about me. We figured, well, I figured if we talked about it before we knew what was going on, it might.... I don't know. Jinx things or overcomplicate matters. So, yes, we kept it a secret, and yes, I hid it from you, but that's kind of what tonight is going to be about. Telling our parents."

"Do Javi's parents not suspect their son is gay?" she asked as she switched her gaze from me to the Castillo house with its brown paint and white shutters.

"No," I said with a shake of my head.

"So I guess I'm here for moral support, then? To tell them it's okay to have a gay son and to love him no matter what?"

I couldn't stop smiling. I had the best mom ever. "That's right." I took my hand out of my warm pocket and reached for hers.

She gripped it tightly. "I know you probably promised Javi not to tell me until you both made the announcement at dinner, but it's better this way. Instead of being taken by surprise and reacting along with everyone else, I can be calm and rational. That's what everyone's going to need."

She was right. Of course, I wasn't exactly telling her the full truth, and she was still going to be taken aback. That couldn't be helped. I had to wait until I was with Javi. My mom would likely not take the news of our going public well after everything I'd already gone through. Likely, neither would Javi's parents, who'd get hit with a one-two punch tonight. To withstand a double-cannon parental-assault of concern and fear with a possible angry kickback, Javi and I had to stand together.

"So, your first boyfriend, huh?" she asked as we stepped onto the front porch. "How's it feel?"

"Like flying," I said before knocking on the front door.

MRS. CASTILLO made us all sit down around the small kitchen table while she prepared the beef enchiladas, refried beans, and Spanish rice. The spicy scent that filled the kitchen usually made me ravenous, but I was so nervous that for the first time I *could* wait to dig in.

"I wish you'd let me help you, Maricela," my mother said. She was not accustomed to being waited on.

"You sit," Mrs. Castillo said while plating the food. Her thick accent had come to sound like home to me. "You serve people most every day of the week. Let someone bring the food to you for a change."

"That's very kind of you," my mom said. "Thank you."

Mrs. Castillo smiled at her from the stove before sweeping her gaze to where I sat next to Javi. Over the past few months, a strange look fell across her features whenever she stared at her son and me for an extended period of time. It was an odd combination of affection and fear. It reminded me of how my mother peered at me while she applied peroxide to a fresh cut from a new bully's fist.

Had her mother's intuition clued her in?

"It's so good to finally meet you, Grace," Mr. Castillo said. The permanent smile Javi's dad wore had never faded, though. Whenever I came over, his lips broadened in welcome and he'd pat me on the back, asking me how things were going in my life. He was a good man, how I imagined my father would be if he were still alive.

"You too, Gustavo," my mother said. "You have all been so kind to my Tru. I can't tell you how much I appreciate it." When she spoke her last few words, her gaze fell upon Javi. Her smile extended to the light in her eyes. It was her way of telling Javi she knew, and she'd be here for us both.

Javi got the message. He reached under the table and squeezed my hand. His touch basically asked, "She knows?" When I patted his hand in response, he understood my answer was yes. The tension in his grip relaxed, and he laced his index finger with mine. It was all good.

"Please call me Gus," Mr. Castillo said. "Most everyone does."

"Thank you, Gus," my mom said as Mrs. Castillo placed a plate before her. "Maricela, this smells wonderful, and it looks delicious."

Mr. Castillo patted his belly. "It's better than delicious," he said. "That's why I'm *gordo*."

All of us laughed at Mr. Castillo's comment. Calling himself fat because of his wife's cooking was his way of warning us we were going to stuff ourselves. Only Javi didn't laugh. Flames of embarrassment licked across his red cheeks. His father was perhaps the only person alive who could mortify him so easily.

"Dad!"

"What?" Mr. Castillo asked. "It's true. Look." Over his button-down shirt, he grabbed more than an inch of skin from his side and presented it to the table. "See?"

"*Dad!*" Javi said again.

"*Ay!*" Mrs. Castillo scolded her son as she put plates in front of Javi and me. "Leave your father alone. It's good that he eats. It means I'm doing my job." She grabbed plates for herself and her husband. "Besides, it gives me something to hold on to," she added with a wink as she sat next to my mom.

Once again, everyone laughed. Javi practically slid under the table.

"The two of you are killing me here." Javi's face turned redder than the enchilada sauce.

"It's what parents do," my mom said. "Embarrassing our children is one of the perks of the job." She then threw her arms around me and planted a big, wet kiss on my cheek. This time everyone laughed but me. I was too busy trying to not crawl under the table with Javi. "Isn't that right, Gus and Maricela?"

Mr. and Mrs. Castillo nodded with glee.

"Now, let's eat," Mr. Castillo said. "But first, we say grace."

We held hands. While Mr. Castillo blessed the food, I offered up a silent prayer that love and understanding might continue to rule our parents' hearts.

OVER THE course of dinner, our parents bonded. Mr. Castillo and my mother traded war stories about working outside the home. Mr. Castillo worked at Brooks Army Base as a manager in one of the departments at the hospital and told my mother if her job with Dr. Torres didn't pan out to give him a call. He was friends with the head of Human Resources and would help her out if she needed.

"That's very kind of you, Gus," she said. "I will definitely remember that."

My mother and Mrs. Castillo talked cooking. She admitted to being awful and pitied me for having to eat whatever she happened to string together. Mrs. Castillo offered to give her a few cooking tips and share some easy recipes to help improve her skills.

"Now I know one of the reasons Tru comes over here so much," my mom said. "The two of you are wonderful!"

Mr. Castillo nodded. "It's true. We are."

Everyone laughed while Javi groaned.

After a few more minutes of small talk about the prospects of my mother's new job, Mr. Castillo turned to Javi and me and asked, "I have one more question, and it's for the two of you."

"What's that, Dad?"

"Not that I haven't enjoyed my wife's wonderful meal or finally meeting Grace, but when are the two of you finally going to tell us why you've brought us all together?"

Javi's jaw hit the table, and he once again found my hand. I gripped onto it just as tightly as he grasped mine. Our scheming hadn't gone unnoticed and now that we were being called on it, neither of us knew how to respond.

Mrs. Castillo nodded as she joined her husband in studying us. She glanced down as if she could see underneath the table before nodding. Did she know we were holding hands? "I've been wondering the same thing," she said before turning to my mother. "How about you, Grace?"

My mother sighed before looking into Mrs. Castillo's eyes. My mother was just like me. She lacked the ability to lie. "I have some idea," she said. "But I think it's important we hear it from the boys."

Mr. Castillo agreed as he sat back in his chair. No anger brewed in his eyes, and no worry crouched at the corners of his big smile. "So tell us. What's going on? Is there some big party you two want to go to? Perhaps out of town, and you think that if you ask us together we'd be more likely to let you go?" He chuckled as if the idea amused him. "I did the same thing when I was your age. My best friend, Jose, and I had been asked to go to this party at a friend's house in Austin.

We were seniors too, and boy, did we want to go. But we knew our parents were likely to turn us down. We had a plan, though. We'd be on our best behavior for weeks, get our parents together, and tell them how we had it all worked out so they wouldn't worry. Is that what's going on here?"

Javi tried to speak but no words came out.

Mr. Castillo glanced from his son to me. Since Javi seemed incapable of answering, he sought a response from the next likely candidate. "It's not quite the same thing, Mr. Castillo, but we do have a plan about something we want to discuss with you."

This got my mother's attention. "A plan? For what?"

Now it was my turn to lose the ability to speak. When Javi squeezed my hand in comfort, the strength we lacked separately coursed between us. Alone we couldn't handle such an adult situation, but together it seemed we'd weather most anything.

"Let me go first," Javi said. His eyebrows arched, asking me if that was okay. After I nodded, he surveyed the table before speaking. "I've been sitting here trying to figure out how I was going to bring this up, and the words just never seemed right. But as we ate and laughed, and you all embarrassed the heck out of Tru and me—" His father chuckled while the moms waited in silence. "Well, I realized no matter how scared I might be, I was surrounded by love. As I've always been. Mom and Dad, you've been the best parents I could have ever asked for. You've always been there for me. No matter what. And I can't thank you enough for that. But—" Javi stuttered, trying to find the words. When I squeezed his hand, he received the required jolt of confidence he needed. "I just hope you'll still be all those things after I say what I have to say."

Mr. Castillo's smile slowly retreated. He switched his gaze to his wife and my mom, who looked back at him. They both waited on his reaction. "Son, I'll always be there for you. I love you and your mother more than anything else in this world. More than my life. So don't ever doubt that, but the way you're talking is scaring me. What's happening? Are you okay?" He stared at his wife. "Is he sick, Maricela?"

She shook her head. "No, *amor*. He's not."

He locked onto Javi's eyes. "Then for the love of God, just tell me what's going on. It can't be worse than what's going through my head right now."

Javi gave my hand one final squeeze. This was it. We had arrived at the point of no return. He stared at me, and I smiled before he turned to his father and said, "I'm gay, and Tru is my boyfriend."

Silence stole all sound from the room. No one moved or even seemed to take a breath. Mr. Castillo sat completely still, unable to stop glancing back and forth from Javi and me.

Mrs. Castillo turned her gaze upward, her lips moving in silent prayer, and my mother scooted her chair closer to mine. She wrapped a reassuring arm around my shoulders, and I leaned into her comforting touch.

"I don't understand," Mr. Castillo finally said as he shook his head. Was he trying to shake off the words as if they hadn't been spoken? "You're what?"

"I'm gay," Javi repeated. "As in—"

"I know what the word means," Mr. Castillo said. The bite in his tone was unmistakable. In the months I'd had dinner with Javi's family, I'd never seen Mr. Castillo upset. He'd seemed incapable of being anything other than happy or positive. I'd clearly been wrong. "Did you know about this, Maricela?"

Mrs. Castillo, who still conversed with God in the heavens above, closed her eyes. When she opened them, she turned to her husband and said, "I didn't know," she said. "But I suspected."

"What?" Javi asked. "Really?"

Mrs. Castillo nodded. "I saw the two of you in the backyard one day a few months ago. You were talking and tossing the ball like you'd done pretty much every day. And I sometimes stood there and watched the two of you because I hadn't seen Javi so happy in so long. I thanked God for bringing Tru into your life, mijo, because when he arrived, that spark that had always been yours came back. As your momma, I could see the sadness you sometimes struggled with. I didn't know what it was. I thought it might be school or thinking about college. Or even the pressure of all the practices and the new baseball season, but there'd always been some part of you that you never shared with anyone. You had friends, but they never really understood you. Your morals. Your strength of character. Or your desire to be who you truly were. So you hid, and in hiding you got lost. But when you and Tru were together, you were a different boy. And it was a sight I cherished. So that was why I would sometimes watch." She took a deep breath, glanced over at her husband, and continued, "And on that day, the two of you wrestled. And when I saw the way you looked at each other. And the way you touched each other, I suddenly realized what you might be hiding. Why you seemed so alone when you had so many friends. After that, I didn't know what to do. So I prayed every night, and finally God answered me. He reminded me I was your mother, and it was my duty to love you. Against that love, nothing else mattered."

Javi wiped the wetness from his eyes before he stood to hug his mother. My mom and I both sniffled, trying to hold back the tears that threatened to turn us both into blubbering messes. That was another trait I'd inherited from her.

"Thank you, Mom," Javi said into his mother's neck as he wept. "I love you so much."

"Let me get this straight," Mr. Castillo said. He pulled back from the table and stood next to his wife. "You suspected our son might be gay, and you didn't say anything to me?"

She glanced over her shoulder at him. "Suspecting and knowing are two different things, Gustavo. You know that. Besides, it wasn't for me to say. After all, you've always said a man has to speak for himself. I figured if it was true, Javi would tell us when and if he was ready."

Mr. Castillo studied his son as if he were a stranger before turning around and walking to the kitchen sink. "I don't know what to do with this," he whispered. "How can my son be gay? What did I do wrong?"

That was my mother's cue. She stood and walked over to Mr. Castillo. "Gus, you didn't do anything wrong. From where I stand, I see a loving, kind-hearted young man any parent should be proud of. It took great strength to tell us what he's told us. And it's taken great courage to overcome the inner demons that kept him from being honest. But most of all, it shows how much he loves and trusts you because he's willing to share what he's kept hidden. *That* is the son you've raised. *That* is the man he's become. You should be proud."

Mr. Castillo turned around, tears streaming from his eyes. "I am proud of him," he said with a sniffle. "But the Bible. It says homosexuality is a sin. We are Catholic, Grace. How do I reconcile what my son is with what my faith has always told me to believe?" His eyes pleaded with my mom for a response, as if her words had the potential to save his son's soul.

"The only advice I can give you is to have faith," she said as she held his hands in hers. "And as you know, having faith isn't easy. But that's what keeps us strong."

"Dad," Javi said as he left his mother's safety for the uncertainty that still warred across Mr. Castillo's features. "I want you to know I haven't changed. I'm still the same boy you played catch with in the backyard. The one you taught how to shave and what it meant to be a man. To own up to my actions. To walk with my head high and my heart open. It was you who taught me being a man means I have to stand on my own but to never be afraid to lean on others when I needed it." My mother stepped away from Mr. Castillo, and Javi filled the space. He placed his hands on his father's shoulders and squeezed them like I'd seen him do countless times in the past. It was how they reassured each other. It was how they said "I love you." "I'm a man of faith too. The same one you and Mom and the Bible taught me. God lives in my soul too, Dad, and I believe He loves me whether I'm gay or straight. Because He's a parent too. Just like Mrs. Cobbler, and just like you and Mom."

"I'm scared," Mr. Castillo uttered, and the words choked in his throat. It wasn't easy for anyone to admit, much less a father to his son. "I don't know what to do. As your father, I'm supposed to have the answers. I'm supposed to be your guide. But with this, I can't help you. And not being there for you terrifies me the most."

"But you will be there for me," Javi said. The tears lodged in his throat caused his words to quaver. "You've always been there for me."

"And we'll all be there for each other," my mother added. She stood behind Javi and patted his back soothingly. "Like you said, Gus. Sometimes a man has to lean on others, and we can be each other's support. Isn't that right, Maricela?"

Mrs. Castillo reached across the table and took my hand. She smiled and gazed upon me with the love she'd always freely given.

"That's right," she said. "Because that is what the Bible teaches us most of all."

Mr. Castillo held out his arms and drew Javi into perhaps the strongest hug I'd ever seen. "I love you, mijo," he said. "And I'm sorry for the way I acted. I was surprised, and I was confused. But I never for one moment stopped loving you. I hope you know that."

Javi nodded in his father's embrace. He buried his face like a child into his father's strong shoulder. "I do."

AFTER THE dishes had been washed and put away, we all sat in the living room. I'd never been more exhausted in my life, and we were only halfway through what we needed to discuss with our parents.

Javi and I chose spots on the floor, facing the couch where our mothers sat. Mr. Castillo had plopped himself into the recliner on the left. His slumped shoulders clearly revealed how spent he was. And even though his typical smile had returned, worry eclipsed its usual light. An unspoken question most likely crouched on the tip of his tongue.

"How do you know you're gay?" he asked. "You're so young, and I know you've had girlfriends, Javi. Are you sure you're not just confused?"

"I'm not confused, Dad," Javi said. He inched closer to me so his right knee rested against my left. We couldn't hold hands in front of our parents. What they had just learned was still too fresh to be so open with our affections, but in order to deal with what came next, we needed the strength contact gave us. "I've always known girls just didn't do it for me. That I was trying to be something others said I should be."

"But how can you know for sure?" he asked again. "I don't understand."

"Can I try to answer this one?" I asked Javi. When he gave me his okay, I turned to Mr. Castillo. "I hope you don't take offense at what I'm about to ask you."

Mr. Castillo waved my words away as Javi had done to me so many times before. "I'm the one who's wanting an answer. Go ahead."

"Well, can you imagine yourself kissing another man?"

Mr. Castillo was taken aback. He sat up in his chair and grimaced. "No," he said quite definitely. "I can't."

"That's how you know you're straight," I said. "And since I can't imagine kissing a girl, that's how I know I'm gay."

"But Javi's kissed girls," Mrs. Castillo said. "At least that's what you've told me."

Javi nodded. "I have, and it never felt right. It always seemed strange. Like I was kissing a rock." He looked at me and smiled. "But when I kiss Tru, it's not like kissing a rock at all. It's like sticking my finger in an electric outlet."

Javi's face turned lobster red when he realized what he'd just admitted to our parents. When we turned back to them, Mr. and Mrs. Castillo glanced away. Listening to their son describing his kiss with another boy wasn't something they were quite ready to hear yet. My mother, however, couldn't hide her smile.

"That's the way I felt when I kissed your dad," my mom said. Her eyes flooded with tears from the memory. "That's how I knew he was the one."

"I wish I could be as positive as you, Grace," Mr. Castillo said from the recliner. "But I'm not. And it's not because you two are gay. It's because the world we live in is a terrible place. People are cruel and vicious, and I fear for your safety."

"Me too," Mrs. Castillo admitted after reaching for the comfort of her husband's hand.

"I won't lie to you, Gus," my mother said. "Life's been tough for Tru. Even though he hasn't come out to anyone, most people assume he's gay because he's smaller than most boys. And he gets teased a lot for it. That's why I've had to move him around so much. To keep him safe."

"That just proves my point," Mr. Castillo said. "I'm sorry kids have been so awful to you, Tru. That makes me very angry, but it also scares me about Javi's safety. We can't afford to move. This is our home, and if word of this gets out, I don't know what kind of reactions people will have."

"That's another thing we wanted to discuss with you," Javi added with a sigh.

Three pairs of parental eyes turned and narrowed in unison.

"There's more?" Mr. Castillo asked. He rested his head in his hand.

Mrs. Castillo made the sign of the cross while my mother locked eyes with me. "I thought you told me everything earlier, Tru." Her low voice told me she wasn't happy. "What have you left out?"

I told everyone what had happened to us that day.

"Fighting, Javi?" Mr. Castillo asked. "I haven't taught you to deal with problems with violence."

"No, you haven't," Javi said. "But you have taught me to stand up for others. To not be afraid to take a stand against people who do wrong, and Oscar was wrong for shoving Tru and trying to hurt him. I couldn't just stand there and watch it. I had to stop it, and I don't regret it." He leaned his knee harder against mine. "And I'll do it again if I have to."

"No," Mrs. Castillo said. Her eyes were steady and serious. I'd never seen such severity in her expression before. "While I'm glad you were there for Tru, I'm not going to have you getting into fights every day at school. It's not safe."

"I have to agree with Gus and Maricela," my mother added. "Reacting as you did today might put both of you in more danger than you expect. The fact that this Oscar was so cruel and hateful tells you the kind of person you are dealing with. It's better to get up and walk away from people like that."

Javi shook his head. "I won't slink away and let the bullies win. That gives them too much power. If they think we're afraid, they'll use that fear to control us. That's not how I'm going to live. I need to be true to myself." He grabbed my hand and held it firmly in front of our parents. "And we have to be true to ourselves. That's why Tru and I have decided not to hide anymore."

"I don't understand," Mr. Castillo said. "You've already told us you're dating. What more hiding are you two doing?"

Mrs. Castillo's crinkled forehead revealed she was just as confused as her husband. The dissatisfied frown that squatted on my mother's lips, however, told me she knew exactly what we were planning. "Gus, I think what the boys are trying to tell us is they're planning on letting their classmates in on what they've told us."

"What?" Mr. Castillo asked as he sprang from his chair. "You can't be serious."

"Mijo, no!" Mrs. Castillo pleaded.

"That's exactly what we're saying," Javi said. "The kids at school are already talking about it. Oscar practically outed me in the hall today anyway. He told me I had to choose either Tru or them. If I don't cast Tru away, which isn't even an option, then everyone is going to assume that I *am* gay, and we *are* together. If they're going to think it anyway, why not just be upfront about it? It's better than hiding in the shadows and hoping we're not caught. This way, we control the situation. It doesn't control us." Our parents remained completely unconvinced. "We've given this a lot of thought."

"That's precisely what you haven't done," Mr. Castillo said. "People can assume what they want all day long. Once something is proven true, there is no more guessing. It becomes fact. And those facts have serious consequences."

"More serious than what we're already facing?" I asked.

"Of course!" Mr. Castillo replied in frustration. "We don't live in the shows you boys watch on TV. We live in the barrio, where life is already dangerous enough as it is."

"He's right," my mother added. "You know how difficult your life has been, Tru. Better than anyone else in this room. And that's just been on the *assumption* you're gay. What do you think will happen to both of you when you announce to the world you're gay and dating? Do you think it's going to magically make things better? As if being honest is going to save you from pain. What you plan on doing is reckless and unnecessary."

"I agree," Mrs. Castillo said. "So what if Oscar Gomez, who I've never really liked, says you have to make a choice? He has no right to tell you such things. Choosing not to be his friend doesn't mean you are gay or that you and Tru are dating. Choosing not to be his friend means you're not choosing the bully. Why would anyone pick the bully anyway? Those people aren't true friends, and you don't need them in your life."

"So you want us to what?" Javi asked. "Keep our relationship a secret? Hide how we feel about each other from everyone and let the rumors define us instead of defining ourselves?"

"No," Mr. Castillo said. He turned to stare at his wife and my mother, who nodded in agreement. "We aren't asking you to do anything. We're telling you, as our boys, that you will *not* reveal your relationship to anyone else."

"You can't do that. I'm eighteen years old," Javi said as he stood in front of his father. "This is our choice. It's our life."

"Not yet, it isn't," he said. "You boys live under our roofs. We make the rules, not the other way around. And you will both continue to be the good boys you've always been before this and mind what we say."

"Or what?" Javi asked. "You can't keep me from talking. This is still a free country last time I checked."

"Javi!" Mrs. Castillo's reprimand struck harder than any punch I'd ever received. She rose from the couch and took her place at her husband's side. "You will *not* speak to your father that way. I will not allow it!"

"And to answer your question," Mr. Castillo began, "there will be consequences for not obeying our wishes."

"Like what?" I asked as I turned to my mother.

"We can't control what you boys say, but as your parents we do have say over what you boys do," she answered. "I think Gus and Maricela will agree with me that as long as you keep things as they are, the two of you can continue to date. But if you out yourselves, there's just no way we can allow this relationship to continue. You'll be restricted to school and then straight home. No more bike rides to the park. No more hanging out. No more phone calls."

Javi and I searched the expressions of every parent in the room. They were locked in complete agreement.

"That's not fair!" Javi said. He turned his back to his parents and faced me, eyes wide, waiting for an answer he expected me to provide. I had none. Earlier that afternoon, our plan had given me strength. Now that it had been ripped out from under us, I had no clue where to go from here.

"It's not fair," Mr. Castillo said. "But that's because life is terribly *unfair*. I know you boys are angry, and that's fine. You don't have to like our decision. Or even like us right now. That's part of being a parent. But we do what we do to protect our children, and right now, this is the only choice we have to make sure you both remain safe."

I glanced at Javi's parents and my mother, everyone waiting to hear how we intended on handling the boom they'd lowered on us. "We don't have a choice," I said to Javi, who sighed in exasperation. He'd clearly been expecting me to put up more of a fight. He sure seemed ready to go a few more rounds, but our parents' minds were made up. We could push the issue and test the boundaries, but when had that ever really worked in any child's favor? "If we don't do what they say, we don't get to be together. How can we be boyfriends if we never see each other? It kind of defeats the purpose."

Javi couldn't argue with my logic. He blew out his frustration before turning to his parents. "Fine. We won't say a word."

His parents' smiles revealed their gratefulness.

My mother wrapped her arms around me and whispered in my ear, "Everything will work out, Tru. I know right now it feels as if we're the bad guys, but we aren't. We love you both so much, and you just have to trust that in this situation, your parents are more familiar with the ways of the world than you are."

Although my mother had intended to ease my troubled mind, her words didn't offer comfort.

What were Javi and I going to do now?

Chapter 11

THE WEEKS after dinner with our parents were tough. The rumor mill continued to churn out gossip about the nature of Javi's and my relationship. The whispering questions that had followed me around the day after Javi's fight with Oscar increased in number and volume.

"Tru's obviously a fag, but do you think Javi is too?"

"Probably. You know how those gays like to parade together."

"How can Javi be gay? He's so hot. And if he is, *why* is he with that funky motherfucker, Tru?"

"One night with me, and I'll turn Javi straight. He just hasn't met the right girl."

"Who would've ever thought Javi Castillo took it up the ass?"

But it wasn't anything I wasn't already familiar with. I'd learned long ago how to tune out the nastiness of others.

Javi hadn't quite mastered the skill yet.

If someone whispered something shitty behind his back, he confronted them and told them to say it to his face. His most recent encounter had been yesterday with some football player named Eddie. He'd been talking smack during lunch while Javi sat with the friends who hadn't jumped over to Oscar's camp.

From the story I heard, Rance had to pull Javi back and escort him outside before the heated exchange attracted the attention of the teachers. Javi never once brought it up on the bike ride home or as we made out on my mother's couch. When I asked him about it after

Claudia called to clue me in, Javi said he hadn't wanted me to worry. That he could take care of himself.

But I was worried. Javi walked around school with a hair trigger. What would happen when the wrong person said or did the wrong thing at the absolute worst time? As crazy as it might seem, the one person who seemed to keep Javi from self-destructing was Rance.

He was one of the few team members Javi had who still talked to him. And even though Rance wanted to kill me, I'd been grateful he could be there for Javi when I wasn't, like at lunch or baseball practice.

Rance gave Javi the friendship he needed to remain levelheaded at school. I just hoped what I gave him fed his heart and soul as much as he fed mine.

Doing that in secret, though, proved difficult, but we stuck with the plan Claudia helped us draw up. We continued our routine of arriving to and leaving from school together to show that we didn't have anything to hide. Completely changing our pattern would be as strong a confirmation as throwing open the closet door and telling the world.

It was the second part that was the toughest.

We had to try to keep physical distance between us at school. According to Claudia, we naturally gravitated to each other. If we stood side by side, we found a reason to touch or lean against the other. That just wouldn't do. So we made certain whenever we were talking at school, we stood opposite each other even though what we wanted was to leap into each other's arms.

We also had to be mindful of our eye contact. Claudia claimed our eyes lit up when we saw each other, and everyone else seemed to vanish. We had to stop that as well, which was pretty damn difficult. Talking to Javi without solely gazing into his eyes had been torture. I had to force myself to look around, and Javi had gotten into the habit of counting to ten, looking around, and smiling at people passing by before returning his gaze to mine.

It wasn't what we wanted, but it was what we had to do. The alternative wasn't acceptable for either of us.

But was I being fair to Javi?

Most people blamed me for Javi's fall from golden child status. Whenever people like Alison passed me in the hall, they twisted their expressions and rolled their eyes. For a while, every time she saw me, she'd screamed, "Selfie!" and taken a picture. Now, she barely justified my existence. Because of me, Javi had lost perhaps half the friends he'd once had, and his life had profoundly changed.

Javi claimed he didn't care, that it was their loss. Claudia said pretty much the same thing. And they were right to some extent.

But should being with someone cause this much pain?

I had my doubts.

"Have you lost your tail or something?"

I switched my attention from the ad layout I was working on in the Mac lab for the yearbook to Claudia, who suddenly stood at my side. Alice in Wonderland decorated her black T-shirt today. Except this Alice had tattooed arm sleeves and wore a Jack Daniels shirt. The playful scowl on Claudia's face told me she believed she'd just made a funny. "What?"

She shook her head and chuckled. "I guess you have," she said. "I shall call you Eeyore from now on!"

"I have no idea what you're talking about," I replied before turning my attention back to adjusting the photo on the template.

"What's the matter with you, Tru?" She plopped down next to me. If she were any more concerned about me, she'd be prescribing happy pills. "You've been mopey all damn day long. You're acting like it's *not* the last school day before spring break. You should be in the other room with us listening to music and winding down."

I shook my head. "I can't. I've got things to do."

"Yeah, well, I'm the boss around here," she said as she turned off my monitor. "I order you to have some fun."

I glared at her before switching the monitor back on. "You can't order someone to do that."

"I believe I just did," she replied, switching the monitor off again.

"Come on, Claudia," I said when she refused to remove her hand from the power button. "I've got to finish this."

She placed her hand on my shoulder until I made eye contact. "What going on?" The playful pain-in-the ass routine had ended. She'd switched on the worry button.

"I've been thinking these past few days that maybe I'm not being fair to Javi."

"I don't understand," she said. "Have your feelings for him changed?"

"Oh, God no!" I said. I didn't even think such a thing was possible. Every time I saw him, I found it hard to breathe. When he touched me, my skin burned and sizzled, and when he kissed me, I swore it was like standing before the gates of heaven. "I'm worried he's paying too high a price to be with me."

"I'm still not following you."

"Look at how many friends he's lost," I said. "In Mr. Rodriguez's class alone, he only speaks to you, me, and Rance. The rest of the Jock Brigade barely gives him the time of day. And how many people has he mouthed off to today? At last count it was, what? Five?"

"Six," she said with a sigh.

I had to rest my head on my hands. "Who now? And when did this happen?"

She shrugged. "All I know is what Lydia told me." Lydia was one of the staff writers for the paper. While she didn't particularly care for me, she liked Javi. He'd once brought her homework to her every day for two weeks when she came down with chicken pox. For Javi's past kindness, she deigned to be coolly cordial to me. "Someone at lunch said something shitty in passing, and Javi about came unglued. Luckily, Rancid was there to pull his butt out of the fire again."

"See, that's what I'm talking about," I said. "Javi's never had to face this kind of crap before. People loved him. They wanted to be his friend. Now they're going out of their way to be nasty to him because of me."

"Javi's not complaining," she said. "So why are you?"

Was Claudia really that blind? "Because it's not right. Javi shouldn't have to lose the life he had because...." I surveyed the room, making sure we were still alone. When I found only computer monitors and silent printers, I whispered, "Because he and I are dating."

"Tru, you're being a dumbass again. Which happens all too often these days. You might want to take something for that."

How was she not seeing what I saw? For that matter, why wasn't Javi? "Would you go through this for someone?" I finally asked.

"No," she said.

I pointed at her as if she'd proved my point. "See?"

"I would for someone I loved, though," she added.

I had to grip the computer table so I wouldn't fall off my chair. Claudia's words sent my world spinning. "You think Javi loves me?"

She laughed as if I was the stupidest person in the world. "Do you really have to ask me that? Don't you know it already?"

I couldn't speak. I was still trying to process.

"Why else do you think Javi is doing this?" she asked. "Because it's fun? Of course it's not. It's awful, and it pisses me off. Every time some idiot opens his mouth and says some shit, I want to staple their mouths shut. But I don't have to. Javi does it for me. And it's one of the most beautiful things I've seen. And if you don't see that, then you're even more of a dumbass than I thought you were."

Claudia was right. I was a dumbass. "Thank you." I stood before giving her a peck on the cheek.

"Fuck!" she said, wiping it away. "How many times do I have to tell you? I don't do mushy crap."

"I know," I said before crossing toward the door. "That's why I did it."

"And where do you think you're going?" she asked.

I stopped at the threshold and peered back over my shoulder at Claudia. "I need to tell him I love him too." And then I sprinted out of the classroom and down the hall to the gym, where Javi was getting ready for one final workout before the break.

MY STUDENT press pass got me by the questioning teachers and administrators who wondered why I wasn't in class. "On a deadline for the paper," I called as I sped past their distrustful gazes on the way to the gym.

I hadn't been there since my first day, when Rance had tried to wipe me from existence, and I'd had no intention of ever going back. If the paper needed a quote or a picture at the gym when there wasn't a game going on, Claudia assigned the task to someone else.

That was just smarter and safer.

But now that Claudia had helped me see the true reason behind Javi's actions, I had to see him no matter where he was. Even if he happened to be in the bowels of hell. And to me that was pretty much what the gym was.

After I exited the main building's side door and crossed to the orange-tinted brick structure that made up the outer exterior of the gym, I found it difficult to contain my glee. Inside, the boy who loved me had no idea I was going to say those three very important words to him for the first time.

Maybe it was too soon to make such statements. We'd only been dating a few months, and I wasn't even eighteen years old yet. Was it possible to be in love at such a young age?

It had worked for my parents. They'd met in high school and would still be together today if my dad hadn't been killed in the line of duty. When I thought about it that way, I realized when it came to love, age didn't matter. Its power transcended such triviality. Because once true love took hold, it never let go.

So whether it was too soon or not, it no longer mattered. All that mattered was how we felt, so I pulled open the heavy metal door that led to the basketball court.

Almost instantly, my nose detected an overwhelming stench of plastic, rubber, and sweaty armpits. How the hell did people breathe in here? I had to switch to drawing breath through my mouth to avoid triggering my gag reflex.

I didn't have to deal with the angry scowls from the general physical education classes that usually occupied the gym at this time. The court was empty. Most of the gym classes had been suspended for the holidays. Those that were still in session had students running laps around the outdoor track about a quarter of a mile away.

That left the gym and the weight room, where Javi had said he would be, to the baseball team, which met during last period. Since the team had planned a Jock Brigade party in Coach Moore's office in the adjacent building, Javi had chosen one last workout before the holidays over pretending to care about most of his teammates.

That meant we'd have the entire place to ourselves.

I shot through the hallway, taking a hard right before the locker room. Unless I had to, I was never setting foot in that tiled room again.

I went straight through the double doors that led to the weight room and surveyed the area.

Javi wasn't there.

Nautilus machines, weight benches, dumbbells, and other monstrosities littered the padded floor. What were some of these machines designed for? They resembled torture devices used during the Spanish Inquisition rather than apparatus designed to sculpt muscle and keep bodies fit.

And what the hell was that stench? It was like someone was trying to cover up the smell of sweaty ass with a truckload of Axe Body Spray.

More importantly, though, where the hell was Javi? Maybe he'd decided to go to the team party after all. Coach Moore could have made attendance mandatory, especially considering the morale problem the team was currently experiencing. He might have believed forced male bonding to be the cure.

When I saw Javi, though, we'd be doing some very special male bonding of our own. It was time to kick our intimacy up a notch. While I still wasn't ready for sex, it was time to leave first base behind, and perhaps round second and head straight for third.

The door behind me swung open. Javi had finally arrived.

As I turned around, my advancing smile retreated. It wasn't Javi at all.

"Well, well," Rance said. The sneer I'd come to know all too well snaked across his lips. If he'd been a cobra, he'd have spit venom at me. "What do we have here?"

"I'm looking for Javi," I said as I backed up. There was no way I was letting him get his hands on me again. "He's going to be here any minute."

Rance laughed. "Nice try, cock breath." He took measured steps toward me as I continued to retreat. I gazed around the room, hoping to spot another exit, but the one behind Rance seemed to be the only way in or out. That made this place a death trap I'd happened to spring. "I saw Javi leave for the main building a few minutes ago."

How was that possible? If he'd gone back inside, I would have seen him. Unless he'd bypassed the side entrance and strolled through the quad. Javi enjoyed treed areas, after all. That was definitely something he'd do.

That oversight was going to cost me a few ounces of spilled blood.

"Let's not do this again, Rance." I rounded the dumbbell rack. Thanks to the weights, I had managed to erect a temporary barrier between us. No matter which side Rance tried to take, I could sprint across the room from the other side and out the door. "Can't we just call a truce?"

"Fuck, no!" His face twisted in disgust at the mere thought. "I've waited for this moment for the past few months. All I had to do was be patient. I knew somehow, some way, we'd find ourselves all alone again, and I could pay you back for getting me thrown into ISS."

Perhaps it was the knowledge that Rance couldn't make a move without giving me an avenue of escape, but a surge of confidence jolted through me I'd live to regret. "It's not my fault you got caught beating me up, you stupid fuck." Rance's eyes turned to thin slits of hate, and he clenched his jaw so tightly, it popped. "It's also not my fault that your pea-sized brain can't stand that Javi's my friend."

"Javi's *my* friend," he mumbled like a child who had not yet learned how to share. He then feigned a move to the left. But the trick didn't work. I stayed put in relative safety behind a waist-high wall that weighed about five hundred pounds.

"Are you kidding?" I was actively taunting him as if I'd not learned one lesson from all my previous beatings. Poking the bear ended only in disaster. "Javi has had other friends besides you for years. We both know that. So what's the fucking deal that he makes one more? Why does him being my friend turn you from a common asswipe to King Asswipe of Shit Mountain?"

"You better watch yourself," Rance warned. He again feinted to the right, but still I didn't move.

"No, really," I said. "What is it? I'd really like to know. I've done nothing to you that I know of. What is it about my friendship with Javi that cheeses you off so bad? The two of you have been best friends since second fucking grade. Are you that insecure?"

"I'm not insecure of shit!" he said. I had worked him into a frenzy. He cracked his knuckles and practically foamed at the mouth.

"What really has you so pissed off?" I asked. "It can't just be my friendship with Javi. There's something going on with you." He snorted as if I was crazy. "Javi's seen it too, you know? He told me. You've changed. Something about summer camp."

Rance didn't react well to that at all. He picked up a ten-pound weight and hurled it. I ducked as it shattered the mirrored wall behind me. I'd never had such reflexes before. Perhaps playing catch with Javi these past few months had its benefits after all. "Fuck!" I surveyed the shattered fragments of glass littering the floor and the volleyball size hole in the wall. "What the hell happened to you at camp?"

"You're so gonna pay," Rance said. He licked his lips in anticipation of smacking me around. His eyes burned with a hatred I'd never seen before in any of my past tormentors. Most of them had enjoyed the thrill of picking on the weaker and more unpopular of the pack, but that wasn't Rance's problem.

His hatred of me cut down to the bone.

He despised everything I was. Everything I represented. As if by existing, I challenged something so basic, so primal within him, his unstable reality teetered on the edge of oblivion.

But what was it about me that caused Rance to act this way?

That was when it finally occurred to me. There could only be one reason that explained Rance's knee-jerk reaction to me and my relationship with Javi. "Are you jealous?"

Clouds of fury gathered in his eyes, and the low growl in his throat rumbled like thunder.

"That's it, isn't it?" Now it all made perfect sense. Rance hated me not just because I was gay, but because I'd been able to do something he likely had wanted to do for years—capture Javi's heart. "You're in love with Javi, aren't you?"

"You are so dead," Rance said through gritted teeth. The vein on his forehead bulged.

"Javi doesn't know," I said, talking more to myself than Rance. "That's what happened at camp. You hooked up with some boy for the first time, and after that, you realized what you'd felt for Javi all these years wasn't friendship. You were in love with him."

Rance's chest heaved, and his fists clenched at his sides.

"But you didn't know what to do with those feelings, did you? So you pulled away. You turned into an even bigger douche than you were before because if you put distance between you two, then you wouldn't have to deal with what you were feeling."

"I'd stop now if I were you," he said. The poison in his voice had vanished. Dead calm now filled his words.

"Then, when you saw me that first day and pegged me as a fag, you hated me because you hate yourself. And when Javi and I got close, when those rumors started circulating that he and I were more than friends, it didn't make you angry. That's not what this is about at all."

"I. Said. Stop."

"It broke your heart."

In one swift motion, Rance hurdled over the weight rack. If his foot hadn't caught on one of the weights, causing him to stumble and the dumbbell to crash to the floor, he would have collided with me before I had a chance to react. While he struggled to regain his balance, I dashed to the right and toward the door.

Fueled by dual motors of anger and heartbreak, Rance would likely overtake me before I'd find help, but we wouldn't be in the isolated weight room when it happened. The scuffle would catch the ears of teachers, who'd be able to pull Rance off me before he inflicted irreparable damage.

All I had to do was make it out the double doors ten feet away and through the gym doors twenty feet down the hall. Only thirty feet stood between me and salvation.

And I wasn't going to make it.

I'D MANAGED to get five feet from the outside gym doors when Rance's hand gripped the collar of my shirt and yanked me backward. I slid along the waxed floor before crashing into the wall. Before I had a chance to get my bearings, Rance pounced again. He grabbed me by both wrists and dragged me toward the weight room.

"Let me go!" I yelled, hoping my cries would catch the attention of someone passing outside or in the locker room.

Rance didn't respond. Drool slid down his chin as if all intelligent thought had been switched off. What appeared to drive him now was instinct and pure hatred, a deadly combination.

He shoved open the double doors and tossed me back into the weight room. I tumbled and skidded across the padded floor. The rough rubber tiles on the floor scraped my flesh, causing a searing fire to spread down my right side as the friction scraped away some of my skin.

I tried to stand again, but Rance shoved me down. I rolled into the thrust and managed to put some distance between us by moving to the other side of the bench press. Once again, a piece of gym equipment separated us, except this time Rance wasn't stopping to talk.

He kept coming.

Whenever I attempted to stand, he was there to send me sprawling once again. It was as if he were herding me somewhere.

A kick from his strong leg sent me forward, toward where Rance had heaved the weight, and that was when it dawned on me. He was leading me back to the glass.

The sharp, ragged shards that littered the ground mocked me by innocently glinting under the fluorescent lights. Nothing pure or good waited for me among their sharp edges. Rolling over them would slice my back, since my shirt now hung about me in tatters, or cut jagged lines across my face.

Or if Rance wanted, he could inflict far more permanent damage with the weapons that lay strewn about the floor.

"Please," I managed before Rance lifted me off the floor by my neck. His big hands wrapped around my passageway, cutting off my ability to speak and breathe.

"You think you're so fucking smart, don't you, Tru? That you have all the answers? That you know me. Or you know Javi. Well, you don't know jack shit, bitch."

He released his stranglehold, dropping me. I fell with a yelp on top of the glass, landing on my back. At least two pieces ripped into my skin, and my back grew warm.

"Let me tell you something," Rance said. "Before you came along, Javi spent all his time with me. I ate dinner with his parents, and we played catch in the backyard. And I waited, and I prayed that one day he'd see it. That one day he'd realize what we could be. And then *you* came."

He placed his foot on my chest and rested all his weight on me. He had me pinned. There was nowhere I could go. No matter how hard I tried to lift his massive size-eleven foot from me, I lacked the strength. To make it worse, Rance bore down. It became more difficult to draw air, and the glass under me continued to bite into my skin.

"Without a second thought, he replaced me," Rance continued as if I weren't struggling for air. "It didn't matter that I'd been there for him for all these years. One look at your funny-looking face, and he was gone. That's how much I meant to Javi. That's how little he fucking thought of me."

Rance increased the pressure, practically standing on my chest on one foot. My breathing became labored, and a fog enveloped my vision. I didn't feel the glass cutting into my back anymore. Had the fragments somehow been swept away?

"And even when the rumors started flying, when it became obvious he had to choose, he didn't choose his teammates. Or me. No matter how many times I kept him from getting into fights, it never mattered. He chose you."

The red mist lifted for a moment. Pools of water welled in Rance's eyes.

But they dried up as quickly as they'd formed, and he reached down for something I could no longer see. I gasped for air, but my lungs couldn't capture enough.

My eyelids grew heavy, and I closed them for a second.

When I opened them again, Rance stood over me, the ten-pound weight held high over his head. This was it. The moment I'd dreaded for years. The funny thing was, I wasn't terrified at all.

I had Javi in my heart, and I'd live forever in his as well. My only regret was that I never had the chance to tell him.

A strange roar suddenly filled the room. I couldn't make out the voice. Had someone said my name?

I tried to focus, but it was like trying to look at the world from under water. Light and forms kept shifting. Something, or someone, was on Rance's back. The surprise attack unsettled him and caused the weight to tumble from his grasp. I closed my eyes, preparing for the inevitable crushing impact, but it landed inches to the left of my head with a deep *clunk*.

A furious growl shook the room. Rance stepped off me and reared back, sending whoever clawed and beat on his head flying backward. There was a thud and a crash.

With Rance's weight no longer on my chest, I sucked in air. I gulped it down as if it were food, and I hadn't eaten in days. As a result, I coughed and hacked as my body once again filled with what it needed to survive.

After a few moments, I breathed normally again. The water, which had previously clouded my vision, retreated, and my world returned to normal.

The first sound I heard was Rance's screams.

"No!" he shouted as he knelt over someone who lay on the floor behind him. "I'm so sorry," he said. "Goddammit, I'm so sorry."

I mouthed the words, "What happened?" But my throat burned. I could see and breathe, but I couldn't yet speak. I struggled to sit up, to see what had changed Rance from an infuriated beast into a hapless kitten.

But Rance's bulky frame hid what lay on the other side.

I crawled forward as Rance sobbed. Moving over broken shards of glass, I inched closer, sending ribbons of pain shooting through my forearms and bare stomach. The pain no longer mattered. All I focused on was getting around Rance. The desire to see what he saw dominated my body and my will.

As I crunched closer, Rance glanced over his shoulder. The madness had departed. Deep regret now strangled his expression. "I didn't mean it, Tru. I swear. I didn't mean it."

"What?" I finally choked out.

And that was when Rance moved out of the way. That was when I saw Javi lying on the ground, his head next to the weight that had caused Rance to stumble earlier. The one that had almost given me time to escape.

The one that now had blood on it.

"Javi?" I rose and half crawled, half walked to where he had fallen. His eyes were closed, a trickle of blood draining from his mouth. "Javi!" I screamed as I knelt over him, trying to wake him up. Javi refused to respond. He lay there, no lopsided grin, no mischievous eye wiggle.

"I'm sorry," Rance cried. "Javi, I'm so sorry."

I turned to Rance. Fury I'd never experienced before exploded in me. "You motherfucker!" I punched him in the face. Blinding pain crushed my small hand while Rance just sat there, crying.

"I'm sorry" was all he'd say.

"Goddammit!" I screamed. I checked to see if Javi had a pulse. It was slow and thready. "Go get some fucking help."

My words forced Rance to his feet, but still he only gazed down at Javi. Tears coursed down his cheeks. Misery wracked him.

"Now!" I said, far more forcefully than before. Rance turned on his heels and tore out of the weight room. His voice echoed off the walls as he ran outside and called desperately for help.

I turned back to my beautiful boy, who slept peacefully on the floor.

I gathered the tattered remains of my shirt and wrapped them carefully around the freely bleeding wound on the side of his head. Rich, red roses bloomed across the pale fabric by the time I'd finished.

When I was done, and while I waited for the help I hoped Rance would find, I kissed Javi's cheek, curled up next to him, and rested my head on his shoulder. It was our routine after school, and I wasn't going to change it now.

"I love you, Javi Castillo," I said before the tears once again stole the world from my vision.

WHEN HELP finally arrived in the form of Coach Moore and a teacher I'd never seen before, they had to practically rip me from Javi's side. I'd refused to leave my place on his shoulder. That was where I belonged.

"Tru," Coach Moore said. His voice low and calm. "I worked as a field medic in the army. I've had some experience with head trauma, but if I'm going to help Javi, I need to be able to work. I can't do that if I'm tripping over you."

I rose and stood about ten feet away while Coach Moore checked Javi's pulse before he told the other teacher to retrieve the first aid kit from the closet.

"Has he been unconscious the whole time?" Coach Moore asked once he had the first aid kit in hand.

I nodded. "Is he going to be okay?"

"We'll know better when he wakes up," he said after he gently removed my bloodied shirt from Javi's head. He tore open packages of gauze from the kit and placed them on the wound before securing it in place with white adhesive tape. "Check Tru's back," he told the other teacher, who rounded me to look at my wounds.

"I'm okay," I told him. "Worry about Javi."

"He's got cuts and some glass embedded in his skin, but he should be fine," the teacher told the coach.

"The paramedics are here," Ms. Garcia said from the double doors. I hadn't even noticed her standing there, or the other administrators who had arrived. The principal, Mr. Valdez, whispered to one of the assistant principals after nodding at me.

Suddenly two paramedics burst into the weight room, carrying a plastic board on top of a collapsible gurney. Without speaking, the two men rushed to Javi's side, assessed the situation, and asked what happened.

"Javi fell and hit his head on that weight," I responded.

They glanced at me and nodded. "Has he been drinking or taking drugs?" one asked.

I got angry. "What? No! Of course not."

They placed the board on the ground next to Javi. "What's his name?" The other asked as they stood at his head and his feet and then lifted him simultaneously onto the blue plastic.

"Javier Castillo," I replied. They used the board to place him on the gurney before raising it and wheeling him toward the exit.

I trailed right behind them.

"Truman, we need to speak with you," Ms. Garcia said. Mr. Valdez stood at her side. On their faces warred fear and anger. They were no doubt worried about a lawsuit.

"Not now," I replied as I trotted past them. The paramedics had just exited the outer gym doors. They sure as hell weren't leaving me behind. I was going with Javi.

Outside, chaos had erupted.

Most of the school had crowded the area. News traveled fast, and everyone had heard that something awful had happened. Upon seeing Javi being loaded into the ambulance, their mouths hung open as if in the middle of a silent scream. Some were taking pictures with their cell phone. No doubt those would wind up on Facebook in the next twenty seconds.

When they saw me emerge, everyone suddenly wanted to talk to me.

"Tru, what the hell happened?"

"Is he okay, Tru? Are you okay?"

"I heard he was shot. Who did it?"

"Did you see who did it, Tru?"

I ignored those questions and all the others they tossed my way. I didn't have time to satisfy their morbid curiosity or decipher the loud buzz their collective voice had created. My boyfriend was about to be taken away. "Wait!" I screamed at the paramedic who had launched himself inside and was about to shut the door. "I'm coming with you."

"Sorry," the paramedic said.

"Fuck that!" I yelled. I ran to the door and held it open. The incessant drone of my classmates grew quiet. "I said I'm coming with you."

"Listen, kid," the paramedic said. His eyes locked onto mine and his lips stretched into a sympathetic smile. "You're a minor, and unless you're a blood relative, we can't take you with us."

"I'm his boyfriend," I said. "I love him." That made our relationship just as strong as the bond of family.

"We're taking him to Christus downtown," the paramedic said. "That's the best I can do." He shut the door. The lights atop the ambulance flashed and its siren wailed before taking off through the parking lot.

"I'll take you," a voice said at my side. "We can go now." I turned to see Claudia. Her hand rested on my shoulder, and tears streamed down her face. She looked at my back and winced. "Are you okay?"

"You're not going anywhere until you tell us what happened."

It was Ms. Garcia. She had her arms crossed, and her bug eyes accused me of being the responsible party. Mr. Valdez, the principal, stood next to her, his cell phone in hand. Who had he called? The police or Javi's parents?

"Holy shit! I need to tell the Castillos!" I turned to Claudia. "Can I use your cell phone?"

She nodded as she fished it out of her pocket, but Ms. Garcia placed her hand on Claudia's arm. "We will handle that," she said. "You need to come with us. Right. Now."

That was when I saw Rance. He stood a few feet from the gathering of my strangely quiet classmates. Their mouths were still agape as if they'd just witnessed the most shocking event of their lives.

"You motherfucker!" I screamed before charging at Rance. I shoved him, and he fell on his ass, which elicited a collective gasp from most of the students who stood only a few feet away.

Rance didn't attempt to fight back. Shoulders slumped, he hung his head in shame. Tears and snot streamed down his face. He was the picture of despair, but I didn't care. He'd hurt Javi, and he had to pay.

But before I could strike him again, Coach Moore wrapped me in his steel arms and held me tight. Ms. Garcia rushed over to Rance to check on him.

"Are you okay?" she asked Rance.

"Are you fucking kidding me?" I asked. I'd never experienced hate or anger this powerful in my life. Not toward any of the previous bullies that had tormented me in the past. Or even to that dipshit Bart.

This was different. Rance hadn't hurt me.

He'd hurt the boy I loved.

That sent lava flowing through my blood. That made me want to rip every limb from Rance's body and shove them down his throat.

"You want to know what happened. Ask Rance," I said, fighting Coach Moore's hold. "This is his fault. *He's* the one who hurt Javi."

Ms. Garcia stepped back, and the excited chatter my outburst had started among the other students fell silent once again. "Is that true, Rance?" she asked.

Rance covered his face with his hands. "It was an accident," he said. "I never meant to hurt Javi."

His admission caused an immediate uproar, and suddenly the administrators and faculty had their hands full trying to contain a mob of angry students. They surged toward where Rance blubbered like a baby, and even Coach Moore had to release me to try and contain the situation.

Claudia grabbed my wrist. "Let's go," she said with a nod toward the parking lot. "While they're distracted."

I didn't need to hear anything else. Claudia and I dashed for her car, and ten seconds later, we were screeching out of the parking lot toward Javi.

I STOOD outside the automatic doors that led to the trauma area of the emergency room at Christus Santa Rosa. My wounds had already been cleaned and bandaged in the triage area. But I didn't care about me. I cared about Javi. On the other side of that door, doctors and nurses rushed from one closed curtain to another, working on the patients whom I couldn't see.

In there somewhere was Javi and his parents. They'd arrived twenty minutes after Claudia and I, and after I briefly told them what happened, they were escorted to the back. I hadn't seen them since.

That had been almost two and a half hours ago. If I didn't hear something soon, I was going to barge back there and get some answers.

"Why don't you come sit down?" my mother asked. On our way to the hospital, I'd called her on Claudia's phone after contacting the Castillos, who had been notified. They were already on their way. When I told my mother, she'd gasped. Since Dr. Torres' office, where she now worked full-time, was only a few blocks away from the hospital, she'd run here as fast as she could. She hadn't left my side once.

Her presence gave me the strength I needed not to break down, but it was a battle I'd ultimately lose. The tears gathered at the edges of my eyes and sobs lodged in my throat. I wasn't going to give in just yet.

I had to be strong. For Javi.

My mom attempted a smile to lighten my spirits, but it faltered. We both knew that only one thing would make me better—news that Javi was okay. Short of that, I'd be strong and miserable until I heard any different.

"I can't," I finally replied. I looked through the small circular window in the door. If I sat down, I might miss seeing Javi. There was no way that was going to happen in this lifetime.

"Standing here won't make time go faster," she said.

"Neither will sitting over there. I'm staying put."

She nodded and walked back to the row of plastic chairs, where Claudia sat in somber silence.

That was when all hell broke loose.

Almost the entire campus of Burbank High filed into the waiting room. Even some of the Jock Brigade, including Oscar, stood around the perimeter. They converged on the reception desk, asking questions about Javi. The annoyed receptionist gave them nothing.

"There's Claudia," Stephanie Gonzales said.

They headed toward Claudia like moths to a flame.

A sudden roar of questions thrummed inside the waiting area, which was quickly reaching maximum capacity as classmate after classmate poured through the automatic doors.

One of the nurses stormed over, saying they had to leave.

"We're not going anywhere," the senior class president said. "We're here for Javi."

"You tell her, Enrique," Selina Perez said at his right. The others in the group echoed their collective commitment to stay and wait on their friend.

Normally such concern would touch my heart. After all, seeing so many people here in support of Javi spoke volumes about the boy he was and how he had touched the hearts and lives of so many.

But at the same time, their worry fed the fire of rage seeing Rance outside the gym had sparked. Where had their concern been the past few weeks? Many of them hadn't even been on speaking terms with Javi after the rumor mill switched into high gear.

They had abandoned him. They didn't deserve to be here. They needed to go.

"All right, that's enough!" I screamed loud enough to be heard over the chaos.

Everyone turned to stare at me, dressed in my blood-stained jeans and a green hospital shirt. Normally, I hated being the center of attention. When all eyes were on me, that usually meant I was being pushed around or on the floor covering my head from the fists that flailed against me. But right now all that mattered was that these fair-weather friends got the hell out of my sight.

"Who the fuck do you think you traitors are?"

"Tru!" my mother gasped. She rose and hurried over to my side. She'd never seen me this upset or this confrontational, but that was who I was now.

I was a new Tru, and I wasn't going to be silent any longer.

I'd finally found my voice in the love I discovered in Javi.

"You all suck," I said. I locked eyes with each and every one. None of them would escape my wrath, not even the Jock Brigade. They had to understand what they had done, and it was up to me to teach them that lesson. "Javi was a friend to each and every one of you, and you turned your backs on him. And why? Because you heard he might be gay. Yeah, well, so fucking what? He is and so the hell am I. That doesn't change him from the guy you all claimed to love so much. The same one who was always nice to you. Who smiled at you every day with that beautiful half grin. Who made you feel as if you were the most special person in the world."

My voice quavered. My mother's hands rested on my shoulders, and Claudia joined her on my other side. They were my bookends of support and the strength I needed to finish what I had started. "That's what Javi did for me. Before him, I didn't think I was worth anything. Most of you sure as hell reminded me of that every day of my miserable life. But from the moment he met me, Javi didn't see the loser that you saw. He saw me, Truman Cobbler. And it was that friendship, that loving heart that made me fall so madly in love with him."

Many of them had heard me announce we were boyfriends back at school. Only a few gawked in surprise at the revelation. "So go ahead and hate me. Hate us. But don't pretend you don't. Be true to the disgusting pieces of shit you are and embrace it. Own it. And don't stand there pretending you care about Javi, or me for that matter, all of a sudden. Because it's just more bullshit. You know it. I know it."

I cleared my throat and took a step forward. "Now get the fuck out of here."

"Tru," someone said behind me. I spun around. It was Mrs. Castillo. Her eyes were red and swollen. "I'll take you back now."

I took her hand, and she led me through the doors.

WHEN I saw Javi lying on the hospital bed, I almost broke down. I swallowed hard, took five deep breaths, and crossed over to where he rested. An orange contraption surrounded his head, keeping it immobilized. Fresh bandages had been draped across the wound on the side of his head, and nasal airway tubes sat on his upper lip, feeding him oxygen.

At least it wasn't a breathing tube. I took that as a good sign.

"Is he going to be okay?" I asked Mr. Castillo, who stood on the other side of the bed. His tanned face was pale with agony.

"The doctors are optimistic," he answered. His voice was barely a whisper, but the Castillo hope still reverberated in his words. "They managed to stop the bleeding, and the CT scans show no dangerous brain swelling at the moment. We'll know more when he wakes up."

"He hasn't woken up at all?" I asked. His mother stood at my side and placed her hand in mine.

"Not yet, but he's a strong boy," she said. A sob choked her words. "He will be fine. I know it."

I nodded. He would be fine. There wasn't any other option as far as I was concerned.

"I'm proud of you, Tru," Mrs. Castillo said.

Her words took me by surprise. I had no clue why on earth she said that. It was because of me that her son was lying there unconscious. "Why?"

"I heard what you said in the waiting room." Tears leaked from her eyes as she squeezed my hand tight. "You stood up not only for yourself, but for my Javi."

Mr. Castillo smiled. He was impressed. "Did you now?"

"I had to," I said. "Javi has had my back for so long, it was the least I could do for him. Seeing them there, pretending to be concerned, when they'd been so cruel to him, made me so mad." I swallowed hard. The dam I'd held back was about to burst. "But not as mad as I am at myself."

"Why are you angry at yourself?" Mr. Castillo asked.

Fat tears slid down my cheeks as I looked back and forth between Javi's parents. "It's my fault he's here. He was trying to protect me when it happened. When he got hurt." I averted my gaze from theirs. I couldn't look them in the eyes as I admitted my guilt. "If I'd never transferred to Burbank, we'd never have met. And Javi wouldn't have gone through everything he has. He'd be out there playing baseball or whistling to the birds he loves so much. He wouldn't be lying in here hurt, hooked up to all these tubes and machines. He'd be safe."

And that was it. The fear and guilt I'd locked inside since I'd first seen Javi bloody on the floor crashed out of me. I fell apart in broken sobs, which racked my body. The horror of the last few hours took control, and the poison it had brought expelled itself as tears crashed onto the floor.

Mrs. Castillo held me to her chest as I let it out. She smoothed my hair and rocked me back and forth, and I clutched onto her for dear life. Mr. Castillo was suddenly behind me. His hands rested on my shoulders while he rubbed them.

That made the misery flow from me ever more. Because I understood what it meant. I'd seen Mr. Castillo do that often enough with Javi. It was how they reassured each other. It was how he expressed his love.

When I stopped shuddering and my cries quieted, Mrs. Castillo placed her thumb under my chin and lifted my head. Whatever she had to say was not only serious but true. "You have nothing to be sorry about," she said. "This wasn't your fault. Not any of it."

"Maricela's right, Tru," Mr. Castillo said with one final rub. He moved to stand next to his wife so he could gaze into my red-rimmed eyes. "You didn't cause this, and you aren't the reason he's here now. Our Javi got hurt, yes. And the reason he did it was to protect you. But Javi wouldn't have had it any other way, and you know that. You've brought such happiness into my son's life. True happiness. How could he not protect someone who is obviously so dear to him? If he didn't, he wouldn't be the young man we all love so much, would he?"

I shook my head. "No, he wouldn't."

"So dry your tears," Mr. Castillo said. "Rejoice that Javi is with us, and he will *continue* to be with us. We must all have faith in that."

I wiped the tears from my face and smiled at them. How wonderful were these two? Their son was hurt and unconscious, and they were the ones trying to make me feel better. "I do have faith in that," I said with a sniffle.

Mrs. Castillo smiled and patted me on the back. "Good. Faith is what is needed right now," she said as she eyed her son. "And love."

Mr. Castillo nodded in agreement.

"I have that too," I said. "I love your son very much."

"I know you do," Mr. Castillo replied. "And together, we will make Javi strong again."

"How about a group hug?" a voice from the bed asked.

The three of us turned our attention to Javi. His big, beautiful, bleary eyes were open and staring at us.

"Mijo!" his mother screeched. She rushed to his side and placed her hands on his arm. "Thank God!"

Mr. Castillo stood next to his wife, wiping a stray tear from the corner of his eye. "I knew you'd wake up. That's my boy."

I walked around the bed and took his hand in mine. The tears that had just stopped once again poured down my cheeks. "You're a sight for sore eyes," I said as I quickly wiped my tears away.

"Why are you crying?" he asked. His words were thick, and he sounded groggy. "I was bound to wake up with as much noise as the three of you were making. Sheesh!"

I laughed as he wiggled his bushy eyebrows at me.

"I'm going to go get the doctor," I said. "And tell Claudia and my mom you're awake."

"Not yet," Javi said. His eyelids were growing heavy. "I have to tell you something first."

"What's that?" I asked as I held his hand to my chest.

A huge happy grin spread across his lips. "I love you too."

And dammit, if I didn't start crying all over again.

Chapter 12

JAVI WAS perhaps the worst patient ever.

It had only been two days since that awful mess at school, and he'd spent the last forty-eight hours complaining to anyone who would listen that he wanted to go home. Never mind that he had a serious concussion and a head wound or that the doctors kept him for observation. All he heard was blah, blah, blah.

"Are they here yet?" he asked from the bed. He'd shed the hospital gown I'd grown to love, mostly because I caught glimpses of his cute butt every time he got up to pee. And with Javi's insanely small bladder, that happened more often than not.

But instead of his peek-a-boo outfit, he was appropriately, and aggravatingly, covered. He had on jeans and a white T-shirt. Even fully clothed and with gauze hanging on the side of his head, he took my breath away.

He was being discharged today, and his parents were on their way to bring him home. Claudia had picked me up early and driven me over so we could be here for Javi's grand escape and help him get ready. He sometimes got a little dizzy still, but the doctors said that would soon pass.

"Do you see them in the room?" Claudia asked. She'd grown annoyed with Javi's whining. "Because unless they've become invisible, I'd say they're not here yet."

"Hey, don't be so rude to me," he said, pouting. "I just suffered a head wound, you know?"

Claudia groaned. If Javi wasn't careful, he was likely to experience another knock upside his head.

"They'll be here in a few minutes," I said. I rose from the chair beside his bed and sat on the mattress next to him. "Then you can go home and drive your parents crazy there instead of all the doctors and nurses here."

He gazed at me out of the corners of his eyes. "Everyone here loves me. I've been an absolute delight."

Claudia snorted. "Only if this was opposite day."

Javi shot Claudia a mock grimace. "I don't like *you* very much, though."

"The feeling's mutual," she replied before sticking out her tongue.

These two were going to drive *me* crazy!

"How about we talk about something else?" I asked. "To make the time pass."

Javi nodded. He grabbed my hand and beamed. His touch sent shivers traveling up and down my body. It was like placing my hand on one of the static electricity balls, where the lines of blue flame arced to meet me. That was what Javi's touch did to me. It sent waves of endless energy shooting through me, giving me the charge I needed to keep going on.

"So why haven't you told me you outed us to the entire school *and* told them off on the same day?"

I hadn't wanted Javi to know all that. He'd had enough to deal with than to fret about the possible fallout of my outburst. I turned my attention to Claudia, who stood by the window, pretending to find something of complete interest outside. "Claudia Zamora!" I said. "You weren't supposed to say anything."

She turned to me, her eyes wide and innocent. "What do you mean?"

I glared at her. I wasn't buying her act. One thing Claudia was not was innocent.

"Fine," she said. "I told him, but you know how it is when Javi wiggles those caterpillar eyebrows at you."

"Hey!" Javi said, clearly not appreciative of the comment.

I nodded. "Yeah, I know what you mean."

"*Hey!*" he said again, this time poking me in my side. "I do *not* have caterpillar eyebrows."

"Yes, you do." I turned to him and kissed each fuzzy eyebrow. "And I love them."

Javi grinned. "Well okay, then. I guess I do."

Claudia made retching noises.

"You're just jealous because you don't have adorable caterpillar eyebrows like me."

"Yeah, that's it," she replied with a roll of her eyes.

"Now answer my question," Javi said as he leaned against my shoulder.

I lay back on the mattress and pulled him closer into me. "You had enough going on," I answered. "I didn't want you to worry."

"Worry?" he asked, turning his killer smile up to me. "I think it's fucking great!"

"You do?"

"Of course, silly. I'm glad you told those jerks off. Someone had to. I'd been taking them all on one by one, but you swooped on in and took them all down at the same time. Talk about a power move!" I'd likely have to cure cancer to make Javi any prouder of me than he was right now. "Besides, telling everyone was what we wanted to do in the first place. It was our parents' bright idea to keep everything hush-hush. In order to keep us safe." He scrunched up his face. "Obviously that didn't work out. But who cares now? We are out, and it doesn't bother me one bit. Hell, I'm glad they know. It means we can stop pretending we don't mean everything to each other." He ran his fingers along my jaw. "I can look at you in the halls again. And even brush up against you if I want to. Maybe even hold your hand."

I craned my head down and pressed my lips against his. "I'd love that."

"Me too," he said before kissing me back.

"I hate to interrupt such a nauseating moment," Claudia said. We turned to where she leaned against the window. She studied us as if we'd gone insane. "But you do realize the world hasn't changed these past few days. Sure, everyone knows, but there are still jerks like Rance roaming the halls of our Neanderthal high school. Just because everyone knows doesn't mean you should flaunt it in their faces."

"So what are you saying? That Tru and I should willingly go back in the closet?"

"Of course not. But I think being careful is smart, considering everything you've been through. You do realize you were both attacked by a homophobic, self-loathing fuckhead, right?"

Javi tensed. Even after what had happened, he didn't like people talking badly about Rance. "Don't say that," he uttered. "He's got demons. It's not his fault. Besides, I'm sure he's beating himself up about this."

Claudia sneered. "He can jump off a bridge for all I fucking care."

"That's not nice," Javi said. The severity in his tone was clear. This was a subject on which they'd never agree. Honestly, it was one Javi and I would not totally agree on either. Sure, I felt for the guy. It had to be difficult hating everything about yourself the way Rance obviously did, but that didn't mean he had go around beating on people or almost killing them. He needed psychiatric help, and hopefully he'd get shipped off somewhere to get just that. If I never saw Rance Parker again, that would be one day too soon.

"And Rance is nice?" Claudia asked. She was in full rant now. "You've got to be fucking kidding me, Javi. He's so screwed up, he practically killed you. And Tru."

"I realize that—"

Before Javi could continue, Claudia rolled on. "And he claimed to do all that out of love? That's just sick. He's sick. And he deserves whatever happens to him. I hope they throw his ass into juvie. Let him get pushed around for a while in there and made some guy's bitch. That'll serve him right for everything he's done."

I patted Javi's hand, trying to calm him down. Though Claudia's anger was justified, as was Javi's inherently protective nature. It was what I loved about them both. "I think we get it, Claudia," I said. "You don't like him."

"No shit!"

"But Javi does. And even though we both understand where you're coming from, it's not going to do any good to punish someone who's already been put through the wringer."

Her black-penciled eyebrows wrinkled. "What the hell are you talking about?"

I turned to Javi, who nodded. It was time to tell Claudia what we'd already discussed together and with our parents. They were proud of our decision. It made us men in their eyes. "Don't get us wrong. We aren't happy with what Rance has done. He's facing some serious consequences because of it." Like being expelled from school and facing two counts of aggravated assault charges. "But doing hard time isn't what he needs. He needs serious psychological help."

"You'll get no argument from me there," she added with a snuff.

"Which is why Javi and I plan on going to the judge to ask for leniency."

Her mouth fell open, and her eyes went wide. Even though her lips moved, she made no sound.

"It's the right thing to do," I said. "I, more than anyone, know what Rance is capable of. I was there when he snapped. But I was also there when he realized what he'd done. All the anger was gone. It was like he was truly looking at himself for the first time. And he didn't like what he saw. That's why we feel he needs help, not revenge."

"You two are unbelievable," she whispered. "How the hell can you be so forgiving? After everything."

Javi shrugged. His half grin snaked across his soft lips. "What can I say? I'm too good to be true."

"That's right," I said. "He's too good to be true, and I am Tru."

She threw up her hands in surrender. "Fine," she said. "You two go on with your angel routine. Do whatever you have to do. But that doesn't mean I have to like it or him."

"Fair enough," Javi said with a nod. "Now I just have one question."

"What is it?" I asked.

"When the hell are my parents going to get here?"

JAVI'S PARENTS arrived in time to save him from Claudia, who'd been ready to smother him with his pillow. Javi was discharged, and an hour later, we were turning onto his street.

I rode in the car with the Castillos since Claudia had gone home to crawl back into bed. After the last few days, I could certainly have used more sleep. Spending most of the last forty-eight hours in the most uncomfortable chair known to man wasn't exactly helping the wounds on my back heal. But there was no other place I'd rather have been than in the backseat holding my boyfriend's hand as we brought him home.

"What's going on?" Javi asked. Cars were lined up and down the street.

"Someone must be having a garage sale," I said.

"I hope not," Mr. Castillo said from the driver's seat. "Because I don't remember putting anything up for sale on our lawn."

"Dad, what are you talking about?"

"Take a look for yourself," he answered with a nod out the windshield.

Javi and I leaned forward to take a look, and we inhaled in surprise at the same time. Dozens of people from our school stood in front of Javi's house or on his lawn, waving at us as we approached. Some held signs that said, "Welcome Home, Javi," while others simply said "We love you."

"What the hell?" Javi asked.

His mother glanced over her shoulder. "Watch your language," she said.

"Is that Alison?" I asked, pointing out my window. She held up a sign that read, "I'm sorry for being a bitch." Stephanie stood beside her with a sign that said, "Me too."

"I see I'm going to have to talk to that girl about her language too," Mrs. Castillo said with a frown.

"What's going on?" Javi asked.

"Well, I'm not an honor roll student like you two," Mr. Castillo said. "But I think this is what they might call a welcome wagon."

Welcome wagon or welcome train? There were people everywhere. I'd totally missed the ones standing on the other side of the street. They hollered and clapped as we passed. When I pointed at them, Javi nodded and smiled. He had obviously seen them before me.

Mr. Castillo honked the horn twice to let them know their presence was appreciated. And to get them out of his way. They had cluttered the driveway and parted to let the car pass.

When Mr. Castillo turned off the engine, Javi said, "I'm not sure I want to go out there."

"Why?" I asked. "They came here for you."

He frowned. "I wasn't the only one who was hurt. They should be here for you too." He refused to meet my eyes, most likely embarrassed that people were making such a big deal about him. "You're the one who actually had to fight off Rance. I just came in at the end."

I placed my hands on either side of his handsome face. "I don't care why they're here. I'm just glad they are." I rested my forehead on his and rubbed our noses together. "Now get out there. Your friends are waiting."

"What about you?" he asked. "Aren't you coming?"

I shook my head. "I'll wait for a minute in here. Give them some time with you. Then when you're done, I'll be in the house with your parents."

"You promise?" he asked. He clearly feared I might get lost in the chaos that swirled around the car, and he'd never see me again.

"Absolutely."

He flashed me the grin that made my tummy quiver and opened the door. Applause and whistles instantly greeted him as everyone converged upon where he stood. They patted him on the back and gave him hugs. Dozens of questions were tossed at him as if he were a famous movie star walking down the red carpet.

It made me smile. Perhaps I hadn't stolen the life Javi enjoyed before me. It would be somewhat different, but maybe, just maybe, it would be kinda the same too.

"I don't think you're getting away that easily," Mr. Castillo said. He and Mrs. Castillo still sat in the car with me.

"What do you mean?" I asked. But before Mr. Castillo could answer, I turned my attention to my side of the car. People stood around my door, waiting for me to come out. They gazed into the car with smiles on their faces.

I'd never had so many people happy to see me in my life.

"You better get out there," Mrs. Castillo said.

I swallowed hard and opened the door, and when I exited the car, hands patted my back. People I didn't even know apologized for being assholes, and everyone seemed genuinely relieved to know I was okay.

Someone tapped me on the shoulder. It was Alison. As usual, Stephanie stood right next to her. "Tru, what you said outside the gym was right. We were all being huge dicks. But after what happened, well...." She looked around at the people who surrounded us. "It's time not to be dicks anymore. I hope you can forgive me."

I nodded. Tears once again stole my vision from me. I was going to have to learn to stop that. "Of course," I said as I gave Alison a hug.

I glanced over her shoulder at Javi, who stood on the other side of the car. He blew me a kiss, and I blew one back.

Yeah, forget different. My life was never going to be the same again.

AFTER THAT day, everything about my life changed.

It wasn't perfect or anything. Javi's and my relationship rocked the school harder than the iceberg that sank the Titanic. But instead of sinking us, Javi and I rose to the new challenges we faced.

Sure, we had to deal with the jerks who didn't approve. There were still plenty of those passing us in the halls, making snide comments or whispering behind our backs. That hadn't changed. It likely never would.

What had changed was me.

Their voices didn't haunt me like they used to. The fear they'd once produced vanished as if the ghosts had been exorcized. How could

I flounder in terror when I had the hottest and best guy at my school as my boyfriend? And who loved me about as much as I loved him?

Against that, nothing else blipped on my radar.

Javi, too, had become someone different. It was easiest to see when he smiled.

The lopsided grin still danced across his face when he played ball and helped our school on its road back to state or when he greeted friends. And even when he dashed in late to precalc. But the grin he wore was no longer a mask. It was genuine, and it wasn't the only smile in his repertoire anymore. That half grin told the world he was in a feisty mood. When he was truly happy, surrounded by his friends or at dinner with his family, his big cheesy grin spread ear to ear. But when Javi glanced at me, I got something special. Something no one else in the world got.

When he smiled at me, he beamed, and the light of his smile warmed me from the inside out.

All that smiling certainly made Javi less angry and confrontational than he had been for a while. If someone got in his face, he got right back in theirs. But for the most part, we just let the haters hate.

They had no power over us.

What was even more surprising was we didn't stand up against those dipshits alone. Claudia had our back like she always did except now, she didn't keep her mouth shut. She said if a pipsqueak like me could stand up to an entire school, she could give any idiot who spouted hate a tongue-lashing.

And she did.

But it wasn't just Claudia who no longer stood for people calling us fags. Others, like Alison and Stephanie, led the charge. They even petitioned the school for a Gay-Straight Alliance, and after what had happened with Rance, administration okayed the new club.

Ms. Garcia volunteered to sponsor it.

I'd judged her far more harshly than she might have judged me. There was a lesson to be learned for everyone.

"Hey, Tru." Destiny Villarreal stopped in front of me in the hall. The final bell had rung, and it was time to get going. Javi and I had an important meeting to get to.

"What's up?"

"Are you not going to the library today?" she asked. She had her precalc book in her hand and a paper with huge red *x*'s all over it. She had plainly not done well on the latest assignment.

"No," I said. "Not today. Javi and I have to head over to—"

"Oh, right," she said with a nod. "That's today, isn't it?"

It seemed the whole school knew my business these days. I'd never get used to that. "Why don't you call me later tonight, and I can help you over the phone."

"Really?" she asked with a sigh of relief. "Because I just don't understand this pair of bowls concept."

I nodded. The first thing I had to teach her was that it was a parabola and not a pair of bowls. "Give me a call around eight."

"Sure thing," she said. "Thanks."

I said good-bye and continued toward my locker. By the time I got there, I'd been stopped three more times. Alison and Stephanie made sure I was coming to the GSA meeting next week, and I promised I would. Naturally, Alison had to take a selfie before she let me leave. After them, a guy from my English class asked if I'd join his group on their project over *The Importance of Being Earnest*. Since I was an Oscar Wilde lover, I naturally said yes, and then Heather Barnes stopped me few feet from my locker to make sure I was going to the party she was throwing that weekend. It apparently would be the party to end all parties.

How could I say no to that?

Once I finally headed down the stairs, the smile that made my heart quicken came into view. Javi stood at the bottom, gazing up at me with a pretend grimace on his face. "I've been waiting for, like, five minutes," he complained.

"Yeah, well, you know the perils of popularity," I said as I descended toward him. "Everyone wants a piece."

He scowled. "Excuse me?" He puffed out his chest and surveyed the halls. "Who is he? I'll tear him to pieces, I will!"

I snickered at his pretend fit of jealousy. When I reached the bottom, I pressed against Javi and whispered in his ear, "The only one who will get the piece that matters is you. I am eighteen now after all, right?"

A wicked grin danced on his lips and in his eyes. "Now that's what I'm talking about!"

"Javier. Truman."

We turned to see Ms. Garcia standing next to us. Her tight face twisted into a snarl.

"Yes, Ms. Garcia," I said.

"You know as well as everyone that PDA in the hall is unacceptable." Javi opened his mouth to respond, but she shook her finger at him. "And don't start giving me this homophobic bull either. I don't care if you're gay, straight, or from Alpha Centauri. There's no kissing, and most certainly no bodies pressed against one another in *my* halls."

She grabbed our shoulders and separated us. When we were the distance apart that was suitable to her rule-loving mind, she stood back and smiled. She was actually quite attractive when she didn't look so constipated. "Much better."

"Well, I don't know about that," Javi said with a grin.

She glared at him out of the corners of her eyes. "If memory serves me, don't you two have some place you're supposed to be?"

I glanced at my watch. If we didn't book it, we were going to be late. "Yes, ma'am," I said before grabbing Javi's hand. "Thank you."

As we sprinted down the hall, her voice echoed all around us. "I'm proud of you boys for doing this," she said. "And don't run in the halls!"

But instead of stopping, we just laughed. And it felt good.

JAVI DROVE us back to my place, where we already had slacks, button-down shirts, and ties laid out on my bed. We only had time for a quick costume change before we had to leave for the Bexar County Juvenile District Court.

"You nervous?" Javi asked. He kicked off his shoes and slid out of his blue polo shirt. How the hell did he expect me to answer questions when he was taking off his clothes? All I could concentrate on were Javi's smooth dark skin, the muscles that strained as he bent down to take off his socks, and the trail of dark fur I'd run my fingers through but had yet to follow all the way to its treasure. "Tru?"

"Um, what?" I asked. "Yes... I mean, no. Well, kinda. Wait... what was the question again?"

Javi chuckled as he walked bare-chested over to where I still ogled him. "You're cute when you get all flushed," he said. He then wrapped his arms around my waist and leaned in for a kiss.

My lips trembled against his, and his strong tongue wound its way into my mouth. I wrapped my arms around his neck, pulling us harder into the kiss, which had grown much stronger and far more passionate over the past few weeks than ever before.

Our kisses had always been wonderful. My flesh burned, and my cock throbbed in both ache and want every time our lips were joined. But after what we'd been through, we discovered a passion that rivaled what we'd had before.

I'd likened it once to a volcano that simmered and bubbled, but under the right conditions, exploded sky high. That was what being with Javi was like. It was an intense building pressure that sought release we'd yet been unable to give to our hearts or our bodies.

And boy, did we both want to blow!

But instead of erupting right there, Javi pulled out of the kiss. His cheeks were flushed, and his breath blew hot across my face. His cock practically thrummed in his jeans and pulsed against my stomach. "It sucks being a good boy," he said with a sigh.

"Yes, it does." I laid my head against his warm chest. A faint hint of musk from his pits mixed with the woody cologne he typically wore. The combined scent almost made me wave bye-bye to the good boy and jump Javi's bones right there.

But we'd both promised our parents and ourselves to not have sex until we were out of high school. That didn't mean we hadn't fooled around or gotten really close to breaking the rules, especially when Javi had dry-humped me on the bed last week. Or smelled the way he smelled right now. During moments like these, the only thing I wanted was our clothes off and his skin against mine as we took possession of each other's body in the way lovers did.

But we'd agreed to wait. To make sure if Javi and I were going to do adult things, we would be in a fully committed adult relationship.

Javi and I didn't need to wait to know that we planned on spending the rest of our lives together, but we gave our parents what they needed.

We were men of our word. But that didn't mean we had to like it.

"Graduation is in a few weeks," Javi said.

I groaned before I kissed his chest and ran my fingers up his lean oblique muscles. "It might as well be next year."

"Oh, hell no," Javi said. He hooked my chin with his thumb and turned my gaze up to his. His beaming smile shooed my gloom away. "There's no way I'm waiting another year to have you in my arms and in my bed. After graduation, you're *all* mine. Every last bit of you."

It was my turn to smile like a goofy kid. I loved the way that sounded. "It's going to be perfect."

"Duh," he said with a playful raspberry. "It's you and me. Since we're perfect for each other, there really is no other choice."

How could I argue with that?

Javi glanced at the clock on my desk, just under the picture of the two of us I'd taken so many months ago. "We better get moving," he said, "or we're going to be late."

Before we could have our perfect ending, we had one loose end to tie up.

And its name was Rance Parker.

JAVI AND I sat in the second row of seats in the courtroom of Judge Anthony Clarke for Rance's sentencing. He'd already been found guilty on two counts of third degree assault, which carried with it a mandatory sentence of at least one year in prison for each charge.

That would be two years of Rance's life lost because he hated himself more than anything else. And since Judge Clarke had a reputation for being tough on juvenile offenders, especially when it involved bullying, chances were high Rance would be remanded to a prison, and not juvenile detention, since Rance had turned eighteen shortly after the crime.

Rance sat next to his attorney at the far right table with its emerald granite top and puke green rollaway chairs. He was dressed in his finest Sunday clothes, no doubt to make a positive impression on the judge, but his suit and tie couldn't hide his expression or his body language.

Dread and fear tracked across his face, and his shoulders slumped. He didn't make eye contact with anyone. He stared straight ahead at the beige wall behind the bench, ready to meet the fate he believed he deserved.

I'd never seen anyone so defeated. It made my heart ache.

His parents didn't look any better. They sat directly behind Rance, and his mother wrung her hands in worry. His father, who was probably twice Rance's mass, sat with his arm around his wife, trying to offer her comfort, but his empty expression said he really had none to give.

Every now and then, Mrs. Parker glanced over at us. Hopeful optimism danced in her pale blue eyes. Her lips trembled. She was either on the verge of tears, or she wanted to say something. Maybe apologize or plead for us to forgive her son. But every time her mouth opened, she'd shut it again just as quickly.

I turned to see if Javi had noticed, and he was already staring at me. A sad smile inched across his face as he nodded. I didn't have to say a word. I reached for his hand, and he held it, both of us squeezing the reassurance we both needed from the other.

My mother sat next to me with her arm around my shoulders and her gaze fixed upon Rance. It was her mother bear move. She feared Rance might go berserk and charge at me again, and if he tried, she'd claw him to pieces before he ever reached me.

The Castillos most likely were concerned about the same thing. Mrs. Castillo sat on the other side of Javi, and Mr. Castillo took the aisle seat.

Our parents had surrounded us to protect us, but nothing bad was going to happen here. Today was about healing, not about anger or revenge.

"All rise," the bailiff said, and we did as instructed. Judge Clarke entered from his chambers. He was a short, pudgy, silver-haired man, who would likely not be seen as an intimidating figure in most settings. But here, his stern eyes and thin lips commanded respect for him, the court, and the law.

After taking his seat behind his wood paneled bench in a flurry of his black robes, he said. "You may be seated."

Everyone sat down in unison. Judge Clarke stared briefly down at the file he'd carried in with him before peering at Rance over his steel-rimmed glasses. "Mr. Parker, you have been found guilty of two counts of assault in the third degree, and you are here today to learn the consequences of your violent behavior. I am of the mind that young men who so blatantly harm others do not portend a positive, constructive contribution to society in adulthood if they do not face the consequences of their actions. And that is where my court comes in. I see it as my duty to force angry young individuals such as yourself to pay for their crimes in hopes of learning a valuable lesson that will be remembered throughout adulthood."

Rance didn't respond, nor did his eyes meet the judge's.

"But before I hand down your sentencing, it is my understanding that the victims of the assault would like to speak." He turned to the prosecuting attorney, Ms. Coronado, who straightened her gray suit before standing.

"That is correct, Your Honor," she said as she motioned for Javi and I to stand.

A quick glance down at the file told him our names. "Mr. Castillo. Mr. Cobbler, is it true you would care to make a statement before this court?"

"Yes, sir," I said after I swallowed. Javi only nodded.

"And do you both have your parents' consent?"

My mother stood at my side. "I'm Grace Cobbler, Tru's mother. And he has my permission to speak."

Judge Clarke turned his attention to the Castillos. "Javier has our blessing," Mr. Castillo responded.

"Then please step forward." He motioned to the podium that stood between the prosecuting and defense tables.

As we made our way to it, Rance never once turned to us. Instead, he closed his eyes and flinched, fearing whatever condemnation might fly from our lips. Mrs. Parker, though, still clung to hope. She sat forward in her chair.

I stood at the microphone and cleared my throat. Then I unfolded a paper from my pocket where I'd written out what I planned to say.

"Your Honor, my name is Truman L. Cobbler, and I was one of the boys Rance assaulted in the weight room of Burbank High. It was probably one of the most terrifying ordeals in the already frightening life I've led. Rance was the boy who tormented me almost from the first moment I set foot in his school, and every day I had to deal with the hate in his eyes and the hurtful words on his lips. It was tough." My voice cracked, and Javi placed his hand on my shoulder. His loving touch wiped the tremor from my speech, and I continued. "That day in the weight room, I had no doubt Rance intended to hurt me as badly as he could. I cannot lie about that."

I glanced over at Rance. His eyes were closed, but the misery and guilt that loomed over him could not be denied.

"But something happened to Rance. The anger that had been there for months vanished when he realized what he'd done, and when Rance cried over Javi, his remorse was real. It wasn't me or Javi he had a problem with. It was himself he hated. And, Your Honor, as a gay teen myself, I understand that feeling. It's like walking around with a voice that taunts you every day. That reminds you you're different from everyone else. That you are some freak, and if you could just change who you are, maybe you'd fit in. Maybe people would like you. And maybe you'd even like yourself. I consider myself lucky. I have my mom. I have my friend Claudia. I have the Castillos. And I have Javi. Rance didn't have any of that because no one in his life knew who he was. Being that alone drives you crazy, and though it wasn't right, I understand the reason why Rance hated me. I was nothing in his eyes, yet I had everything he wanted. He didn't know how to handle that. But that Rance is gone, Your Honor. I saw him die the moment Javi hit the ground. The new Rance doesn't hold on to that anger anymore. Call it a moment of insanity or whatever legal term best fits, but Rance doesn't deserve to lose two years of his life any more than Javi or I deserved to lose ours. He should have a second chance. To change. To become the Rance he started to be. The one who took responsibility for his actions. The one who didn't run away. The one who got help and the one who confessed what he'd done. That Rance deserves a chance to grow."

I stepped away from the microphone and noticed that Rance had shifted in his seat. He no longer stared blankly into space. His mouth hung open, and he stared at me in surprise.

Javi took my place at the podium and said, "I don't have a speech like Tru because I'm not that kind of guy. What I want to say is short and sweet." He turned from the judge and stared at Rance. "I'm angry at you, Rance. For what you did to me. And to Tru." Rance closed his eyes. A tear rolled slowly down his cheek. "But I want you to know that no matter how angry I am, you have always been like a brother to me. I love you and I forgive you. And more than anything else, I don't want you to go to jail. But I do want you to get some help. You need it, man. You really do. I hope you realize that."

When Javi was finished, we walked back to our seats. Judge Clarke sat in stunned silence.

"I am shocked. In all my time on the bench, I have never heard such words uttered. You should both be commended," he said with a nod. He then turned to Rance. "Mr. Parker, please rise."

Rance and his attorney stood up. Tears flowed freely down his face, and his shoulders heaved as he sobbed.

"You should know, Mr. Parker, that when I walked into this courtroom, I fully intended to send you to jail for the maximum sentence the state of Texas affords me in such matters. But after what Mr. Cobbler and Mr. Castillo have said, and after seeing your reaction to their words, I realize my previous decision would not be justice served after all." He pointed his gavel at Rance. "That doesn't mean you're off the hook. Not by a long shot. I'm sentencing you to two years of conditional imprisonment."

Mrs. Parker cried out in relief, and Mr. Parker hid his head in his hands. This was what everyone had hoped for. The lessened sentence meant that as long as Rance did as the judge said and followed the court's orders to the letter of the law, he would not see the inside of a prison.

"For the next two years, you will do twenty hours of community service each week, and you will enroll in court-ordered anger management classes. You will also see a court-appointed therapist to help you deal with the demons that haunt you, as well as work with the local chapter of the Parents, Families, and Friends of Lesbians and Gays to familiarize yourself with the community you are a part of and should embrace. It is my hope these small steps will turn your feet onto the right path. But if you do not follow each and every one of this court's orders, you will be taken to prison where you will sit out the rest of your sentence in a jail cell. Do you understand me, Mr. Parker?"

Rance nodded. The sobs racking his body made it impossible for him to speak.

Judge Clarke nodded at the court before pounding his gavel.

"It's over," my mom said as she ran her hand through my hair. "At last."

"Thank God," I said.

"Yes, thank God," Mrs. Castillo chimed in.

"I'm proud of you both," Mr. Castillo said. His smile stretched across his tan face.

"We all are," my mother agreed.

"Let's go get something to eat," said Mrs. Castillo. "I'm starving."

Mr. Castillo patted his belly. "I'm always willing to eat."

We all laughed as we filed down the aisle. Javi's hand found mine and pulled me back. "What?" I asked when I saw a strange look I'd never seen in his eyes before.

"Thank you," he said as he drew me into a hug.

"For what?"

"For being you."

"It ain't no big thing," I said, waving his words away as he so often did to me.

Javi frowned. "You're right. That *is* annoying."

"I know!" I said. "Now let's go eat."

I grabbed Javi's hand and headed for the exit, but before we left, we both turned back and glanced at Rance. His parents, who had huge smiles on their faces, stood around him, but he didn't hear what they were saying to him. He stared after us, and when our eyes locked, he nodded his head once in thanks.

We turned around and left.

Now, it was truly over.

Epilogue

BURNT-ORANGE CAPS and gowns crowded the reception area after graduation. Everyone resembled a life-sized Cheeto. I'd be glad never to see the horrid school color again, but I surprised myself by tearing up as I gazed at the wet eyes of the classmates around me who hung on to each other, saying one final good-bye.

And it was a farewell. Most of us would likely never see each other again once we went our separate ways through life.

I wouldn't miss the pricks like Oscar, who hated Javi and me for being gay. I was going to miss the people who'd become my friends.

Who would have ever thought that would happen to me?

"Tru!" Destiny Villarreal ran up and jumped in my arms. She gave me a big hug and kissed my cheek. "I would never have made it through precalc without you." And that was the God's honest truth. She understood advanced math about as well as I understood batting averages, but I'd tutored her to a respectable C+.

"What am I going to do without you?"

She was going to Texas State in San Marcos, where she planned on getting her teacher's certificate to teach math of all subjects. For the sake of her future students, I hoped she stuck to simple arithmetic. "You'll be fine," I said. "You'll see."

She smiled and nodded before throwing her arms around the person to my left. I continued on, searching the packed room for Javi. He and I had a date, and it was one I didn't intend to put off a moment longer.

How the hell had I lost him? He'd sat next to me in the auditorium, but once we filed in here, the great orange crush began, and we'd gotten separated.

"Dude!" a voice behind me said. It was Enrique Fuentes, the guy I'd beat out for valedictorian. "That was an awesome speech." He bumped my hand and gave me a sideways straight-guy hug, where your hips never touch and you're patted on the back three times before being released.

"Thanks." I hadn't believed my words to be anything special, just honest and straight from the heart. But from the sound of all the sniffles as I spoke, I had strummed the heartstrings of the audience. That had been unexpected, but my time at this school had been such an experience, I had to share what I'd learned from my classmates, my mom, and the Castillos, from Rance, and from Javi.

Being true to who we were and what we wanted in life was the only way to truly succeed. And when life got rough, as it inevitably would, we had to look back at our years here, remember where we came from and what was in our hearts at this moment, and then use that knowledge to move forward, whether it was in baby steps or giant leaps.

"Have you decided where you're going to college?" he asked.

"UT." As valedictorian, I was granted automatic admission to every public school in the state, and with the scholarships I'd been awarded to the University of Texas in Austin, I'd be able to pursue my dream of becoming a lawyer at one of the best schools in the state without further bankrupting my mother.

"Awesome!" he said, and we bumped fists again. "I'm off to Louisiana State next month. My dad went there, and I've always wanted to follow in his footsteps."

Like mine, Enrique's father had passed some years ago. He understood the need to keep the memory of his father as close as possible. "Good for you, I hope you enjoy Baton Rouge."

"I will," he said with a wink. "Those Cajun girls be nasty." He chuckled and went on his way, leaving me standing there shaking my head and laughing.

I proceeded on, cutting through the surging orange on my hunt for Javi. I ran into Oscar instead. Quite literally. He'd been dashing through the crowd and bumped right into me. He apologized before realizing it was me he'd practically mowed down.

"No worries," I said. I tried to move past him, but I didn't get far. His hand on my shoulder stopped me. I glanced at him.

"I don't like gays. I think it's gross, and it goes against God, but you've got balls, Tru. And I respect that." He then continued his mad dash through the crowd to whatever or whoever waited for him on the other side.

I stood there for a few minutes, stunned. Maybe it was possible for everyone to change. Tolerance sure beat bigotry any day. Perhaps that was a lesson Oscar had learned. Whatever it was, it made me smile.

"There's my future UT buddy," Alison shrieked behind me.

When I turned to face her and Stephanie, who naturally was at her side, she squealed and gave me a big kiss. Her affection for me had grown over the past few weeks, and when she'd learned we'd both be going to UT, it had gotten worse. She practically hung all over me and declared me her college BFF, which pissed Claudia off something fierce and also made poor Stephanie frown more. Stephanie didn't have the grades to get into a four-year university, so instead she was getting a full-time job and starting community college in the fall. She'd been following Alison for over four years. How was she going to handle choosing her own path now?

"I'm *so* excited we will still be seeing each other come fall," Alison said before giving me another peck on my cheek. "We are, like, going to do *everything* together."

I quietly sighed. Alison had become a good friend and a great gay ally, but she was a little much at times. She was better in small doses. "I can't wait to see what August brings."

"I hope you guys have fun together," Stephanie said, pouting.

I put my arm around her. "You can come up and visit."

"That's what I've been telling her too," Alison said with an eye roll. She was apparently tired of Stephanie being such a downer. "Are you and Javi coming to Heather's party tonight?"

"I think we might drop by," I answered, even though I already knew we were likely not going to make it. Javi and I had already made other plans.

"You better!" she said after delivering a wet kiss on my lips. "Before I go, you know what we gotta do, right?"

I groaned inwardly. "Take a selfie?"

"Damn straight!" She took the picture before tugging Stephanie through the orange swarm.

After she left, I stood on tiptoes, trying to see if I could get a bead on where Javi was, and saw Claudia making her way toward me with a big-ass grin on her face. All day long she'd worn that smile, partially because she was happy to get away from the majority of our classmates, but mostly because she'd finally decided on making journalism her career. She'd be going to Texas A&M University, which was about a three-hour drive from Austin.

Being without each other every day was going to take a major adjustment.

"I've been looking for you all over!" she said once she finally parted the sea of Cheetos. "And who do I see you talking to but your new BFF, Alison." She arched her left eyebrow and stuck out her tongue.

I'd likely be teased about this for the next four years of my life, if not forever. "You know no one can replace you in my heart."

She sighed. "What have I told you about mushy crap, Tru?"

"Don't hate me because I love you." I hugged her and gave her a big, fat kiss. But instead of pushing me away or calling me a dumbass, she wrapped her arms around me and squeezed.

"I love you too," she said with a sniffle. We held each other for a few minutes, knowing our lives were rapidly changing. We also knew high school friendships sometimes didn't last the distance college placed between best friends, but we'd both promised the other to do our damnedest to keep that from happening to us. And as Claudia knew, when I made a promise, I kept my word. She pulled out of the embrace and smiled. "Dumbass."

I laughed. Some things would never change.

"I take it you and Javi are skipping the soiree at Heather's?"

"Most likely," I said with a nod. "I'm sure you are too."

She lifted her nose to the air with great satisfaction before saying, "I'm actually going."

"What? Claudia Zamora is going to a high school party by herself?"

"Well, it's time these bastards get a glimpse of what they've been missing all these years." She unzipped her gown. No oversized T-shirt hid her body. She wore a tight black mini-skirt with a purple V-neck button-down blouse, which naturally had a huge skull and crossbones on the front. The more things change, the more they stayed the same.

"Damn!" I said. "You're smoking!"

"I know," she replied with a grin. "And pretty soon so will everyone else."

"But why the change? You've always enjoyed being different from everyone else at school."

She zipped up her gown and replied, "I was doing it for all the wrong reasons. Trying not to fit in is not being true to myself. And it's just as bad as trying to become what everyone else wants you to be. You taught me that."

I pulled her into my arms again.

"My look may have slightly changed," she said as she smacked me on the back of my head. "But I still don't do mushy."

I quickly released her before she hit me again. For a little thing, she had a heavy hand. "Yeah, well, I still love you," I said as I rubbed my head.

"I know you do," she grinned. "Now you go to your man while I get myself to that party."

"I've been trying to find him." I once again surveyed the crowd.

Claudia sighed in exasperation. Why was she always so frustrated with me? She grabbed my head and turned it to my left, pointing across the room.

Javi stood by the side door, his robe slung over his shoulder and a full grin stretched across his face. Had he been watching me this whole time?

Claudia kissed my cheek and gave me a gentle shove in his direction. "Go get him," she said. "Just don't forget we have plans next weekend."

I blew her a kiss. "I can't wait."

I set my sights once again on Javi and the night we'd been anticipating for far too long.

JAVI AND I stood at the reception desk of the San Antonio Marriott on the Riverwalk. Thanks to Claudia's cousin, Brian, we had a room booked for the evening, and we planned on using graduation money we'd been raking in to pay him back. But as we got closer to the front of the line, Javi's fidgeting started to get out of control.

He'd begun by constantly shifting his weight from one leg to another. It then progressed to moving his overnight bag from his right shoulder to his left and then back again. When it progressed to long, irritated sighs along with all the hopping back and forth, it was time to calm him down. "Will you stop?" I asked him. "You look like a two year old who has to pee."

He grinned down at me. "Well, I do have to pee."

"I told you to go before we left the convention center."

"I didn't have to go when we left the convention center," he said, grazing his thumb along my jaw. The burning desire in his dark brown eyes almost made me strip him naked right there.

When I spoke next, my voice had gotten low and husky. "Well, we'll be in our room in a few minutes."

"I know," he said. He placed his hand at the curve of my back. "Why do you think I can't stand still? I've been waiting for this moment for months."

God, me too!

"I can help the next guest," the twenty-something Hispanic man at the counter announced. As we headed to where he stood, I couldn't help but hope he was gay. It would make checking in to our room a lot less awkward, and judging by the guy's perfect hairdo, manicured nails, and the high pitch of his voice, all signs seemed in our favor.

"We have a reservation under Castillo," Javi said.

The man entered the information in his computer as he grinned. He'd most likely figured out why we were there. "I see from my notes that the room has been taken care of by Mr. Zamora, and we have been instructed to give you whatever you two may need." When he gazed back and forth between us, his smile widened. "But I'm assuming you have everything you need already?"

Javi's cheeks turned scarlet red. "Yes," he mumbled.

The man nodded as he asked for Javi's driver's license. After stroking the keyboard a few more times, he handed back the license, processed our keys, and told us our room number. "Enjoy your stay," he said before we turned and went down the corridor to the elevators.

"He knew, didn't he?" Javi asked.

"Yup."

"Good," Javi said. The embarrassment from before had vanished. On his cheeks burned an entirely different emotion. "I want everyone to know you're mine."

I pressed the up button and leaned into him. His breath rushed hot against my face. "I am yours," I said. "And after tonight, you'll own every part of me."

A tortured groan escaped Javi's lips. He reached around me to push the up button five more times. "Hurry up, dammit!"

When the elevator finally arrived, Javi and I dashed inside and hit the button corresponding to our room number.

Once the doors shut, Javi dropped his bag and enveloped me in his arms. He kissed the top of my head as I nuzzled into his chest. I'd never felt so loved or safe in my life. In Javi's arms, I was Superman, invulnerable to anything the world might throw at me.

"You do realize our parents know what we're doing tonight, right?"

I nodded. "They didn't quite buy my story for some reason."

"Well, it doesn't help that you can't lie worth shit," Javi said in pretend annoyance. "Who comes up with such an elaborate tale?"

"What was wrong with it?" I'd given it thought for days. I'd told my mom, and also mentioned it over dinner a few nights ago at the Castillo's that Heather Barnes was throwing a big graduation party. That certainly wasn't going to raise suspicions since that was what Heather was known for. Then I'd said Heather's mother was doing some home renovation that had knocked out the landline and even interfered with the cell tower somehow. The entire place had become like a dead zone, which was why we might not be able to call them or why they might not be able to contact us. It had seemed like the perfect answer to everything.

"Are you serious?" he asked as the door opened on our floor. He grabbed my hand and led me down the hall. "That was a taller tale than Paul Bunyan and his blue ox. They saw through it right away. The rambling didn't help either."

"I don't ramble."

"Of course you don't. You just speak real fast and make no real sense when you're trying to cover something up."

"I do not!"

"Oh, yes you do," Javi sang in reply as he inserted the key and opened the door.

My response died in my throat when I walked into the room. It wasn't that it was anything grand or spectacular. We couldn't exactly afford five-star accommodations. Still, it was a nice room with a huge wooden desk and armoire with a flat screen television sitting on a swiveling console. From the window, the San Antonio skyline stretched in the distance. The view was quite lovely, especially with the low rumble of the Riverwalk traffic below.

What I couldn't believe was that the room was decorated in mostly burnt orange. It was everywhere! On the couch, on the funky wallpaper that covered the wall opposite the bed, and on the bed. Was this disgusting shade of orange going to haunt me until the end of my days?

"What?" Javi asked with a snicker.

"You knew, didn't you?" I glared at him, hands on my hips. He knew how much I detested this color.

He replied with a devious giggle as he tossed his bag onto the couch. "Maybe."

"How?"

"When I was researching hotels in our price range, I took a look at all the rooms to make sure I found the right one." He held his hands wide and gestured to the entire area. "And when I saw this, well, how could I pass it up?"

I dropped my bag to the side of the king-sized bed. "I don't know if I'm in the mood anymore," I said, being difficult and loving it.

"Aw." He crossed over to me. He pulled me against him and ran his hands up and down my back. "I think it's perfect. We never would have met if it weren't for the old orange and white."

He had a point. The color was awful, but it had managed to bring me to the man I loved. "Fine. I forgive you."

The smile on Javi's lips gave way to a seductive grin, and the hands that had been patting my back in comfort now massaged my flesh in need. "I've been waiting for this for so long, I can't believe it's finally here."

I wrapped my arms around his neck and stood on my tiptoes. I wasn't as tall as Javi, but elevated like this, I could reach his lips without him practically bending in half. "I know what you mean."

But no matter how much I wanted this to happen, I couldn't help the nerves that made my stomach do flip-flops. We'd both prepared for tonight. Although we understood the mechanics, we'd never had sex with anyone before. Luckily, there was enough porn on the Internet to give us a place to start. Among the videos and naughty Tumblr pictures, we'd accidentally stumbled upon some scenes we didn't plan on trying any time soon. Some of that stuff made us both squeamish.

And the idea of Javi entering me, which made me rock hard, also scared me to death. I'd never had anything but my fingers up my butt, and Javi's cock was definitely bigger than my index and middle finger.

"Are you nervous?" I asked.

He nodded. "But not about doing this. I want to be with you. I just want to be good for you."

"You won't be good," I said. "You'll be great because it's you."

I brushed my nose against his chin, and he dipped downward to rub against mine. He kissed my nose and then my cheek before his trembling lips found mine. With one kiss, most of the anxiety blew away, and the swirling breeze of passion swept us up in its brewing storm.

My body suddenly came to life. We'd kissed before, and it had always been great. Well, fucking fantastic to be quite honest, but this was entirely different. In the past, the reins of our passion had been held tight, pulling us back from crossing a line our parents didn't want us to pass.

But now the line had been erased. I opened up like a seedling underneath Javi's life-giving downpour. There was nothing keeping Javi and I apart anymore. We were free to experience, cherish, and explore each other the way no one else had or would.

The passion I'd held back for so long surged forward in my kisses. I twirled my tongue inside Javi's mouth, and my hands traveled across his muscular back. I gripped on to each sinewy curve before dipping lower and grabbing his ass. He moaned into my mouth in response.

But then I must've squeezed his cheeks just a bit too hard. "Ow," he said with a delicious grin on his lips. "I'm gonna need my ass after we're done, you know?"

I laughed. "Remember that later, when it's you *in* my ass."

I pulled him closer against me, and he cupped my face in his big hands. "I will," he whispered. As we kissed, his fingers scraped against my delicate flesh, scratching down over my shoulders until he rested them on my slim hips before clutching my waist and grinding his groin against mine. Our erections rubbed against each other from within the confines of our slacks.

So far, this was like a bazillion times better than jerking off together.

Javi brought his right hand back up to my lips, where he traced the outline of my mouth. My lips quivered as I drew his finger inside with a swirl of my tongue. The salty tang of his finger and the feel of him inside my mouth caused me to thrust my hips forward.

He panted and thrust back against me as I nibbled and sucked on his finger. "God, that feels great."

I smiled, his finger still in my mouth.

But in his excitement, he shoved his finger too far down my throat, and I gagged.

"Sorry about that. I guess I'm just as enthusiastic as you are."

"I'd say so," I replied as I coughed one final time. "But that's okay. We're gonna learn how to do this together." I drew him into another kiss, and I attempted to fumble the buttons of his dress shirt open. What were they fastened with? Steel? No matter how hard I tried to undo them, they refused to budge.

"Want some help?"

"I've got this," I told him before finally undoing the first button. His breathing grew more ragged with each new button opened, and when they were all undone, I spread the fabric apart and danced my fingertips across his flesh.

"You feel great," I mumbled as I turned my gaze to his smooth chest. I watched in amazement as I trailed my fingers across his pecs and circled his tanned, perky nipples, which grew taut. Javi's flesh jumped under my touch.

"Fuck," he whispered before his lips once again molded against mine. With fingers far nimbler than mine, he quickly undid my shirt as I pushed his from his body. He paused long enough to yank his hands free, but once it drifted to the carpet, he continued to unwrap me before he pulled my top from me.

We gazed at each other, our bare chests touching, heaving. Our eyes followed our hands as we scratched and clawed at each other. Javi dove into my neck, biting and licking his way up to my ears while he flicked his fingers across my nipples. I moaned and gasped at the same time in response to his feathery touch.

While Javi teased my neck and nipples, I wound my hands down his chest, over his tight, shuddering stomach, to his belt, which I easily unfastened. I was getting better at this already! As I undid the clasp and the zipper, Javi's cock lurched in his pants. My own dick throbbed in response.

In one motion I shoved them from his hips. Javi leaned into me. His hard cock pressing against me, its pulsating heat digging against my still clothed skin.

"These must come off," he growled. His fingers made short work of my pants before they joined Javi's at our feet. We held on to each other, my arms around his waist, his around my shoulders as we both stepped out of our trousers.

Now only one final barrier stood between us.

"Are you still nervous?" I asked, gazing up into his burning eyes.

He shook his head. "I want this. I want you."

"Me too."

Javi craned downward and brushed his lips across mine again. He slid his tongue inside my mouth as he surfed his hands down my skin and dipped beneath the waistband of my boxers. I whimpered when his fingers slid over my ass, and he took my bare flesh in his hands. No one had ever touched me there before, and to have Javi be the only one I'd ever feel against me, who'd ever touch those parts of my body, only increased my desire to experience him as he did me.

I slid my fingertips down his sides, his flesh twitching as I advanced. I dug my fingers under the fabric and gripped Javi's hard, muscled butt far more gently than my first attempt. Javi panted in my mouth as I touched him. His ass was wonderful, firm and tight, and I suddenly desired to not only feel it but taste his center as we'd seen in some of the porn that had so entranced us a few weeks ago.

"I want to tell you something," Javi said, his words breathy and thick.

"What's that?" I asked, gazing into his loving eyes, delighting in his almost naked flesh against me.

"I know we're young and most people don't think we'll make it." That was true. Some friends who accepted us as a couple also believed it was their right to tell us we'd never last through college. "And I know the odds are against us, but I don't care about the odds, Tru. All I care about is what I feel when I see you. How my body and my soul ache to touch you and kiss you and hold you like I am now. I may be too young for a lot of things, but I'm old enough to know my heart. And there's no one in this world who will ever be with me like I am with you now. This is for us. *Only* us. I just wanted you to know that."

I rose up on my toes and pressed my lips against Javi's, inhaling the promise he'd just given me and safeguarding it within my soul. "And there'll only ever be us. As far as I'm concerned, we've found what people spend a lifetime searching for. And I'm never giving that up. I just want you to know that."

Javi's big smile crept across his face as he leaned back into my lips. He inhaled my breath, taking the promise I'd just given him.

"Now, enough talking," I said. I lowered my hands and slipped Javi's briefs from his body.

"Damn straight," he replied as he did the same with my boxers.

We gazed between us at our nakedness, and it was even more beautiful than I'd ever hoped it to be. Javi's cock, heavy with desire, sprouted from a thick nest of black hair that trailed a line up to his belly button and fanned down toward his hairy legs. My body was practically hairless, except for the dusting of dark brown hair from which sprang my dick, which was thinner and paler but also about an inch longer.

"Damn," he said with a chuckle. "Skinny white boy is packing. *Very* nice."

I reached out and grabbed his cock. He inhaled sharply as I stroked his shaft. My grip was a bit rough at first, judging by Javi's slight wince, but after I loosened my fingers a bit, I squeezed the shaft all the way to the head to coax out a drop of sweetness at the tip.

Javi's eyes about rolled in the back of his head.

"Holy shit!" he said. I rubbed the clear liquid over the fat head and lapped at my fingertip. Javi arched one eyebrow. It was his way of asking me how he tasted.

"Better than anything I've tasted so far," I told him.

"I'll just have to be the judge of that," he said before taking my hardness in his hand. My entire body tensed as his warm grip gently wrapped around my cock. For the last few years, I'd been the only one to touch it, and it had been nice. Having Javi's fingers clutching me, tugging at my sensitive skin, made me never want to jerk off again.

Javi brought his hand to his lips and sampled what he'd managed to coax from me. His eyes grew wide and bright. "I think you taste much better."

"What happens when we do this?" I asked and lunged upon his lips. Our tongues still coated with each other's precum slid and slithered from my mouth to his. The sticky sweetness amplified even more as our mouths churned our body fluids into one delicious treat.

"Fuck!" he said after I pulled away. His eyes were mad with desire, and his face burned hot. He moved me to the edge of the bed and gently lowered me onto my back. I lay there, legs and arms spread, waiting for him.

He knelt over me on the bed, hovering a painful few inches from mine. His cock throbbed above me before brushing against my skin.

Wherever it touched, it left a trail of Javi liquid on me I just couldn't wait to try again.

"You're too far away from me," I whined, reaching up and wrapping my arms around his neck. I tried to force him onto me, but he was too strong. He simply braced himself and smiled.

"What's that smile for?"

"You're just so beautiful," he said before lowering himself.

His words, and the weight and heat of his body on mine, sent all rational thought from my brain. I clawed at his back, wrapped my legs around his waist, and thrust up against him. I couldn't feel enough of his body on mine. I needed more.

"God," I moaned as Javi licked my neck. He clutched at my sides as he thrust against me. "This feels better than anything I'd ever imagined."

"Oh, yes," Javi muttered before his mouth was on mine again. His hands slid from my sides to my head. He gripped the side of my face and my chin, locking me into a passionate kiss. While we attempted to devour each other, Javi's hard cock slid over mine with each thrust. The friction it created was incredible. It made my vision spin, and the cum in my balls started to churn.

"Please," I begged as I thrust my hips upward to force our sweat slick cocks harder and faster together. "Please stop."

Javi lifted himself up on one arm and stared down at me. The passion from before had been replaced with growing concern. "What's wrong?" he asked. "Am I doing something wrong?"

"Are you fucking kidding me?" I asked. I grabbed his ass and continued to thrust against him. He had stopped because I asked him to. My body, however, had no intention of following my commands. I was getting close. Too close. "It's wonderful. Too wonderful."

"Oh," he said. His half grin tugged his lips up to the right. "So I shouldn't do this, then?" he asked before kissing my neck and then licking a trail down my chest to my nipples.

I moaned and thrust upward again as he flitted his tongue across my sensitive flesh, causing it to pebble. After he'd managed to work both nipples into rigid attention, he circled his tongue around them once again before lapping up the sweat all the way to my groin.

"Oh, Javi," I panted when he buried his face in my crotch, licking and gnawing at my flesh and drawing in a lungful of my scent. When he took my leaking cock in his hand once again, I about came off the bed. I arched into his grip and called out for him to stop. If he continued touching me, I wouldn't be able to keep from blowing my load.

"Tasty," Javi said as he swirled his tongue around my cockhead. He lapped up the clear liquid weeping from the slit, and his mouth grew slack in ecstasy.

"You've got to stop," I warned. "It's too much."

The devious smile on his lips also reflected in his eyes. Javi had no intention of listening to what I had to say. Instead, he flicked his tongue around the head again before grabbing me by the base. He slowly drew back his lips and took my cock into his mouth.

I gasped and shuddered as Javi's tongue slid around my shaft. His pursed lips gripped the sides, and it was like sticking my cock in warm butter on the down stroke. When Javi pulled up, a stray tooth scratched along the edge. I winced and inhaled sharply.

"Sorry," he said. A cheesy grin danced across his lips. "First time and all."

"Mine too," I replied with a wink. "Just remember I'm going to need to use it later."

Javi chuckled.

"And it feels great, by the way."

"Really?" he asked.

I nodded. "Really."

He then dove back on my cock, and I clutched the sheets. "Fuck!" He slid up and down my shaft. He worked his hands, doing crazy circles around my erection, as he bobbed on my dick. My breathing grew labored, and sweat poured down my forehead.

I thrust upward against his mouth as he continued to feast upon me, completely lost in the pleasure he was giving me. And when he moaned, the reverberations strummed across my sensitive flesh. It started me falling over the edge I couldn't wait to tumble over. I'd have to remember that when it was Javi's turn.

He pulled off, his eyes crazed with passion as he jacked me closer and closer. I thrust upward, harder and faster against his grip, before I could hold back no more. "Shit!" I screamed as the first jet of cum arced into the air and splattered across his chin. Javi immediately swallowed me once again, catching the remaining spurts I emptied into his hot mouth.

When my convulsions stopped, Javi kept sucking me, lapping his tongue over the increasingly sensitive head until I had to beg him to stop.

"Damn, that was hot," he said. He still stroked my cock as he wiped the spit and cum from his face.

I couldn't speak yet. I had to nod in reply.

He kissed my shaft and then my head before he licked a trail back up to my lips. Once there, his lips were on mine again, and this time our kiss tasted of sweat, cock, and cum.

My dick immediately flared back to life. Javi gazed between us at my hard dick and grinned. "Ready for round two?"

"Yes," I said. Except it was Javi's turn. I rolled him off me and onto his back as I straddled his middle. "But this time I'm in control."

Javi placed his hands under his head and grinned up at me. "Yes, sir," he said. "I'm all yours."

"Yes," I said as I bent over and kissed his lips. "You are."

I lingered upon his lips, outlining a path around his mouth with my tongue while I ground my butt against his hardness. Javi groaned into my kiss when I moved my hands to his chest and pinched his nipples. I twisted and released, and then twisted again. Thank God for porn. I'd learned that move from the countless videos we watched, and Javi appeared to appreciate it. He writhed under my touch, his top half wiggling while his bottom half thrust against my ass.

After I'd worked him into a sexual frenzy, I left his lips and nibbled my way along his smooth chin, nipping at his neck before gnawing my way down to his stomach. I lingered across his treasure trail, darting in and out of his belly button with each circular pass around his tummy. Another lesson learned. That one was from Cocky Boys, and Javi enjoyed it as much as he loved the nipple play. He moaned and pushed up against me until my mouth finally found his pulsing shaft.

I gripped him, and he was so thick around the middle my fingers didn't touch around his circumference. I stroked him slowly and then picked up speed. Every time a pearl of clear liquid squeezed from the slit, I swirled my tongue around the head and slurped it up. Javi whined and begged me not to stop. It was exactly what the blond from Raging Stallion did.

And like the blond's scene partner, I had no intention of stopping.

After a few moments of alternating my strokes, I hovered over his cock, mouth open as I rested my tongue against the swollen head. I jacked his cock as fast as I could before I popped the head in my mouth.

Javi cried out as I sucked on his head. I tried to mimic his actions from before. I swirled my tongue, moaned to produce the right vibration, and stroked his shaft until a steady stream of precum flowed from his cock.

"I'm so fucking close," he mumbled.

That was what I was waiting to hear.

I took a deep breath and choked down as much of his cock as I could. I made it three quarters of the way in one motion, which made his entire body tense. He groaned and gripped my shoulders. He forced himself in and out of my throat. I gagged and forced his cock out of my mouth, but I wasn't letting involuntary body functions stop me. I gobbled his dick back up and increased suction, practically gripping his shaft with my tongue.

When he came, I planned on drinking it all down. There was no way I'd ever let a drop of him go to waste.

"Oh, Tru," he said. His grip on my shoulders tightened, and he went rigid. "I'm gonna come."

And with a roar, he came, quickly flooding my mouth with his spunk. I slobbered and swallowed as much of the volley as I could, but I wasn't experienced enough to get it all. Some dribbled down his shaft, and I had to chase after the runaway stream with my tongue.

"Holy fuck!" he panted as he wiped his brow. I smiled up at him from his crotch. This was a vantage point I'd never get tired of experiencing. Looking up across his body was like gazing upon the most special of God's creations. And to me, that was exactly what Javi was.

"Come here," he said, reaching out for me.

I rose and lay back in his arms. We placed our heads upon the same pillow and rested our foreheads against each other as we'd done countless times before. As we gazed into each other's eyes, words not only seemed unnecessary but insufficient. They had yet to come up with anything that could accurately describe the joy in my heart and the fullness in my soul.

"I love you so much," Javi said.

"I love you so much too."

Javi kissed my lips once and then twice before our tongues were once again sliding between our lips, and our spent cocks once again sprang back to life.

"I just can't get enough of you," Javi said before he pressed his lips against mine and crawled on top of me.

The pressure of his lean body, his strong chest, and his thick cock drove me wild. I clutched at his back, grabbing handfuls of muscle as I ground against him and bit at his shoulder. "You could have as much of me as you want," I panted. But what I really wanted now was for Javi to claim my body as his. No matter how much it scared me, I wanted him inside me because only then would we truly belong to each other.

I placed my hands on the sides of his head and pulled out of our kiss. My eyes were wild, and my breath left my body in broken pants. "Please, Javi. Do it," I said before diving onto his mouth again. "I need you inside me."

Javi broke our kiss, his breathing short and quick. "Are you sure?" he asked.

We'd discussed the possibility of anal sex prior to tonight. In theory we were both for it, but we'd been nervous. It was going to hurt, and Javi didn't want to hurt me. That was why I'd been practicing at home. Every night before bed, I jerked off with as many of my fingers up my ass as I could take. My ass had some idea of what was going to happen. But right now, the future pain didn't matter. Not when I craved for Javi to crawl inside me and make himself a home. "Yes," I answered. "Please."

Javi reached into my duffel bag. We both had purchased bottles of lube just in case, and when he came back up he had the bottle in his hand. "Lube ready," he said. "But we both know what has to happen first, right?"

I did. Thank God for research. And what was coming next was an experience I'd been curiously drawn to since we first read about it and saw the pictures.

Javi kissed me gently on the lips before sliding down my body. He raised my legs and positioned his head between them. "Everything about you is so beautiful," he said as he stared at my ass.

"That's because you love me."

Javi gazed up at me, and his smile made my heart flutter. "Yes, I do."

He then dove between my cheeks. I practically screamed as Javi's tongue lapped around my hole. I had thought sucking my cock was the most sensitive place Javi's tongue could travel.

Boy, had I been wrong!

Each slide of his tongue along the rim or flutter across the opening sent waves of pleasure rippling through me. I couldn't lay still. He'd obviously been doing his research on rimming. How the hell did he know how to do all that with his tongue? I thrashed and backed up against his face. What exactly I hoped to accomplish with that was beyond me, but my body had suddenly developed a mind of its own.

When Javi nibbled up and down the crack, I mewled. Then he started blowing short puffs of air across my hole, and my ass responded by twitching.

"Does it feel good?" he asked before he resumed munching on my ass.

"Fuck, yes," I panted. I grabbed my legs and pulled them to my chest to give him whatever access he needed. I'd seen actors do that in pretty much every video we watched.

"Good," he said as he came up for air. "Now let's see what you think about this."

Before I could ask, he was nibbling at my center before pushing his way past the ring of muscle. I screeched and almost crawled up the wall.

His tongue squirmed and wiggled before retreating. He then pushed the tip back inside before shoving almost his entire face up my butt. Why the fuck hadn't we been doing this the whole time we'd known each other?

"I need you," I managed to force out between gasps. "Please."

"Almost," Javi replied. He then inserted a finger inside me and drew circles inside my ass. I had to bite my lip to keep from yelling at the top of my lungs. The pain was sharp, and I had to focus all my thoughts on relaxing my muscles. And remembering to breathe. That was pretty important too.

He withdrew his finger before inserting two and repeating the same pattern.

With each new finger, my body tensed, and my ass burned, but after a few minutes of Javi twisting around inside me, the pain gave way to a pleasure that made me practically leap out of my own skin.

I moaned and bucked against his fingers, staring down between my legs. Javi knelt between them, stroking his throbbing, red cock. "Now?" The pleading in my question was unmistakable.

He nodded and withdrew from me. He retrieved the bottle, squirted an overly generous portion on his cock and then slathered even more around and in my hole. After tossing the bottle of lube on the bed, he placed my legs on his chest and mounted me.

He nudged his cock against my hole, teasing me with the entire length as he slid it along my crack. "Please," I begged, thrusting my hips upward, trying to force him inside me. My previous apprehension had all but vanished.

Javi gripped my hips, steadying me with his hands. "I love you, Tru," he said before he gripped his cock and placed it at my entrance.

"Oh God, I love you too," I whimpered as he nudged forward.

The pleasure his tongue and fingers had started quickly turned into blinding pain. I gritted my teeth and threw back my head as fire scorched across my asshole.

"Are you okay?" Javi asked, keeping completely still.

I nodded. Words couldn't form on my lips, and the world had suddenly gone white. Fuck, it hurt having a cock shoved up your ass. "Are you in?"

He giggled. "Just the tip."

"Are you fucking serious?" It felt like a Buick was making its way inside my butt. It seemed my at-home lessons were never going to prepare me for this.

"Yes," he said. "Do you need me to stop?"

I shook my head. "Just give me a minute. I need to get used to it," I replied, taking several deep breaths. "But whatever you do, don't fucking move!" I focused on relaxing, envisioning every muscle in my body releasing all the tension. Javi remained statue still above. After a few seconds, I nodded for him to continue.

Javi kissed my legs and ran his hands lovingly up and down my chest before pushing forward again. Sweat immediately coated every inch of my flesh as Javi's head popped past the first ring of muscle, and my previously relaxed body tensed up again.

"Relax," Javi whispered. He caressed my face, tracing my lips and my nose.

"I'm trying," I replied.

"I know you are, and I don't know about you, but this feels great."

"It does?"

Javi nodded slowly and bit his lip. "It's wonderful. And looking at my cock sliding inside you is fucking hot."

For whatever reason, those words caused a sense of calm to drift over me, and I relaxed. My body pulled Javi farther within me, and I reached out to grab his butt. When my hands were full of his ass, I gripped him and pulled him gently all the way in until his pubic hair tickled my ass.

"Holy shit!" he gasped. His mouth hung open in silent ecstasy.

The pain that had ripped through me began to fade. All that was left was a sense of being full of Javi, his throbbing cock lodged inside me and making us one. "Do it," I told him.

Javi slowly pulled out, and my ass gripped him tight, fighting against him leaving my body. When he pushed all the way back in, I groaned and clawed at his shoulders and grabbed on to his biceps. "Oh, Javi," I said as he continued working himself in and out of me. "You feel so good inside me."

"No, baby," he said. "It's all you."

"It's us," I replied as I craned up to meet his lips.

Once our lips reconnected, Javi picked up the pace. Faster and harder he fucked me, pulling his cock out almost entirely before he dug once again inside my flesh. I had to wrap my arms around him and bury myself in his chest so his body would muffle the sounds of moans and curses.

Forget being sucked off or rimmed, this was by *far* the most intense and loving experience there could possibly be.

"Oh fuck," he repeated over and over again as he forced himself in and out. I kissed his chest and surfed my hands down his back and across his chest as he fucked me slowly and then faster. He alternated speeds, gyrating his hips in circular motions while I ground against him to increase the friction.

Whatever we were doing was getting him closer to coming again, and I wasn't too far behind.

My cock throbbed as if my heart had suddenly fallen to my groin, and a clear pool of liquid had collected on my stomach.

"I'm getting close," I told him. I took my cock in my hand. I couldn't help myself. Javi had brought me right to the edge and just a little push was going to send me over.

"Me too," he grunted.

In a few strokes, I tensed again and my toes flexed wide as my cock exploded. White streams of spunk blew across my chest as I convulsed underneath Javi.

"*Fuck!*" Javi bellowed as my contracting internal muscles and his quick thrusts milked the cum from his cock. His dick pulsed inside me as Javi filled my body with a second dose of his juices in a span of a few minutes.

I was going to be sloshing by the time we headed home tomorrow.

Javi's retreating cock slipped from me, and he collapsed on top of me.

"That. Was. Awesome," Javi panted. His body shook from the after-tremors of his orgasm, and I caressed the back of his head and kissed his temples.

"Yes, it was," I said. "You were awesome."

He rose up briefly from the crook of my neck and smiled his lopsided grin. "I could tell. You were about to crawl out of your skin. Based on that reaction, I was fucking incredible."

I laughed and rolled my eyes. "Just you wait. In a few minutes, I get my shot in your ass."

Javi lingered on my lips and rubbed our noses together. I loved when he did that. "And it's gonna be fucking incredible too. Because it's you."

He slid off me and wrapped his arms around me, drawing me close. A few seconds later, Javi's low snore filled the room, and though I didn't want to fall asleep because I wanted to bask in this moment forever, my eyes grew heavy, and I drifted off into perhaps the soundest and most peaceful sleep of my life.

MY EYES fluttered open when a crushing weight pressed along my body. Javi had climbed on top of me, a grin wide across his face, and I wrapped my arms around his shoulders and my legs around his waist. "I could get used to waking up like this."

"Fuck, me too!" he said with a kiss. "I don't know how I'm going to fall asleep alone in my bed from now on."

I nodded. That was definitely going to be difficult. We'd crossed the line, and there was no going back. I wanted Javi naked in bed with me 24/7. Anything else just wasn't acceptable.

That wasn't going to happen. We might be eighteen now, but we still had a whole summer in our parents' houses. Sleepovers weren't going to be condoned, no matter how much they loved us or accepted our relationship. Parents were so lame sometimes.

"Once we get to college, though, that'll be a whole other story."

I couldn't wait. He had gotten a baseball scholarship to several colleges, thanks to his successful return trip to state. He could have gone to the University of California or even Penn State, but he had chosen the University of Texas, so we could go to school together. I'd told him not to just follow me. If he wanted to go to California or Pennsylvania, we would work it out. We'd be fine.

He wouldn't hear of it. It was UT, and the decision was final.

I certainly wasn't going to argue with that.

"Yeah, but you'll likely be in your jock dorm," I said, jutting out my lower lip in a pout.

He kissed my fat lip before saying, "Well, that's where my stuff will be, yes. But unless you're in that bed too, I'm going to be wherever your ass lies down for the night."

"Yay!" I said with a big grin. I must've looked like an idiot, but I didn't care. I was an idiot, an idiot for Javi.

All of a sudden, his face grew serious. His mouth puckered to one side. He had a question, but he didn't know how to ask.

"What?" I asked.

"Well, there's something I've always wanted to know, but I'd been afraid to ask."

"Why would you be afraid to ask me a question?"

"Okay, well, maybe I've not been afraid of asking, but more of you not wanting to answer."

I squinted at him. "What are you talking about?"

"Will you tell me what the L in your name stands for?"

I groaned and looked away.

"Aw, come on," he said. He nuzzled his cheek into my neck and kissed me gently. His lips resparked the fire that once again seared my flesh. Round three and Javi's ass were just around the bend. "I figured, since we've seen each other naked, tasted each other's cum, and just had the hottest sex in the world," he added with an eyebrow wiggle, "it's finally okay for me to ask and for you to tell me."

He had a point. "Fine," I said with a sigh. "You're going to think it's stupid, so I'm warning you now."

He frowned. "I'd never think anything about you was stupid."

"Wait till you hear what it is."

He stared. After a few seconds of silence, he poked me in the chest. "Out with it already."

"My middle name is my mother's maiden name. It's a family tradition on my mother's side of the family."

Javi rolled his eyes. "That doesn't exactly answer my question. What's your mother's maiden name?"

I exhaled all the air in my lungs before I replied. "Love."

"Aww, how sweet," he said with a kiss. But then his eyes fluttered open. "Wait a minute."

Here it came.

"Your name is Truman Love Cobbler?"

"Yes," I admitted with a mortified shake of my head. I buried my face in his neck. My name couldn't have been worse. Well, that wasn't necessarily the truth. If Bart had adopted me, I'd have been Truman Love Cox. Even though as a gay young man it was technically true, I didn't need to advertise my love for a hard stiff one with my name.

"I can see why you've kept that to yourself," he said.

"Can you imagine what my life would've been like if everyone knew?"

Javi shook his head. "It would've been even tougher. But who fucking cares now? All that matters is what I think, right?" When I nodded, he continued, "And I think your name is perfect for you."

Oh, please. Just because he loved me didn't mean he had to placate me. My name was awful. Even if he admitted that, I wouldn't love him any less. "How so?"

"Because you are *my* Tru," he said. "*My* true love."

Could he be any more perfect? He knew exactly what to say every single time. "And you, Javier Castillo, are my true love."

Javi once again rested his forehead against mine.

It was where he belonged, against me, on top of me, inside me.

Forever by my side.

And though our future had just started to unfold before us, it was one he and I were destined to walk together.

If the hot jock and the weird-looking geek could make it through high school, life was going to be a piece of cake.

JACOB Z. FLORES lives a double life. During the day, he is a respected college English professor and midlevel administrator. At night and during his summer vacation, he loosens the tie and tosses aside the trendy sports coat to write man on man fiction, where the hardass assessor of freshmen level composition turns his attention to the firm posteriors and other rigid appendages of the characters in his fictional world.

Summers in Provincetown, Massachusetts, provide Jacob with inspiration for his fiction. The abundance of barely clothed man flesh and daily debauchery stimulates his personal muse. When he isn't stroking the keyboard, Jacob spends time with his daughter. They both represent a bright blue blip in an otherwise predominantly red swath in south Texas.

You can follow Jacob's musings on his blog at http://jacobzflores.com or become a part of his social media network by visiting http://www.facebook.com/jacob.flores2 or http://twitter.com/#!/JacobZFlores.

Provincetown Series

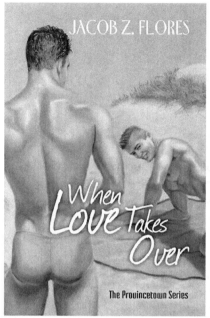

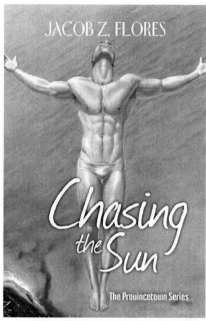

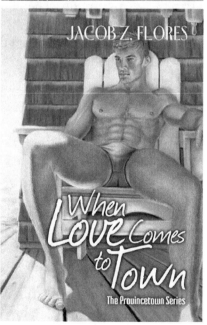

JACOB Z. FLORES

http://www.dreamspinnerpress.com

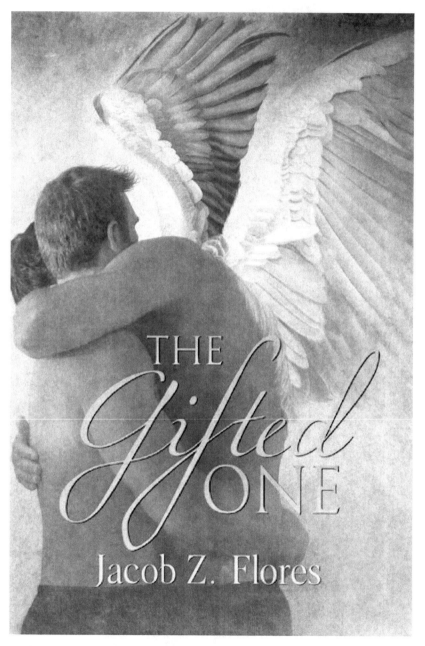

http://www.dreamspinnerpress.com

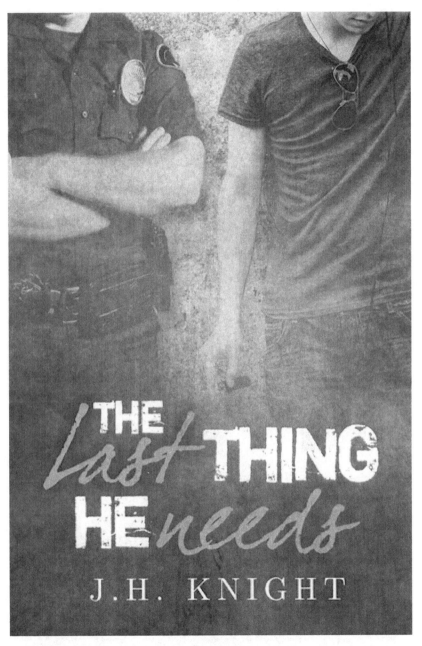

THE Last THING HE needs

J.H. KNIGHT

http://www.dreamspinnerpress.com

CPSIA information can be obtained
at www.ICGtesting.com
Printed in the USA
FFOW01n0607300914
7687FF

9 781632 163790